Other Ross Duncan Titles

They Die Alone
Sleep Not, My Child
For A Sin Offering
To Catch Is Not To Hold
Unto The Daughters Of Men

THEY DIE ALONE

A Ross Duncan Novel

Christopher Bartley

PEACH PUBLISHING

ISBN 978-1-78036-185-7

Published by
Peach Publishing

Dedication

For Karen, who is my happiness.

And for my parents and grandparents who encouraged the habits of reading, writing, and questioning everything.

Author's Note

This novel is a work of fiction set within a specific historical context. The main characters in the story never existed, although their life histories and activities share similarities with people who actually lived during this era. Some of the characters in the story are real, and some of the peripheral events described actually happened. Apart from its fictional elements, I have done my best to ensure that this novel is historically accurate to the period in which it is set. I apologize in advance for the inevitable mistakes and inaccuracies, which are my fault alone. Please feel free to let me know if you spot any.

My email address is rossduncan32@gmail.com.

In its early days the Federal Bureau of Investigation, directed by a young J. Edgar Hoover, built a reputation for law enforcement by glamorizing, demonizing, and then hunting down the independent bank robbers who emerged in the wake of the Great Depression, while carefully ignoring the far more powerful and insidious elements of organized crime. Few people are aware of the interconnections between these two disparate elements of the criminal underworld. The bank robbers' era ended suddenly in 1934. That year Bonnie and Clyde, John Dillinger, Pretty Boy Floyd, Homer Van Meter, Baby Face Nelson and several others were all gunned down by law enforcement officers, resulting in national headlines and guaranteeing the continued existence and expanding budget of the fledgling FBI. While several brave special agents lost their lives in the line of duty, in at least two instances law enforcement officers appear to have summarily executed this new breed of criminals called Public Enemies.

Chapter One

Chicago: April 1934

I stepped over the curb and headed across the street towards the red door, cinching my overcoat under my chin. Before opening the door I paused for a moment to look up at the sky and suck in a deep breath. Traffic sounds echoed harshly around me as I stood there, exposed.

I exhaled and reached for the handle on the door. It was cold to the touch. A shiver ran up my arm, rattling a bell inside me.

It was the middle of another harsh April in the Windy City. I'd come into town less than two days before to look for a girl – and they'd already found me. The eyes of the underworld saw everything. My invitation to a late lunch had come via telegram, delivered while I was still finishing a breakfast of corned beef hash and reading the obituary column of the *Tribune*. It was an invitation a man in my shoes couldn't turn down.

Inside the restaurant I quickly spotted the man I was looking for. He was seated in a dark booth towards the back of a long rectangular room, leaning sideways against a wall. Ancient flecked mirrors lined the interior wall. It was mid-afternoon and we were the only customers. The man did not stand when I approached the table. We did not shake hands. His eyes drooped wearily, as though life disinterested him and had for some time.

"You know who you look like?" he said to me in a flat, nudging accent. "You look like John Dillinger himself."

I merely shrugged. I'd heard that one before and it never led to anything I liked. Quietly, I took a seat in the booth across from him and rested my forearms on the table. The air in the joint was dry and stifling with the acrid scent of fried onions and garlic that had hung around too long.

The man nodded his head up and down slowly, as if confirming his own observation, then took a large swallow of chianti. With the back of his wrist he wiped a thin sheen of deep red juice from his upper lip before slowly sitting back, sighing quietly as his eyes drifted upwards. The pale aura of failure and exhaustion haunted the long stare he directed towards the ceiling. I waited for the paint above us to curl and peel.

Lou Alvarini was Old Italian, he probably came over on a ship near the turn of the century with his parents and maybe a few uncles and aunts. Everybody knew he worked for Frank Nitti now that Al Capone was recuperating in Alcatraz. I studied him. He wore a dark blue silk suit with ghostly pinstripes and a monogrammed white silk handkerchief peeked out from his breast pocket. A black felt Stetson was on the table near the wall. There was a slight bulge under his left shoulder where, it was rumored, he carried a large revolver just in case he needed one. Having now seen the bulge I was inclined to believe the rumor, but wondered if he would have the energy to draw it if the need arose.

According to the word on the street, he was one of the most feared killers in the city, a reputation he'd earned in Five Points before coming out to Chicago in the early '30s. Now the pale graceless aura of illness and advancing age lingered inexorably, filling the crevice of every deep, yellowed line in his face. He coughed dispassionately and fumbled for a cigarette.

"You said there might be a job for me." I phrased the words carefully and then waited.

Alvarini nodded and his eyes slowly traveled down until they were level with my face, but I still wasn't quite sure where they focused. "Do you see the specter watching over my shoulder?"

"No," I lied. "What specter?"

He sighed and shook his head dismissively. "Yeah, we might have need for a man of your talents."

"Which talents are those?"

"You rob banks, and you're good at your job according to the newspapers and the police blotters."

"Only if you believe them."

"Why wouldn't I?"

"No reason I can think of."

"Maybe they got it wrong?"

I looked away, noncommittal. We both knew what I did and we both knew there was nothing to be gained by denial or acknowledgement. "You want me to rob a bank for you?"

"No. We own the banks in this town. But we like your talent. It takes nerve to walk into a bank flashing a Tommy gun."

I sat quiet, still noncommittal. I had never carried a Tommy gun.

That was an invention of the boys trying to sell dailies, but I didn't see any point in mentioning this. We all have our stereotypes and theirs served me fine for the moment. "So what is it that you want me to do?"

"We'd like you to kill a man for us. Can you do that?"

"I'm not a killer."

"You're a bank robber aren't you? What's the difference?"

"I'm one of the new-style bank robbers, we go with a soft touch."

His eyes focused bluntly. "That ain't what I hear. Regardless, we'd like you to kill a man for us." He mixed in several foul words to make sure I got his point.

"Isn't that your expertise?"

Alvarini shook his head. "Sometimes we can't do it, sometimes we need outside help."

"Didn't know the boys ever needed help."

"Now and again we do. It would pave your way in the city as far as we're concerned."

I considered the question. "So, it's sensitive. Does he have a name?"

Alvarini sighed and paused. "O'Farrell," he said softly; it seemed to take all he had to get that one word out. His eyes drooped further and he reached for his chianti, holding it beneath his chin in a still pose.

I whistled lightly, knowing I was supposed to be impressed. I'd only been in town a few days and even I knew who O'Farrell was. Everybody knew. The Chicago newspapers had led off every day, above the fold, with the latest speculations. O'Farrell was a special prosecutor forced on the city by a runaway grand jury to investigate the rackets. It was the next big story. Capone's sensational trial and conviction had emboldened citizens tired of the corruption and bloodshed in the city, and with Prohibition over there was sentiment that it was time to drive the old bootleggers out. The prosecutor had empanelled his own, separate grand jury and indictments were expected by the summer.

"Why me? There are plenty of others. You must have friends in New York."

"We do … But New York has its own problems. Can't ask them. Figured it would be good to have somebody from outside this thing of ours altogether, if you know what I mean."

I didn't really, but I let it pass.

He drank some of the dark red wine and wiped his mouth again. "It's not every day that we kill a special prosecutor," Alvarini said, his voice still soft. "You need to know why we want him aced?"

"Probably obvious: he's Irish, you are not."

Alvarini seemed to laugh silently without mirth, nodding his head slowly. He finished the remaining chianti in his glass and raised a finger towards the waiter. The boy folded an apron over the table he was clearing and came over with a large carafe and a glass for me. As he carefully poured the wine I noticed his hands shook slightly and a vein in his neck throbbed.

*

We were eating veal with pan-fried potatoes, spaghetti, and breaded squash. I sipped my wine carefully and listened to Lou Alvarini tell stories about the old days in a low, sloppy voice. He liked to talk more than I would have guessed.

"Back in the day, Joe the Boss, he ate four, five huge meals every day, with side bowls of pasta, splattering red sauce all over the place as he ate, always talking with his mouth full. He loved to eat. Behind his back, we called him 'Joe the Glutton.' He was eating when they hit him."

"Before dessert?" I replied.

Alvarini ignored my quip. "How many banks you robbed?" he asked with his own mouth nearly full. He had found new energy to invest in the meal.

I tasted the veal and gravy, putting a cautious bite into my mouth. It was fine, but I had little appetite. "Enough to know better," I replied.

Alvarini stared at me for a moment, as if trying to decide what I meant. His eyeballs were small in their sockets, and the flesh around them sagged coldly. He finished chewing and swallowed the food in his mouth before he spoke again. "I've never robbed banks, at least not yet. Too busy selling booze, running the tables and girls, and paying off police and politicians in this town. The rackets are great – at least they were. God, we loved the Volstead Act, it was good to us. We started out making rotgut, with alky-cookers in the basement, and finished up with our own distilleries in Pennsylvania and Canada. All that while the rest of the country was waiting in bread lines and eating in soup kitchens. Too bad about Repeal. Those were good old times for us. We're okay, though, there are still ways to make a buck in this town, but it's not like it was. You have to be careful because there's always somebody who wants to cut into what's yours. I guess you know about what happened

Valentine's Day a few years back?"

I nodded.

"It was bad business," Alvarini said, shaking his head. His eyes focused remotely beyond my left shoulder as though he was seeing the past from some neutral perspective, and then suddenly his eyes were sad and tired again. They drooped down. "People won't learn. I guess it's their nature, especially those North-Siders. Your business and my business aren't so different are they?"

I could think of a few differences, but I saw nothing to be gained by saying so.

Alvarini chewed on a large bite of veal and took another swallow of chianti. He wiped his mouth, with the cloth napkin this time, and stared beyond me again. His fatigue was palpable. It was as if his own words hung over him in a thick blanket of dread.

"We're both men who take what we want and aren't afraid to risk being shot at, if that's what it takes. 'Course I never been famous like you, being one of those new Public Enemies – I'm thinking the dames like that." He laughed mirthlessly, again without sound, and stopped suddenly. He put more veal into his mouth and chewed without pleasure. His eyes rolled partially up in his head as he ate. "I bet you tell them who you are, wave the Tommy gun and they're unrolling their stockings before you can take your hat off."

"I usually take my hat off before I wave the Tommy gun."

He grunted. "You know what I'm talking about."

"Yeah, being hunted by the FBI is a terrific way to live."

Alvarini gave another exaggerated sigh. "Don't worry about the Feds here. They won't bother you in Chicago, not if Big Al says not to."

"That's good to know."

"He may be in prison, but Big Al still runs this town." Alvarini nodded, making eye contact with me now. His eyes narrowed with a clarity I had not yet seen. "How come you're not Public Enemy Number One?"

I shrugged, as if modest. "It doesn't pay any better to be Number One."

"We're gonna have to see about this. Maybe have a little talk with Mr. Hoover. Man like yourself ought to get more respect." Alvarini made small noises from the side of his mouth, as if he didn't enjoy his own attempted joke.

"Number Sixteen has been lucky for me."

"Yeah?"

"At least I haven't been shot since moving up from Nineteen."

"Oh?"

"I took two bullets at Nineteen."

Alvarini's eyes drifted up again towards the ceiling as he sat back from the table. "Really?"

I made a sour face that he didn't seem to notice. "What do you think?"

He considered this for a moment. "You're shining me on. There's no such rankings anyway, except for Dillinger at number one. Bonnie and Clyde probably next, and those two clowns will get theirs soon enough. They're small-time punks, and they got no style."

I shrugged. "I don't need the fame. Hoover's only looking to set up some trophies for himself."

"Okay. The G-men stay quiet in Chicago. I guess the glory is in catching bank robbers. They know better than to interfere with the rackets: booze, girls, the tables, the labor unions … Hoover doesn't care about any of that. Guess he knows better."

"Guess so," I said.

"You got a woman here?" Alvarini asked apparently with only mild interest

I thought about this for a moment. "No," I said.

"I heard Pretty Boy Floyd travels with his girl, that she keeps the car running for him."

"I don't have one."

"Probably got girls waiting for you in six states."

"That'd be five too many."

Alvarini nodded solemnly.

"It's best that way," he said, raising his chianti. "What you gonna do? Stick around here awhile? The dames in Chicago are the best."

"Best at what?"

Alvarini laughed, harder this time and with a high wheezing sound, but still without any suggestion of mirth. His fat lips were almost purple and his neck quivered. "That's right," he said. "That's the important question. I'll let you find out for yourself." His face was suddenly impassive and his eyes flickered, as if quickly coming to life.

I grinned. I could pretend to enjoy myself.

Alvarini's eyes narrowed, focused on mine again. "Where'd you come up as a kid, anyway?"

"Minnesota."

"Farm boy?"

I shook my head. "Twin Cities."

"That's a wide open town. I grew up in New York City, Hell's Kitchen on the West Side, mixing it with the Irish gangs there, then worked all over East Harlem until the unpleasantness started between Masseria and Maranzano. Came out here to help out with Al's thing that he'd got going on. We've done all right. It ain't New York, but it ain't bad. Sure, it hasn't always been easy, but we've done all right, and Al will be back in a few years. He can do his time standing on his head with an all-day sucker in his mouth. Income tax evasion – what a weak rap. Why'd you rob banks anyway?"

"I think somebody once said: because that's where the money is."

Alvarini sat back and smiled without pleasure. "That's kind of funny … 'where the money is.' Who said that? Probably some guy in the last century, huh?" He didn't seem to have the energy to invest in his version of laughter. He twirled some pasta on his fork without showing any intention of putting it in his mouth. Tiny drops of marinara landed on the tablecloth between us. "And now you're looking to change professions, in a manner of speaking?"

"Maybe."

"We can use you. If the O'Farrell business goes okay, we'll have other work for you. Always room for a good man."

"Stable employment'd be nice."

Alvarini nodded seriously. "Yeah, there's opportunities in this town. But tell me something. We can't match the thrills of bank robbing, especially now that the beer wars are over, or the quick money that comes in stacked piles. Why give it up?"

"Seems probable," I said, and paused to reflect for a moment, "that independent bank robbers don't have much of a future anymore."

"You really believe that?"

I nodded. It was at least part of the truth.

"No. I guess they probably don't. I heard your partner got shot up on a job."

My face became a stone.

"It's a shame. Heard he was a stand-up guy. Figure you're right about it. Robbing banks is not like the rackets. You're making a smart play there. But what are you gonna do? You can't just give it up and live like any other crumb. A gangster, with the right connections and not too much ambition for his own good, can live the high life forever. Maybe, anyway."

"I can be patient, while I figure something out."

Alvarini paused for a moment and when he spoke again his voice was a register lower. "I'm going to say something," he told me. "Just try to listen without thinking too much about it or saying anything about it while I'm talking. You're in Chi-Town now, which is our town, but Chi-Town isn't quite like it was before, last time you were here. Things are different and they're changing fast, nothing moves like it used to and the people you think you know here aren't the same people anymore. Maranzano used to think he was fucking Julius Caesar, but he's gone and nobody thinks of themselves that way any more. Sorrows have been heavy and our thing, along with the rest of society, is going through a period of transition and after this period, if we survive – and we probably will, in the general sense of things – nothing is going to be the same again. You can't go back to the day and you can't reclaim the innocence of youth in the old neighborhood, so you have to go forward and make what you can with the ingredients you have to work with. It's the only choice, and it ain't a great one, but you gotta recognize what it is and proceed with that understanding..." He stopped speaking to take a drink.

"... and he rode a pale horse," I injected into the pause.

Alvarini set the wine glass down. "You read the Bible?"

It wasn't a question one answered casually.

"Yeah, sure, get Biblical. Whatever. Maybe I confused you earlier, talking about the specter. You're not Sicilian, so maybe you can't ever understand. But hear what I'm saying right now. Things are different. Sure, the beer wars are over and maybe we won. We've consolidated the businesses, and pushed most of the old greasers and the Irish out, with a few exceptions they're gone or retired. Or they work for us. So we won. But that ain't necessarily all for the good. There used to be a way that you did things and if you followed that way you were a stand-up guy, and that mattered, it meant something. There used to be honor, and there were Men of Honor, and their word meant something. Like I said, there was a right way to do things. But don't count on it no more. We didn't adopt the same code as New York and in the end, we're gonna be sorry, we're gonna pay for it. Our whole family will. This city is unclean, and before you leave here you may be sorry you ever came."

He leaned back with his mouth half open and his hands splayed flatly on the table before him as though he had more to say. I waited without speaking, but no further words followed. After awhile, he sighed and stared back up towards the ceiling, arching his head slowly as though he was gradually turning a winch.

*

After the plates had been cleared Lou Alvarini stood up from the table, and brushed the breadcrumbs off his suit. "I've got to take a leak," he said hoarsely. "Go ahead and order some cannoli, they have the best mascarpone in the city, and some brandy if you like."

"Maybe just coffee," I said with a lazy wave as he turned away.

"Yeah, whatever. Jesus, but you look like Dillinger," he said with his back to me, shaking his head as he walked slowly down a narrow hallway towards the men's room. "Fuckin' dead ringer."

Alvarini had not been gone more than a minute when two men came into Antonio's through the main entrance, walked briskly past the booth where I sat, and headed towards the back. They wore beige overcoats with gray Stetsons pulled low over their foreheads. Their eyes looked straight ahead with determination. I had just noticed that the waiters had all disappeared when I heard the gunshots coming from the back. There were three or four of them, spaced closely together – two different guns – followed by a brief moan. It didn't carry far.

I could have made a run for the door, but I never would have gotten there in time. Besides, there was no reason for anyone to shoot me. I had only been in Chicago for three days and hadn't had enough time to cross anyone yet. Unless having lunch with Lou Alvarini was enough to piss someone off. Or someone wanted to collect on a reward. I drew the 1911 model .45 semi-automatic that I carried in a shoulder rig and held it beneath the table. The ambidextrous thumb safety was off and I squeezed the grip gently, caressing the trigger guard with my forefinger. I was finishing the chianti and trying to look casual when the two men came out from the back of the restaurant. The first one walked past me without even glancing in my direction. The second one stopped at the booth. He used his thumb to push the brim of his hat back slightly.

"The Irishman would like to speak with you," he said. His tone was polite and unhurried. His pale-gray eyes were opaquely tightened with visible crow's feet at the corners. They revealed little indication of anything much at all.

I nodded patiently and waited.

"At your convenience." The man handed me a card. I took it and looked at it. It had the phone number of a flower shop on it.

"I'll call."

"He really would like to speak with you."

I stared at him. "Nuts," I replied quietly.

"Please do call," he said, and then he smiled coldly without allowing his eyes to reveal anything more than the nothing they were already showing. His teeth were disconcertingly perfect and I could smell his uptown cologne, unaffected by the hot scent of cordite and gunpowder. "Maybe we'll see you at Lou's funeral. Should be a swinging affair – he was a swell guy."

"I'll probably just send flowers," I replied, pocketing the card. I didn't replace the safety on the .45 until after he had left the restaurant.

Then I got out of there fast.

Chapter Two

In the late afternoon I kept an appointment I'd made earlier that day. I needed a place to stay and I'd heard of a room that was for rent over near the Cicero line. It was an old, gray neighborhood still mired in the depths of a barren winter that seemed to have lasted more than the one season. Elm trees with sagging, empty branches lined the street, towered up from inside the sidewalk and dotted dry, brown lawns. Most of the houses were old, faded brick two-stories that could have withstood new coats of trim paint. A lonely dog barked half-heartedly from some back yard, working through his tired situation with an unheeded appeal.

The cabbie dropped me off at the corner. After I got out of the Ford I paid the fare through the window and tipped him a dime. He grinned at me and blew cheap cigar smoke in my direction, along with the hint of not-too-stale rye that emanated like pollen.

"Thanks, Mac," he said.

I forced a smile and held up a dollar. The solitary bill crinkled in the wind. "I need a ride back into town. Will you wait?"

He thought about this for a moment. "In this sad old neighborhood? For a buck, I can wait. Don't take forever."

I nodded. He held out his hand and I placed the dollar in it.

"You know," he said then, as he folded the bill, "when you first got in, for a moment I thought you were Johnnie Dillinger."

"Yeah?"

"Yeah. Right down to the mustache and hard look in your eyes. Bet you get that a lot though, huh?"

"Yeah, I do." I shrugged and backed away from the cab.

"You got twenty minutes," he rasped as I was walking away.

"Nuts."

*

I walked slowly down Prairie Avenue and studied the houses on each side of the street, until I came to number 7125. It was a modest, two-story brick house with a discolored and badly chipped sidewalk leading up to the front door. The white paint on the porch rails was peeling rapidly and the screen door hung at a crooked angle. Maybe it had never been square. I went up the steps and knocked twice. The door was opened almost immediately. I found myself looking at a short woman in a bluish dress with small yellow flowers on it. A pair of owl-like reading glasses hung from a silver chain around her neck. She squinted at me. Her expression was cautious without being hostile.

"You saw me coming up the walk," I said.

"We don't get many visitors here."

"Mrs. Giacalone?"

"Yes, that's me."

Her hair was a lazy auburn, with wisps of gray in it, and she wore it long and loosely pulled back. I guessed her age as somewhere on the wrong side of 35 and she had put on a little weight in recent years, but you could tell she had once been very pretty. Hazel eyes and a short, upturned nose led down to a wider than usual mouth. Her lower lip was plump and slightly extended, giving her a look of vulnerable curiosity. She smiled tentatively and it seemed that her eyes were suddenly soft and kind in a way that I had not quite expected in a landlady.

"I'm here about the room."

"Of course. Please come in," she said. She held the door open for me as I stepped into the foyer. "Perhaps we should sit in the drawing room for a moment, or would you prefer to see the room first?"

"We can sit for a moment if you like. That would be fine. I imagine you have some questions for me."

I followed her just off the foyer, into a front parlor. It was filled with green plants and had several gilt-framed landscapes on the walls. From up close I could see the landscapes were all original watercolors, done mostly in pale browns and yellows. I didn't recognize the artist's name. The furniture was old, but neat and well cared for. Everything about the room suggested order and a constant effort at control. She gestured toward a sofa covered in light red terrycloth. I sat down and crossed my legs.

"May I offer you tea?" Mrs. Giacalone asked. She perched on a straight-backed chair, with a wicker seat, positioned beside a reading table and angled at ninety degrees to the sofa. She fidgeted nervously with her hands in her lap. A wedding ring caught what little natural light there was coming through the window.

"No thank you," I replied.

A small charcoal colored cat appeared at the other end of the sofa

12

and silently looked at me with bright eyes. She had a white chin, with black and cream markings around her eyes and muzzle. Her gaze was inscrutable and I felt suddenly very small and unprepared.

"This is Miss Charlotte," Mrs. Giacalone said. "She found us at a lake in Wisconsin two summers back and came home with us. She's a bit shy, but really very sweet. Best to watch your fingers. She has all her claws and on occasion she likes to use them."

I reached out towards the cat and rubbed my fingers together. She did not approach me.

"Do you like cats?"

I nodded, still holding my hand out. "Pretty girl," I whispered.

"It's no use. She'll only come to you when she's ready."

I nodded and looked back towards Mrs. Giacalone, thinking it was a common pattern of female behavior. "She's a smart girl," I said instead.

"I also have a child, a 9-year old boy. His name is Tad. It's just the two of us. You would have the back bedroom, above the kitchen. I never take more than one tenant at a time, so the house will be quiet. I provide breakfast every morning at six-thirty, and dinner every evening at seven. Most people think I'm a decent cook. If you wish to eat mid-day, you'll have to manage that on your own. Sunday dinner is at one. You can join us for church in the morning if you wish – it's not required. I change the linens and clean your room every week, on Mondays. You're not allowed to drink alcohol or curse in the house, and I don't allow visitors. If you plan to stay out late I will leave the front light on for you, but if you make noise when you return or appear to be drunk at any time I will ask you to leave my house. Those are my rules. I have my son to think of."

"I understand. Your rules are quite fair and reasonable."

"You will abide by them without challenge?" Her eyes were set hard.

"Yes, of course."

"Might you be interested?"

"What's the price?"

"How long will you stay?"

My vision blurred slightly as I thought about it. "At least a month, possibly longer."

Mrs. Giacalone thought about it for a moment, and then named a weekly price. "It's due at the start of each week, and I'd like the first week's rent in advance—before you move in."

I nodded. "That is fair."

I felt a tingle on the back of my neck and turned halfway to look.

13

Miss Charlotte had crept along the back of the sofa and now leaned in against me. She was purring. Her cheek was against mine and her whiskers tickled my nose. Her charcoal striped tail wrapped around my neck and rested on my shoulder. Suddenly I felt very much at home.

Mrs. Giacalone smiled and her hands relaxed for the first time. She opened and clasped them once, and then let them lie flat on her thighs. "I think Charlotte likes you."

I smiled as I rubbed the small cat's forehead, gently with the tips of my fingers. "I like her too."

"Would you like to see the room now?"

"No. There's no need." From my wallet I handed Mrs. Giacalone several bills. "This should cover the first two months."

"Oh," she said. There was a mild look of surprise on her face that pleased me in a strange sort of way. She counted the money quickly and then looked up at me. "I only need a week in advance."

"I know. Take it anyway." I had learned that paying a little extra in advance might buy a little confidence and loyalty if I needed it later.

"When will you move in?"

"Tomorrow afternoon. I only have one suitcase and a duffel bag."

"Yes. I'll expect you for dinner tomorrow then."

"That would be fine."

We both stood up and I said goodbye to Miss Charlotte, who then flopped down on the sofa in the very spot where I'd been sitting and proceeded to assiduously groom her left front paw. The small cat looked very pleased with herself as she soaked up the warmth of the body heat that I'd left behind. Mrs. Giacalone walked me to the door and came out onto the front steps with me.

"Mister Duncan, I don't know who you are. You have a gentle way about you, but your eyes are dangerous and this town has a bad way about it. Please don't bring any of the commonness that's out there into our home. We've had a tough go these past couple years."

"No," I said. "I won't."

She smiled sadly as if she only half believed me. Her hazel eyes had that vulnerable look to them again. I shook her hand and turned towards the street, sensing her gaze watching me carefully from behind as I moved under the elms, past the boundary of her front hedges onto the sidewalk and out into the settling dusk.

*

The cab was still waiting where I'd left it. I got in the back and the cabbie started up the motor. As we drove slowly down the street he pointed at a brick two-story that had a wide stone staircase and a single narrow tree out front. The shades were drawn and there was a darkness that permeated the house and floated over the street like smoke on water.

"That's Al Capone's house," the cabbie said as we passed by. "He's in stir, but his mother and wife still live there."

I looked away from the house, toward the street in front of us.

The cabbie was shaking his head. "7244 Prairie Avenue. You believe it? With all his money, he could live in a fuckin' mansion and he lives in that dump."

Above us the sky was rumbling softly and a curtain of dark clouds moved swiftly across our path as we drove back into the forlorn city.

Chapter Three

It was just past five o'clock by the time I returned to my hotel. It was a creaking, second rate joint, not too bad, but not too nice – certainly not as luxurious as The Blackstone. I'd learned long ago to resist instinct and so I avoided the better hotels.

My room was on the sixth floor. Going up I took the lift – a mildly rickety affair made entirely of cheap metal, complete with folding parts, bare rivets and exposed cables. With the door of my room closed and locked behind me, I removed my jacket, untied my shoes, and washed my face in water that wasn't hot enough. I was vaguely uncomfortable with the eyes that looked out at me from the mirror when I lowered the towel, then I lay down on the too soft bed and tried to decide whether I needed a nap. Before I could decide, I was awakened by sharp raps on the door. I sat up slowly, until I was balanced on the edge of the bed, and peered around in the faint light. Outside the window it had somehow become dusk. I looked at my watch and discovered it was half past six. The shoulder rig was chafing painfully into my neck.

"Yeah?"

"There's a message, sir."

I stood up and pulled my jacket on over the shoulder rig, adjusting it off my neck.

When I opened the door the bellboy handed me the envelope and I tipped him a nickel. I closed the door again and stepped over to the window to read the message. It was written in pencil with telegraphic brevity on the hotel's stationary.

"I'm waiting – lobby – must speak with you. Gino Torresi"

I pondered this for a moment. Torresi was a gunman for Frank Nitti's outfit, one of Capone's oldest lieutenants and, I understood, a friend of Alvarini's. There wasn't anything to be gained by avoiding him, so I tied my shoes, combed my hair back and took the stairs down to the lobby, by-passing the lift.

*

Gino Torresi was a very large man with large jowls and thick lips. He wore a freshly pressed linen suit of navy blue, a black Stetson, and fresh spats over black shoes that were polished to a hard shine. He sat in the lobby with a dark gray overcoat folded over his lap and one hand pushed down into the folds of the coat as if he were holding a gun. The coat was so big it could have concealed a Howitzer.

As I came off the last step, I saw him in profile watching the lift.

"Torresi?" I said with my hand inside my own jacket.

He turned without urgency and raised his chin up slowly to study me as I walked across the tiled floor towards him. The sounds of my steps echoed in the near empty lobby, soft taps on a snare kit, heightening my sense of the moment. As I drew close he stood up, set his coat on the chair behind him and reached out to meet me with the hand that had been buried under the folds of the coat. There was no gun in the hand, so I shook it and then we stood staring at each other.

"Good to meet you," he said finally, as if unsure of how to begin.

I nodded.

"I didn't know if you were alone … Well, you know, we need to talk."

I nodded again.

"Perhaps we could walk over to a little place I know. It's over in the next block. We can have coffee and a little privacy."

I looked around. The lobby was more or less empty, but that didn't mean there wasn't a guy with a Tommy gun waiting for me on the street. I looked back at Torresi and nodded.

"Hey," he said, following my thoughts blandly. He held his open palms up for me. "If this was a bump, they'd be wiping you off the floor by now."

I shrugged. "Maybe so. Okay, let's get some coffee."

I followed him out the door, vigilant to any movement on the street. Nobody shot at me, so we walked together for about a block and then entered a small, narrow restaurant that was half a flight below street level. Inside it was dim with smoke and the noise was gathering momentum. We were greeted by a man in a cheap black suit who was deferential to Torresi and he led us to a table in the back. A bald waiter appeared almost immediately and stood with his hands folded in front of him, waiting for our order. He smiled impatiently and I caught a flash of two gold teeth as he chewed the inner corner of his mouth.

18

"We don't have to drink coffee," Torresi said to me.

"Didn't think we would. Make mine a Martini."

"Two." Torresi held up two fingers in case the waiter didn't listen well.

When the waiter returned with the drinks he asked if we were interested in seeing a menu. Torresi looked at me and I shook my head.

"Bring us bread and the soup," Torresi told the waiter, waving his hand afterward.

I didn't bother to tell him I wasn't very hungry. He wouldn't have cared. "Salute," I said instead. We drank the Martinis. They were very cold and mixed with just the right amount of vermouth, which is to say, very little. The waiter brought us a loaf of bread and Torresi ordered two more drinks. I pushed my empty glass away from me and the waiter took it with him as he departed.

"You were with Alvarini when he got hit this afternoon," Torresi said. He was busy with the bread, tearing it into four large pieces of roughly equal sizes. We could have been discussing bus schedules for all the urgency in his tone.

"Not exactly," I replied. "We had lunch together. But he went to the can by himself."

Torresi ignored me. He spread a lot of butter on one piece of the bread and took a very large bite. The waiter brought fresh drinks. I looked at the beads of condensation that had formed on the outside of the glass. I took a sip. It was good, almost as good as the first one, but then again you could never quite beat that first one of the day.

"You get a look at the shooters?"

"You're sure there were more than one?"

"Alvarini had a lot of bullets in him – heard there was more than one caliber used."

I nodded. "There were two men."

"Who were they?"

"I didn't know them."

"Italian or Irish?"

"Well," I said. "They weren't wearing signs."

"They were Irish."

"Probably."

"You scared?"

I let him have the hard stare.

"They could've popped you too."

"Yeah, but like I said, I didn't know them."

Torresi finished with the bread and drank most of his second Martini. The bald waiter brought the soup. It looked like clams, scallops, and carrots in a tomato broth. I hate seafood and pushed the bowl away from me.

"Have some bread," Torresi said.

"Thanks," I told him. "The Martini will be fine without company."

He shrugged and dipped a spoon into the soup, slurping loudly as he brought it up to his mouth. It must have been very hot. I lit a Chesterfield and smoked quietly while he ate more of the soup. The waiter brought a third round of drinks without being asked and also another loaf of bread. He collected the empty glasses and flashed his crooked grin at us as he backed away with nervous energy. Presently Torresi set the spoon down in the bowl and looked at me with stern eyes and pursed lips.

"The fuckin' Irish. Somebody needs to drop them in a hole. Did Alvarini talk to you about that?"

"He said something about killing a man named O'Farrell."

"He's special prosecutor, you probably read about him in the headlines."

I nodded.

"Crooked Irish bastard. He's cramping our operations."

"Too bad."

"It will be – for him. The beer wars are long over now, but there's still a few of these independent operators hanging around. New York has the Jew, we have the Irishman."

"You still want to hire me?"

Torresi swallowed the last of his Martini. "Yeah … maybe."

"To kill O'Farrell?"

"Yeah, but not tonight. There's something else you could help us with."

I stubbed out my cigarette and lit another one. "Oh?"

"We've got a convoy of trucks coming down from Green Bay tonight, one of the last. Alvarini was supposed to take some men and go over the state line to meet them."

"What's the idea?"

"Our trucks have been getting hijacked by the Irish lately and the idea is to stop them."

I swallowed some gin and vermouth. "You want me to ride shotgun

20

for your convoy?"

Torresi nodded. "I want you to ride with me."

"I don't know the country up there. I don't know what's out there."

"You know how to work a pump gun?"

"Yeah."

"That's all you need to know."

"What's in it for me?"

"Might square you with us, for the Alvarini bump."

"So that's the way it is?"

Torresi didn't answer. He gestured toward the waiter and pushed his chair back from the table.

"Nuts," I said to no one in particular.

I tossed the butt of my cigarette into the seafood broth and followed him out.

Chapter Four

The sky was black as pitch and the air was still. Silent flashes of lightning blinked periodically along the horizon. Torresi drove a big Dodge truck fast over the hard country road, sliding forward into the darkness in front of us. Headlight beams bounced ahead, only partially illuminating the way. We were second in the convoy. Behind us there were three more trucks and seven other men.

About twenty miles from town Torresi gestured toward the shotgun. "You know how to use that thing?" he asked casually. His voice sounded like a whisper over the engine's hum.

"You asked that question earlier."

"So, I'm asking again. Do you?"

"Yeah, but I'm not crazy about it."

"We got Tommy guns in the back if you prefer."

"I'll be okay."

"This should be a pip."

I nodded. The last time somebody had said that about a job I was on there had been gunplay, and lots of it. I slid the thought away.

"This is a new route. Nobody knows we're coming in tonight. Its gonna be a smooth run."

"Then why do I need to know how to work a pump gun?"

Torresi looked over at me in the dark with a strange twist to his lips. "Just in case," he said. "Just in case."

I didn't respond and we drove on in silence. I stared out at the grim shadows that raced by, dancing faintly in the periphery of the light shed by our convoy. Song fragments floated through my mind and I thought about a girl I once knew, a girl I had felt responsibility for and failed in a distant sort of way, a girl I still needed to find. Almost an hour passed before Torresi spoke again.

"He was my friend, you know." He spoke in a low voice.

I glanced over in the darkened cab, mildly surprised by the unexpected sentiment. Torresi's wide jaw was set impassively, but his eyes looked feverish in the dim glow of the dashboard.

"I'm sorry," I told him.

"Lou was okay – not really a very nice guy, but okay if you knew him. Sad, in the way that people get when they think that life has failed them. He was morose. We come up together a long time ago from the old neighborhood: Hell's Kitchen. You work closely with somebody for a lot of years like that and you really get to know him, even if there's not much there to like. We played cards every Thursday, but he always cheated. He didn't like women, except the whores. He even hated dogs. But he took care of his sister and she loves him – probably the only one who does. I hate to think how she's gonna take this."

"It's something, I guess."

"What is?"

"A man who's loved by his sister – means something."

"Yeah, you got a point there."

We drove quietly for a few minutes. Night shadows flitted by rapidly.

"Well," Torresi said after a while, "what're ya gonna do about it? He wasn't going to live forever, was he?"

"But who does?"

"You got that right," Torresi said in agreement. His knuckles were tight on the wheel and he stared straight ahead into the creeping blackness before us.

*

On the return, less than twenty minutes after we met the convoy from Milwaukee, we heard the first shots. They came from a copse of trees a hundred yards off to our left. The truck in front of us had rolled over and landed sideways in the middle of the road. Its tires were still spinning in the air amid the flames that came from the underbelly. Torresi pumped the brakes hard and we skidded up against the overturned truck. Several shots hit our hood and then we were bathed in the brilliant light of a spotlight that swept along our front windshield, passed over, and then down along the convoy of trucks behind us. Another beam played over us almost immediately after the first. A shot hit the windshield and shattered it. I had already dived halfway out my door and was rolling onto the grass by the side of the road when it hit.

Torresi was right behind me. "Get the pump gun!" he shouted, waving his hands.

I ignored him and brought up the .45, using both hands. Behind us, along the roadside, men fired wildly into the night. I squeezed off four shots and both spotlights went out. The firing continued for a moment and then tapered off. The night was suddenly almost silent. It would have been dark too except that one of the truck's headlights had not been shot out. Another spotlight came on and swept over our heads. Instantly, there was more rapid-firing as two Tommy guns started up from the copse of trees. A man from the next truck went down screaming and kicking, clutching at his throat.

Torresi was yelling in my ear about the shotgun again and waving a large revolver that he pointed toward the unfettering sky. I sucked in some air, held it in, and raised myself up onto one knee. This time I emptied the magazine and the last spotlight went out. I dropped down, ejected the empty magazine onto the ground, hammered in a fresh one, and released the slide catch. The firing had stopped again, but there was a lot of confusion along the road. Men shouted angrily at each other and somebody retched in the ditch behind us.

"Get 'em moving," I said loudly to Torresi.

He nodded quickly and jumped to his feet. "Let's go, boys! Let's go!"

Six of the men got behind the roof of the overturned truck that was blocking the road and pushed it off to the side. Several shots were fired over their heads in the dark. We jumped back into our truck. There were more shots. Several rounds from a Tommy gun glanced off our rear fender.

"Jesus, that was some shooting!" Torresi said as he gunned the Dodge forward, seeking the safety of darkness and distance from the site of the ambush.

*

We pulled into a large garage that was in an alley just off Clark Street. Signs along the street front advertised vegetables and canned goods, and the entire street smelled of stale wine, vomit, and rotting wood. The other three trucks pulled in behind us and men jumped out, still excited. Torresi pointed me towards a back room as the others began to unload the trucks. We went in and closed the door. It was a small office, with only a couple of chairs and a desk in the way of furniture. Last year's calendar hung on the wall. It had a section for the days of the month at the bottom and the photograph of a woman doing something on the top. After I studied the photograph and realized what the lady was doing I understood why they hadn't updated the calendar.

"Have a seat and a drink," Torresi said. He handed me a bottle of Canadian whiskey and pointed toward a tumbler on the desk. "Try a little of what we brought over tonight. There's also cartons of cigarettes and a few other things if you wanna sample them. I'll be right back."

"When I smoke, I prefer Chesterfields," I said, "but I don't mind a drop of the Canadian."

I sat down in one of the chairs and poured a little of the whiskey into the tumbler, about one finger, just enough to taste. Without pause, I tossed it back and, as it burned down my throat, I poured a little more into the glass, just another finger. Then I got the pack of Chesterfields from my left breast pocket and extracted a cigarette. I lit it up, smoked a little and then drank more of the whiskey, sipping it this time, mixing the heat of the alcohol with the heat of the smoke. My hand shook, just a little, as it always did afterwards, when the adrenaline had worn off and I was able to smell the fear in my own dried, putrid sweat.

Torresi came back into the office and closed the door behind him. His face was flushed with excitement and pleasure. Waving the cigarette in an arc, I brought it briefly to my lips, then set it quickly over the other hand in my lap. Resting with my palms up and the cigarette held upside-down between my thumb and forefinger, the slight tremor wouldn't be noticed. I exhaled a thin stream of smoke towards the ceiling and leaned back in my chair. My eyes were irritated and felt as though they might drop from their sockets.

"Not bad," he said, looking at me with expectation.

"Yeah?"

"We only lost one truck and one man. A couple of the guys got hit and some of the booze is spilt. Nothing serious there, we made out okay."

"Which do we care more about, the booze or the men?"

Torresi stared at me for a moment. He passed a thick-fingered hand over his head, smoothing the hair back. "Pass me that bottle," he said finally.

I handed it to him and he poured a bit into a glass. Without pausing, he took several long swallows. I raised my glass.

"I don't care for the lip, but I'm glad you were with us tonight."

I nodded. "The lip and the trigger finger go together. Two for the price of one."

Torresi wiped his mouth with the back of his hand and set the glass down on the desk. His fat lips seemed to quiver afterward.

"You're good with that gun."

I made a few slow motions with my shoulders and chin.

"You don't have to be so fucking modest."

"Lucky shot."

"Three times? Like hell."

"What else?" I asked, more patient with the booze inside me now.

"Nobody," he said. "Nobody knew about the route we took."

I took a long drag. As I held the smoke in my lungs, I studied the hand that held the cigarette. It was steady again – another thing that the booze helped with.

"Somebody knew," I said. "We didn't imagine those machine gun bullets warming the air around our ears."

"Yeah. Nitti will turn purple when he hears about this. Somebody's tipping our play."

"Is that how they hit Alvarini?"

Torresi looked at me. Then he nodded and picked up the bottle again, and poured sloppily with his right hand until his glass was half-full. Drops of Canadian whiskey splashed over the rim. Lifting the glass with his left hand, he took another swallow and held the bottle out as though he were holding a cross up to the sky. "Not many people knew where he was meeting you."

"I knew."

Torresi nodded slowly. "Yeah," he said without meaning. His expression was blank. "I thought of that. But you didn't know about the route our trucks were taking."

"No," I replied. "I didn't."

"So if you ratted out Alvarini – and I say if – you couldn't have tipped them to the truck route."

I nodded.

"Maybe they followed us from your hotel."

"Doesn't figure," I said.

"Why not?"

"You tell me."

"Because we would have seen their headlights if they had tailed us over those dark country roads."

"If they had their lights on."

"Yeah. But even if they hadn't, they couldn't have set up that ambush without knowing the route in advance. Those spotlights would take

27

some work to get in place."

"True."

"And if they had followed us, they couldn't have known our return route – we didn't go back the same way we came."

I nodded.

"So, somebody tipped our play."

I nodded again.

"Okay," he said, after thinking about this for a bit. "We're through for now."

"Yeah?"

"And this is for your trouble." He handed me a thin stack of fifties. I put them in my coat pocket and stood up.

"Does this mean I'm off the hook for Alvarini? Can we give up on the fiction that it was my handiwork?"

We all knew by now the Alvarini hit was not my doing, and certainly not my fault – just bad timing that I happened to be there when they got him. Of course they had to be wary, but it had to be obvious to everyone now that I had nothing to do with it. In any case, I could hardly refuse guys like these and I had other reasons to think they would be useful to me. There was still a girl out there I had to find.

Torresi stroked the round softness of his chin for a moment, considering the question. "We'll have to see about that," he said though he put little effort into sounding like he meant it. His eyes were far off and I guessed he was preoccupied with thoughts of Alvarini's bereaved sister.

*

When I got back to my room on the sixth floor, I spread the morning's newspaper across the small desk and field stripped the 1911. Using pieces of a clean T-shirt and a squeeze bottle of gun oil, I wiped down every part and every surface of the gun, except for the barrel. I took my time and worked carefully. It took me almost five minutes to clean out the narrow crevices of the slide rail cuts and the breech face. Next, I polished the ebony grips with a chamois cloth and laid them on the bed. Finally, I coated a special brush with oil and pushed that through the barrel several times and then ran dry patches through to wipe out the oil. I kept doing this until the last one came out dry. Then I held the tube up to the light to admire the shiny interior, staring all the way throughout it without any hope of seeing something happy on the other side.

Before putting it all back together, I slid a new recoil spring over the guide rod. After I reassembled the pistol, I racked the slide back and forth several times to check the spring. It felt comfortably tight so I loaded seven shells into one of the magazines and inserted it into the receiver. I racked the slide back again to chamber a round and then pushed the thumb safety up, leaving the hammer back. The gun felt solid as I hefted it in my hand. Satisfied, I placed the 1911 back in its holster and hung the rig over the back of a chair, next to the head of the bed. I wiped down the other magazines, loaded each one, put three in the special loops on the shoulder rig, and stacked the others in a pocket of my gun kit.

A short time later, I turned out the light and slept fitfully for almost three hours, unable to keep my mind off all those things that cleaning the gun had held at bay so easily. In the grim light of dawn I sat on the edge of the bed with a Chesterfield and coughed steadily, as I seemed to do more and more often now at the start of each new day.

My chest ached. I didn't dare look in the mirror.

Chapter Five

Two days later, at eight o'clock the next morning, after a cup of coffee and three cigarettes, I called the number of the Irishman's flower shop on the North Side and was told to come by at nine o'clock. When I arrived, the shop was in a bustle. Large flower arrangements and scattered cuttings of green and yellow crêpe paper were everywhere.

A pretty girl wearing stiff beige flannel and too much lipstick greeted me and insincerely asked how she could help me. Her eyes revealed that she was bored and she never quite managed to look at me.

"A man with nice teeth asked me to stop by," I told her.

"I'm sorry?"

"He had a rather persuasive manner about him."

Her eyes came up, almost level to mine. "I'm not sure I understand."

I smiled sadly at her. "No, you probably don't. I've got an appointment with your boss."

The color in her gray-green eyes floated lighter. "Oh, I'm sorry. What was your name?"

I gave her the name I had been using now for so long it seemed like my own.

"I'll just be a moment, Mister Duncan," she said before she turned away.

She was only gone a short while and when she came back she seemed to be trying a little harder. Her eyes found mine this time and she smiled, genuinely, showing me soft dimples that must have already broken their fair share of hearts. "If you'll come with me, sir."

I followed her to a door at the back of the shop. She opened it for me, but did not follow me in. Inside, I discovered the room was surprisingly large, windowless, and had crushed green velvet draped over the walls. Flower arrangements were lined up two rows deep along the wall to my right. Many of them said things like "Farewell to our pal, Lou" spelled out in roses. There was a sickly-sweet odor drifting up from the floor – the smell of too many flowers wilting into eternity in a too-warm room. It stank not so much of grief and loss or even of that dark wet pain one might experience when contemplating the general human condition, but of the cheap and hurried disappoints we pile on the dead in our rushed effort to be able to say "we did something" before putting them deep in the ground. I thought about how quickly our dead are forgotten and whether our motives were rooted in sympathy or if it was merely part of a collective effort to avoid uncomfortable thoughts about our own mortality?

In the very middle of the room there was a large mahogany desk with two high-backed chairs in front of it and one behind it. Standing next to the desk was a man of medium build, with thin lips, small ears, and eyes that were close together. His hair was a light red and his face was heavily freckled. He wore a dark silk suit and a navy-blue tie with rows of shiny white silk diamonds spilling down its length. Everything he wore was expensive, from the patent leather shoes to the large cut diamond tie clip he wore up close to his throat to hold the knot out over his collar. There was nothing casual about him, not even the pose he had struck while he awaited my arrival. His close-set eyes were inert puddles of something dark and sinister, as if some primordial creature might emerge from them.

"Good day, sir," he said. His accent was heavily Irish and he rolled the "sirrrrr" mightily. "I do not think we have met before."

I shook his hand. "I don't believe we have."

"You must forgive the commotion. It is a very busy day for us today."

"I'm sure Lou would be touched to know so many people cared."

"Oh, yes. You were acquainted with Lou?" His tone was one of feigned surprise.

"Right up to the very end," I said.

The Irishman smiled knowingly, but without comment. "Please, have a seat." He gestured toward a heavy chair.

I sat down and tapped a pack of Chesterfields. The Irishman walked slowly around the desk and sat down behind it. He leaned back in his chair and interlaced his fingers behind his head. I lit a cigarette and casually examined the items on top of the desk – there were only two: one was an ashtray, broad and empty, made of deep black obsidian, and the other was a Thompson machine gun with a varnished wooden handle and stock. It sat at an angle, with the muzzle pointing towards the wall that held Lou's flower arrangements. There was nothing particularly threatening about it other than the fact that it could kill fifty men in a minute without even heating up.

We sat in silence for a long moment. The Irishman studied me while I smoked and I grinned back at him like I hadn't a care in the world.

Before too long, the door opened behind me and the girl in the beige flannel came past and set a tray on the edge of the desk. She poured coffee into two cups, set one, with a saucer, on the other side of the desk and then set another saucer on my side, within easy reach. She smiled as she handed me the cup. It was her good smile, the one with the dimples and full eye contact. I noticed for the first time how long her eyelashes were as she batted them in my direction. She offered sugar and milk from a small pitcher. I took both and stirred vigorously. The Irishman drank his coffee black.

After the girl left, I took a sip of my coffee. It was very good. I took another sip and looked up at the Irishman. He was waiting for my reaction, an expression of pride on his face. I made noises of approval.

"It is a special blend from Egypt," he said proudly, with just a momentary hint of vain humanity peering out at me from the puddles that were his eyes.

"Very good."

"There is an import shop down the street, two blocks from here. They roast it daily."

"It's really very good." And it really was.

"The beans are grown and cured in Egypt, and then roasted here every day. They take great care in selecting the beans."

I nodded.

"You must use the beans the same day they are roasted, otherwise the taste is not fresh."

I sipped my coffee and nodded again.

"I can send a girl down to pick up a packet for you if you like."

"Thanks," I replied. "I'll find it later myself."

I drank more of the coffee.

The Irishman picked up his cup and sipped, holding the saucer in his other hand, just below his chin, posing again. It could have been for my benefit, but I was starting to suspect it was an affectation he maintained even when he was alone. I finished my cigarette and leaned forward to stub out the butt. The cigarette practically disappeared within the vast obsidian ashtray. I drank more of the coffee, holding it in my mouth and savoring it for just a moment before I swallowed.

"You like it, though?"

"Yes," I said. "It's very good."

I finished the coffee and set the cup on the saucer. Leaning back in my chair, I lit another cigarette and blew smoke towards the ceiling. It rose quietly for a period and then disappeared as it passed the backdrop of green velvet on the walls and blended in against a sprawling green Greco-Roman relief on his high ornate tin ceiling.

"I forgot that you knew Lou."

"No you didn't," I told him.

"Well, really …"

"Don't bother yourself with it," I said then. "I only met him the one time."

"Yes. But you will never forget him."

"Or the man with the nice teeth who sent him off."

"You speak very plainly."

"No reason not to."

"Would you like more coffee?"

"No thank you."

"Do you have children?"

"Who has time for them?"

"I have two – a young boy and daughter. She is at that age where she is interested in boys and spends lots of time in her room crying over things I don't understand."

"Perhaps the boy won't disappoint you."

"Perhaps."

"We were discussing the man with the nice teeth. Actually, I think they were perfect."

The Irishman smiled politely and sipped his coffee.

"You might be referring to Eugene. He does things for me."

"He kills people."

The Irishman stared at me for a moment. "Yes, sometimes he does." The puddles of his eyes were the only color that remained in his face, and he lowered his voice as he looked down to study an insignificant spot on the floor. "You do not seem disconcerted by the machine gun on my desk."

I shrugged.

"I've seen a few of them along the way. Never seen one used as a paper weight before."

The Irishman was still staring at me. I didn't melt. He finished his coffee and set the cup and saucer carefully on the desk in front of him. "It is not actually my machine gun."

"Oh," I said, aware of the obvious question I was supposed to ask. I waited a moment, but he did not speak again. "Who's is it?" I asked finally.

"It once belonged to a gentleman named Paddy McLarren."

I was quiet for a moment. "Don't know him."

"No?"

"No."

"It is too bad. He was a very good fellow. Everybody liked him."

"Past tense," I said. I didn't make it a question.

The Irishman nodded. His eyes were suddenly opaque now, as if he could will them to change to human form if it suited his purpose. "Sadly so. There was a spot of trouble up in Wisconsin two nights ago. Perhaps you heard about it, Laddie?"

I shook my head. "Haven't read the papers yet."

"Just a spot of trouble, but poor Paddy ... Well, he did not come home with the boys."

"Poor Paddy. Just bad luck, huh?"

"Yes. Actually, from what I understand there was some rather remarkable shooting. A fellow with an automatic pistol shot out three spotlights from a quarter mile away. Just Paddy's luck to be standing behind one of them."

"Oh, poor Paddy."

"You had not heard about it?"

I shrugged and a tight knot formed in my stomach.

"We are speaking plainly here."

I shrugged again and brought the cigarette up to my lips.

"That is right. You said you had not read the newspapers yet this morning, but of course it was not in the newspapers. I wonder if, perhaps, you had been there yourself? The shooting really was a remarkable feat. The boys were upset, but very impressed with the one shooter – apparently it was just one talented fellow doing the shooting. So you were not there?"

I blew smoke towards the ceiling and stared back at him without response.

The Irishman shook his head slowly, as if in amazement. "Like I say, it really was a remarkable feat – a quarter mile off with an automatic pistol, a .45 I believe."

I didn't think it had been anywhere near a quarter mile, but I didn't say so. Instead, I remarked: "I wonder if Paddy will get a send-off anything like Lou's."

"It is doubtful." The Irishman frowned. "Everyone liked Paddy, but his closest friends did not carry the weight of Mr. Alvarini. His funeral will be, shall we say, perhaps, a wee bit smaller, less grand." He rolled the "r" in "grand" dramatically and paused for my reaction.

I only nodded.

"Would you like more coffee, Laddie?"

"Still no."

"And you are certain you were not in Wisconsin last night?"

I did not respond and after a moment he nodded.

"Of course. But it really was a remarkable shooting feat, with a .45, much like the one I heard you carry. You are proficient with the .45, no?"

I nodded. "I think you invited me here for a purpose other than to discuss coffee and marksmanship."

The Irishman smiled. His eyes were black disks that emitted no light. "So I did, so I did, Laddie. And I can see you are not a man for idle chatter, just plain speaking. So, this is the crux: you are a man that might cause other men to worry, if you take my meaning. I would prefer not to need to be worried about you. The most certain way for me not to be worried by you is to keep you close to me."

"I hope this isn't a marriage proposal."

He smiled hollowly and the eye puddles formed again. He slowly shook his head and rigidly crossed his arms, creasing sharp lines into the silk jacket he wore. "No. It is not. It is a business proposition."

"And what is the business?"

"Making money."

"Of course."

The Irishman stood up and came around the desk, slowly. He moved as if on short wobbly stilts. He carefully picked up the Thompson machine gun and held it as if preparing to fire it at the tin ceiling. Instead, he studied it intently, not without tenderness, and then relaxed his grip on the front handle, caressing the full length of the barrel with his fingers.

"You can see poor Paddy's blood on the stock. Right over here." He held it out for me to see, but I did not take it and I did not lean forward to inspect it. He was right, of course. Even without close examination I could see there was dried blood on the stock and a fresh chip, cracking the varnish, where a bullet might have nicked it.

I nodded. "I see."

"Yes, well … We will be laying young Paddy McLarren to rest the day after tomorrow. Perhaps you will attend?"

I shook my head. "I'm busy that day."

"I understand. Will you consider my business proposal?"

"You have not specifically explained yet, what my end of the business is to be."

"More than you can dream of," he replied with a causal tone that belied the deadliness of any business he was likely to need me for. "More, much, much more."

I grinned at him because I knew, by reputation, that was what I was supposed to do and he confirmed this with a nod. It didn't hurt me any to allow him to believe I was as venal as he had reason to believe I was.

"Yes," he said, smilingly back at me with an expression filled with emptiness. "I thought so."

The Irishman returned the Thompson gun to its place on the desk and set it down carefully, gently. I wasn't sure if this was out of reverence to Paddy, or so that he wouldn't scratch the finish on the desk. Maybe it was neither. When he was satisfied that he had it set just right, he looked up at me and his empty smile vanished.

"Can you come for a proper drink tonight? At the Nightingale Club, say about ten?"

"I might be there."

"I want you to meet Eugene again."

"Lovely."

"Excellent Laddie, cheers."

The Irishman stood up slowly and shook my hand while I was still sitting down.

On my way out, I passed by the girl in the beige flannel. She stood behind a long counter showing yellow roses to a customer draped in fur. Perhaps it was only my imagination, but it seemed she batted her long eyelids in my direction again and showed me her dimples for just the thinnest part of a second. I tossed her the gunner's salute and walked out of the shop.

Brilliant sunshine danced on the sidewalk around me like rainfall as I stood there, letting the warmth erase the inner chill that had developed inside me. I had the scent of fresh yellow roses in my nostrils, and a beautiful girl in beige flannel with gray-green eyes had just smiled at me.

Then it occurred to me I'd been in Chicago four days, and already been invited to two funerals.

Chapter Six

I was halfway through a hot pastrami sandwich with extra horseradish and bread pickles when Gino Torresi and another man came into the luncheon counter and waved at me. Bent sunlight reflected off the large pane of glass that fronted the street.

"Come on, lets grab a booth," Torresi said.

I picked up my plate, spun around ninety degrees on the counter stool, and followed the two men to a table all the way at the back of the narrow diner. Torresi was dressed the same as he had been the previous evening, except he had on a fresh collar and his suit had been pressed.

The other man would never stand accused of being a thoughtful dresser. He wore a wrinkled white shirt with wine stains down the front and a wool jacket that was wearing thin at the elbows and sleeves. His left hand was wrapped in a soiled bandage that looked like it should have been changed two days ago. A soft, wet toothpick hung from the corner of his mouth. He was even heavier than Torresi and smelled like fried sausage and cabbage. There was a look about his eyes that caught my attention. They seemed intentionally dull, but could not quite conceal the contrary truth – that they were hard, angry, cruel, treacherous eyes that saw everything and trusted nothing. His eyes seemed like a potent mixture of Etruscan, Phoenician, Roman, and Carthaginian bloodlines. They were eyes that had spent centuries in the Sicilian mountains, descending only recently to the more civilized areas where humans gathered to form an evolving society. They were eyes that were trained and hardened through the ages to watch for both predators and prey, to decipher subtle movements at their periphery, to watch the actions of their enemies and potential enemies without ever seeming to. Most of all they were dangerous, jealous eyes that were not to be trusted and suggested you should not turn your back for even the barest of moments.

Torresi's entire face drooped with fatigue, but he grinned gamely at me.

"This here is Vincent Reina. Some call him Vinnie, but the boys don't really like that name for him."

I nodded. "What name do the boys prefer?"

"Go ahead, tell him."

Reina looked at me with the dull eyes that didn't fool me.

Torresi laughed. "Luke! The boys prefer Luke."

"Luke?"

Torresi chortled. "Tell him why. You wanna know why?"

"Yes, why?"

"Because it sounds more American," Torresi said.

"Well, yes it does."

"Ain't that a hoot?" Torresi said. "Vinnie's been in this country for only two years. Still does most of his work with the *lupara* – the shotgun. And we call him Luke."

"Haitch not funny," Reina said in broken English. "I hate 'Luke.'"

"Yeah, it's funny alright," Torresi said. "He needs a name that isn't so much from the old country. We think he looks like a Luke so we call him Luke."

"I don't think it's funny," I said. "I think a man should choose any name he wants."

Torresi laughed at this. "Yeah, well, you should know. What name are you using today?"

I grinned at him and took a bite of pastrami. A middle-aged waitress with a hairnet and blue eye shadow came over and asked the two men what they wanted. They both ordered coffee and pastrami sandwiches. I also ordered a cup of coffee.

"How's your hand?" Torresi asked Reina, nodding at the bandage.

"Don'ch worry," Reina said. His hard mountain eyes seemed to dilate as I looked at him.

"What happened?" I inquired.

Torresi chortled, "Vinnie was with us the other night. Go ahead and tell him what happened to your hand."

Reina just shook his head angrily and his eyes involuntarily flashed, revealing all that I suspected.

"Guy stepped on it," Torresi said. "When the bullets were flying he was hugging the ground so tight one of the other boys stumbled right over it."

"I tripped."

"Sure you did."

I finished eating my sandwich just as the waitress brought the coffees. She smacked her chewing gum loudly as she set the cups down carelessly in front of us. Some coffee from Torresi's cup spilled over the rim and formed a semi-circle on the Formica tabletop. She cursed softly and dabbed at it with a small, checkered towel that she then wadded and secured in her apron pouch. I watched as Torresi stared at her and sighed, but he didn't say anything while she was still within earshot of the table.

"*Puttana*," Reina muttered after she went away. "Her job is simple, and we get this?" His Sicilian accent was so heavy it took me a moment to process the meaning of his words after he spoke.

Torresi nodded and stirred sugar into his cup. "Relax. As long as it's hot, what do you care?"

I sipped my coffee. It wasn't as good as the Irishman's. I stirred in a little more sugar and milk and tried it again. It still wasn't as good. I drank it anyway.

"We should talk about the other night," Torresi said.

I nodded.

"You did good. Real good. That was some shooting – never seen anything like it. We got another run in two nights. Will you come?"

My grin felt plastered to my face. "We'll see."

"Yeah?"

"Yeah."

"Hmmm. What about tonight? I got some guys I want you to meet. We'll make it fun: have some drinks, some chuckles, meet a few girls – nice girls, you know, the kind you'd want to meet, the kind your mother would like you to bring home." He winked, just in case I didn't catch that he meant rather the opposite of his words.

I took another sip of coffee and thought about this for a moment. "Can't tonight."

"What do you mean you can't?"

"I mean I can't. I'm busy. I already have plans."

"With what?"

I gave him the look. "Things."

"I thought you wanted to work for us."

"Maybe I do."

"Maybe?"

"Maybe after last night I'm not so sure you're the ones I should be working for."

"Meaning what?"

"Meaning I might have other options."

"Huh, huh."

Reina's pupils grew larger and his face beamed stop-sign red. The toothpick had disappeared somewhere without my noticing it. If he'd been a large dog he might have growled. As it was, he didn't make a sound. He just stared at me and panted angrily. His eyes became glassy and more blood-shot and I thought for a moment he would lose control.

"Easy," Torresi said, with a hand on Reina's forearm. He was a master, calming an agitated hunting dog. Torresi took a moment to slurp some coffee. "You don't want to make Luke mad," he said to me with a straight face. "Come have a drink with us tonight."

"I don't want to make anybody mad, but I'm still busy tonight."

Torresi nodded and slurped more coffee, as if we were discussing our favorite fishing spots. He set the cup down hard though, spilling more coffee on the Formica, and a look of rare frustration was starting to form. "Okay, we'll talk with you again soon. We'll see how things sit then."

Reina continued to stare at me and then he blinked several times without swallowing.

I successfully resisted the urge to say, "Down, boy."

Torresi stood up and fished a couple of coins from his front right pocket, flicking his wrist from hip level. A nickel and a dime rolled across the counter and tipped over in the coffee spill area with a slight *kerplunk*. Reina scowled and pushed his chair back too harshly, hitting the empty chair behind him. Then the two men walked out in single file, with Reina going first and holding the door from outside long enough to accommodate an elderly couple walking in after Torresi had stepped out. They were just a couple of quiet thugs with troubles on their mind.

Through a wide, dirty window at the front of the diner I could see them standing on the pavement, conferring together for almost two minutes. The sun had sprung, at least momentarily, from behind a gossamer shroud of light cloud cover and the wind had picked up. Torresi cupped his hands around a match, lighting a large cigar and turned his body slightly away from the wind, so that he stared back at me through the window for as long as it took for the cigar to catch. Maybe it was just my imagination, but I shivered as I noted what seemed to be a puzzled and uncertain challenge in his expression as he watched me watching him.

That's when the waitress arrived with their hot pastrami sandwiches and a saucer of bread pickles.

Chapter Seven

Mrs. Giacalone whispered a short, formal grace and served dinner promptly at seven o'clock. There was a large pot-roast with gravy, new potatoes, carrots, celery and peppercorns in a pan on the table. The heavy metal lid of the pan rested behind her on a hand-carved wooden serving board. The scent of pepper, vinegar, and delicately cooked meat dominated the room and prompted the first hard pangs of hunger I could remember since the day I'd lost my partner a few weeks back.

With a metal ladle, Mrs. Giacalone put most of the food onto a plate that she handed to me and then carefully divided the remainder in half. She and I were drinking coffee. Tad had a small glass of buttermilk set before him, but he had not yet touched it, and the unsettled eyes he aimed at it periodically suggested he was in no hurry. I could sense the bitter, thick-curdled flavor from across the table and I didn't like it anymore than he did.

"You've found the room to your liking?" Mrs. Giacalone asked. She sat very straight in her chair with her hands folded in her lap and her head bowed slightly as though she were still saying another, more intimate grace that neither Tad nor I could detect. I watched her without speaking, searching myself for an appropriate sympathetic reaction.

"Yes, ma'am," I said at last. "It suits me fine. It's peaceful in the back. Thank you."

She nodded and looked up from her private trance with eyes that seemed to register little awareness that any words had been spoken. Without any change in her expression, she picked up a spoon and pointed it at her son. As if responding to a cue, Tad handed me a plate of fresh biscuits, still warm and emitting small puffs of steam. I took two, broke each in half, and covered them in butter and currant jam, allowing them to sit in the vinegar-laden pot roast gravy that pooled at the edges of my plate.

"You slept this afternoon," Mrs. Giacalone said with a vague hint of slight disapproval. Her eyes were focused again on the table and she looked at me, slowly, raising her chin. Small half-crescents swelled beneath each eye. She appeared fatigued, but her pupils were clear and direct as she studied me, waiting for my response.

It wasn't exactly a question that she had asked, but I nodded anyway. Tad did not look up from his plate, where he was swirling a slice of carrot slowly through the gravy in an ever-widening circle that would not hold as he got closer to the edge of the plate. At the last moment, just before gravy would have splattered over onto the table he paused, looked at his mother, and then quickly looked down again, lifting the carrot off the plate with his fork.

"I took a nap too," he said quietly as he brought the carrot up to his mouth. Gravy dripped on the tablecloth in small, dark brown dots that grew larger and somewhat faded as they bled into the cloth. He got the forkful of carrot into his mouth before it dripped gravy onto his pants and shirt too.

I nodded at Tad and started to eat.

"It was an early morning," Mrs. Giacalone said on my behalf, offering redemption with an apologetic smile that broke through the fatigue in her expression and in her voice.

"Yes, it often is, and I must go out later tonight," I replied. "I have work I must do."

She didn't say anything. The smile faded slowly like a sad, distant memory and she looked down at her own plate, suddenly concentrating on the food there. She cut small pieces that she then moved slowly up to her mouth, chewing them deliberately without looking up. I was hungry and the food was good. I ate with purpose, and cut my food with economy. I put each new bite into my mouth as soon as the last one was chewed and swallowed. We did not talk or look about at each other. We ate quietly for several minutes before Tad set his fork down and moved his chair back. He had eaten barely half his meal. More gravy had landed on the tablecloth, but his mother did not seem to notice.

He cleared his throat dramatically and asked in a grown-up voice, "Sir, what's your work?"

"Tad," Mrs. Giacalone said sharply. "Drink up your buttermilk."

"I was just asking."

"And pull your chair back to the table. You're not excused yet."

"I was just asking," he repeated in protest. He pulled his chair forward as he had been told to and rested his wrists on the edge of the table. His face was held tightly by a serious frown.

"It's okay," I said. "I don't mind. I'm in insurance."

Mrs. Giacalone looked at me, as if expecting more now that I had volunteered information, a faint hint of skepticism fronting the top of her brow. She brushed the hair back from her forehead with the back of her fingers and then set her fork down with the other hand. Her lips pursed and her hazel eyes, direct and tired, watched me patiently.

"I sell insurance."

"At night?" Tad asked.

"Some of my clients require meetings in the evenings."

"What kind of insurance?" he asked.

"Several kinds, mostly life and business guarantees."

"What's that?"

"Tad!"

"It's okay. A boy has a right to ask questions about the world."

"But we don't impose like that. Its not our business."

"No. I don't mind. The only way to learn about things is to ask. Insurance policies are a way to protect your family or your business in case something goes wrong. You buy a policy and then pay a little each year. In case you get sick or die, or have a fire. Lots of people have them."

"My dad was a policeman," Tad said solemnly.

I nodded.

"They shot him."

"Tad!"

"They did. They shot him."

"Mister Duncan, you must excuse my son. It's been less than a year."

"They shot him in the alley. He's dead." There was no trace of emotion on the child's face. He spoke the words with stoicism, as though he were describing a mundane event that had happened to someone he didn't know. "He died there."

I nodded. After a moment I said, "I'm sorry." But my words were for the lady of the house who now had silent tears on her cheeks, as she sat stiffly in her chair with her shoulders bunched towards her ears. A lock of hair had fallen down over her forehead.

Tad sighed and drank a small amount of buttermilk in concession, ambivalently ignoring his mother's silent pain. "Well," he said as he carefully set the glass of buttermilk down next to his plate, "they shot him, they did, and he's buried now. We went to his funeral and three men shot rifles into the air behind us and then a man played a song on a trumpet."

We finished the meal without any further words. As I scraped my plate with the last biscuit, Mrs. Giacalone poured out the coffee and cleared her throat: "Tad, you can go out to the yard."

As if chastised, the boy pushed his chair back from the table and left the room without looking at either of us. Mrs. Giacalone sat forward in her chair and leant on her elbows, with moist eyes softly looking off to a distant place behind me.

"He never cried," she said, "not even at the funeral."

I nodded. "I know. Sometimes they don't know how. He'll be okay."

"I worry about him so."

"Mrs. Giacalone, how can you not?"

"He's only nine years old, eight when his father died. I can see a difference in him, a change. He's my son. It breaks my heart to see him struggling with this."

"He'll be okay."

"You can't know that."

"No. I can't." My voice sounded small to me, almost as small as the meaning of the words themselves.

She brushed at the lock of hair over her forehead, without quite managing to push it back. Lines of weariness showed around her eyes as she sighed. "Last week was our anniversary. It would have been our tenth. We didn't wait long before having Tad. Sometimes I look back and I think that you just can't know. You think you can, but you can't. I thought I had my whole life before me, that my husband would always be there and together we'd watch Tad grow up, get married, and have children of his own. I thought we'd grow old together and always have each other, sit on the porch out back in the autumn and watch the leaves turn and live in the grace of the Lord. And now he's gone and my life is so different than what I expected … All I can do is pray and trust that there is a larger plan that has not yet been revealed to me."

I didn't know what to say, so I didn't say anything. Mrs. Giacalone stared off into her lost dreams. After a while of silence, she looked at me.

"Mister Duncan," she said, "I don't know what kind of insurance you're selling or who you're selling it to. I hope you'll carry the Lord's blessing with you tonight and that your efforts won't keep you out too late this evening or cause you to stray too, too far from the straight path of the Lord."

She lowered her sad eyes and sat in even sadder repose, ignoring the tears that continued to well there. My lips pursed in hesitation. An apparition that was probably Miss Charlotte glided across the floor at the periphery of my vision, and headed towards the kitchen. By the time I turned my head, she was gone from my sight and I wondered if she had been real or merely a figment of my imagination. I kept quiet and waited patiently.

Chapter Eight

Shortly before ten o'clock that night, down on Madison Street the air was heavy with moisture and the scent of gasoline fumes. It was misting lightly and heavy raindrops occasionally fell around me, splattering the street that was slick with oil. Flickering headlamps from moving cars and streetlights reflected off the shiny surface, which created an atmospheric glow of slow motion sparkle and despair.

I entered The Nightingale Club through a side door from an alley that bent around and cut through to State Street. The goon who opened the door for me must have been 6' 5", and 325 pounds, with the shoulders of a stevedore. He had a scar across his forehead and one of his eyes drifted off to the left. He bit his lip as he stared at me.

"I know you," he said with an Irish accent, as he stepped back from the doorway to allow me room to pass. A shadow closed behind me and the door clicked. "They said you looked like Dillinger. I don't see it."

I grinned at him and shook the water off my umbrella. "Brother, it's the nicest thing anyone's said to me all day."

"Well, you don't."

I slotted the umbrella into a bin beside the door and offered him a Chesterfield. I took one myself and lit it with a match.

"My mother doesn't think so either," I told him.

He lit his cigarette off the last of my match and stood smoking, almost thoughtfully, with his eyes focused somewhere in the past. "My mother died back in '26," he said. "She never got to see the Exposition, she would have loved it."

"Tough losing a mother."

"They're the only ones who really love you."

"And sometimes not even them."

The big man nodded and took a long drag from his cigarette. He didn't say anything, but just stared at me through the smoke with eyes that were softer than they should have been given his line of work. I didn't speak either. I hadn't expected to find myself in a sentimental conversation with a thug. He took another drag and dropped the butt on the floor, mashing it beneath his foot.

"Come on," he said then. His voice was hoarse. "You probably didn't come here to see me get all wobbly. The Irishman's this way."

I followed him down the dark hallway, up a half-flight of stairs, down another hallway, through two right turns, and then down another half-flight of stairs. From somewhere ahead of us came the advancing sounds of live music and people having fun, very expensive fun.

An elevator took us to the seventeenth floor. The hallway was library-quiet and strewn with expensive narrow oriental rugs in a variety of colors and designs. Hand-fitted wooden panels lined the walls and each heavy door we passed was surrounded by elaborate molding and fitted with a shiny brass knocker, handle, and hallway lamp with a low wattage bulb. Most, but not all, of the doors were unnumbered. Some had a small white ivory plaque with a name painted on it in a blue flourish.

The small shuffles of our footsteps were nearly absorbed by the oriental rugs. They registered no more than a slight padding sound as we moved. The watery murk of the street seemed suddenly remote and distant. Without speaking, we walked a remarkably long way before we stopped at an unmarked door that had a delicate, narrow nightstand of polished cherry-wood set up next to it. A single yellow rose bloomed from an expensive crystal vase that was centered on the flat surface of the nightstand. Even in the dull light of the corridor, the hard angles of the vase twinkled undeniably and cradled the simple petals of the flower.

The thug nodded at the door, then at me. "When you're done," he said "just take the elevator to the third floor. If you want a drink, if you want a girl, try the fifth floor. Thanks for the cigarette."

He knocked once on the door and then turned the brass handle.

*

I was let into an interior room that had an extremely heavy door, no windows, and a second door on the other side of the room, opposite where I entered. Like the hallway, only more so, the entire room was covered in dark hand-fitted panels of walnut veneer with intricate molding at every angle and joint along the ceiling and around the doors. The quality of the wood and the workmanship clearly exceeded that of the hallway décor. A large, heavy desk that complemented the walnut theme dominated one half of the room, and a group of over-sized dark brown leather wing-backed chairs dominated the other. In one corner a small dry sink cabinet, with a row of partially concealed crystal bottles, offered the promise of fine whiskey, brandy, or decanted red wine. Above it all, two wide gold chandeliers hung down lower than they should have, spreading a sickly soft yellow haze from low wattage bulbs. A crystal vase, identical to the one in the hallway held another single yellow rose on one corner of the desk. There was little else in the room to suggest human presence. The expansive desktop was otherwise bare – there were no small tables, photographs, paintings, books, or any of the other touches that someone might furnish an office with.

The Irishman was already standing in his formal pose, with his chin tilted upwards, when I stepped through the door. He wore a black tuxedo with a black silk bowtie, a heavy white silk shirt, and pearl cufflinks that seemed to shine an odd pink in the dull light of the room. He raised a hand to the side of his face and dramatically swept it over the back of his neck and then back down over his cheek and mouth. In an effort to make a welcoming gesture, he took two small steps toward me and gave a slight bow. His manner was formal, stiff even, but without a single element of any real grace.

Another man was present in the room. He remained seated in one of the leather wingbacks, with an ankle crossed over his knee. He also wore a black tuxedo and a black silk bowtie, but in a casual and offhand manner. His top button was undone.

"Mr. Duncan," the Irishman said, commanding my attention, "cheers and welcome." He gave me a tight and soulless smile, with thin pale lips, and then extended his open hand towards me with the palm turned up. I shook it and then followed his gesture as he half-turned towards the other man. "This is Mr. Eugene Robinson. I believe you met the other day at Antonio's. Although he's not Irish, Eugene is one of my most trusted confidantes; he handles our toughest situations."

Robinson stood up quickly, with a startling economy of motion, and shook my hand. I guessed he was probably in his early forties, but I could have been off by ten years in either direction. His hair had a faint reddish tint and was clipped extremely short above the ears. He had no facial hair – not even beard stubble or sideburns. He did not smile or speak. If he was surprised to see me, he didn't show it. His pale-gray eyes were relaxed, and yet conveyed no emotion whatsoever. To look into his eyes was to drop a small stone into a well a mile-deep, empty and black.

"I remember," I said.

Robinson nodded courteously, without speaking. Somehow, without smiling, he managed to show me his perfect teeth again. I couldn't be sure, but I wondered if it was meant to ensure I fully recalled our first meeting.

The Irishman nodded to himself, as if pleased that Robinson and I had finally been formally introduced. "Please sit," he said as his open hand gestured towards one of the wingbacks. "Can I offer you a drink, Mr. Duncan? Perhaps something a little stronger than what we shared this morning?"

I sat in the offered chair. "It would be tough to beat that Egyptian coffee."

"How about a sniff of some genuine Irish whiskey, Laddie?"

That caught my attention. "I don't mind."

The Irishman went over to the corner dry sink, paused for a moment, and surveyed the bottles stored there. Then he selected one and poured a couple of fingers into a short crystal tumbler. He came over, handed me the glass, and then returned to the corner where he poured one for himself. Robinson wasn't drinking anything, nothing was offered to him.

"How are you enjoying our Windy City spring so far?" the Irishman asked me when he was seated with his drink. He smiled without warmth and sipped his whiskey. I looked at mine and admired the dark amber of the liquid in the pale yellow light of the room. The glass felt solid and heavy in my hand. I took a pull and nodded with satisfaction as a small, blessed, pagan warmth spread within my chest and then passed on down. I took another, larger swallow.

"It's very good," I said, as I nodded slightly towards the glass so that he would know I was not referring to the Windy City spring.

"And you enjoy the city too?"

"It's only my fourth day in town. We'll see."

"Visitors to our city sometimes struggle with the cold, wet air this time of year and the harsh wind that drives right through their clothing. You have to be careful not to catch a chill, which would be very bad for your health. We knew a man, Eugene and I, several years ago that went about on a spring night in this city without an adequate coat to ward off the air. In fact, he went for a dip in the lake, tempted by the romantic notion that a springtime bathe in the cool waters under starlight would be healing. Afterwards, he drank three hot-toddies in a row that his wife had brought up to their hotel room, in a futile effort to ward off the chill that had set in. Within a week they were placing orders from my shop to decorate his casket for the train ride home."

He hesitated, as if to reflect, and while he was doing so, sipped his whiskey.

"One thing that confronts you in my business, Laddie," he continued, "is the strange and myriad ways that people manage to die, especially here in Chicago. I do hope you'll be careful while you're in our town. Have you had a chance to consider my business proposition?"

I held out an open palm. "I'm still not sure just what it is, yet."

"I want you to work for me in the business that I have to do."

"Now we're getting someplace. What is the business?"

"Making vast sums of money for myself and all of my associates."

"Meaning what, specifically, for me?"

He sniffed at his whiskey and considered my question. "There are several possible configurations, starting with a retainer arrangement. I could pay you three hundred a week for exclusive rights to your services, barring, of course, any freelance banking business you care to conduct strictly for yourself as long as that business does not take place within certain areas of this town."

"In other words, three hundred to me so that I don't work for your competitors, and I can rob all the banks I want so long as they're not in your territory?"

"That is correct."

"What else?"

"In addition to the three hundred, I think we could promise you plenty of additional contractual opportunities."

"Such as?"

"Use your imagination."

"No, spell it for me."

"We often have need of security work – for our trucks, our establishment here, my own person."

"You mean bodyguard duties?"

"I don't wish to seem immodest, but there are people who think their chances at making a fortune would improve if I were not in competition with them. That pays a hundred a day."

I shook my head. "I don't get out of bed unless a job offers promise of at least two grand. What else have you got?"

"There is one particular inconvenience you might handle for us?"

"What is it?"

"Not what, but whom. His name is Vincent Reina. Do you know him?"

I did not so much as blink.

"It would be of considerable assistance to our endeavors if Mr. Reina were to disappear. That job would pay enough to get you out of bed."

I drank more Irish whisky. "What's the point of acing Reina?"

"The point is we need it done, simply that."

"Murder is never simple."

"Yes, Mr. Duncan, in Chicago it usually is."

"I don't follow. He's dumb muscle. You don't need expensive independents for that."

The Irishman sat quietly and stared down as though contemplating the whiskey in his glass. He frowned. He then took a small sip from his glass, but his frown did not dissipate. When he spoke again his voice was soft and highly controlled. "I believe that some of our Italian friends are enjoying themselves downstairs tonight. A celebration of sorts, it appears to be – maybe a recent success, or maybe a farewell to one of theirs. Maybe they would welcome you at their table?"

"Maybe they would."

"Why not join them? You can give my most sincere regards to Mr. Reina if you should see him."

I swallowed the last of the whisky and sat with my head inclined upwards for a moment, savoring the final bit of Irish heat in the back of my throat. Then I stood up and crossed the room to the dry sink. I could hear the ticking of a clock from somewhere.

"Can I offer you more whiskey?" the Irishman asked patiently. "You may help yourself."

I shook my head and set the empty crystal glass on the board, gently so it wouldn't clink. "No thank you," I told him as I turned to face him. I stared into the vast, dark expanse of his unblinking eyes.

"I will need your answer," he said, pausing to stand up slowly, "within three days."

I nodded. Robinson stood too and looked at me without expression. He had not said a word during my entire visit.

As I was opening the door, the Irishman cleared his throat. The abrupt noise was harsh and seemed to echo in the confined space of the windowless library. "And Laddie, if Reina is still around after three days, I'll have my answer. Cheers."

I walked out of the room without response and allowed the door to shut hard behind me. Before I started down the long narrow hallway, I pulled the yellow rose from its vase on the hallway table and brought it up to my nose.

In the elevator I told the attendant to take me to the third floor.

Chapter Nine

I skirted the dance floor and the shrieks of the trumpets, and made my way to Torresi's table at the back of the room. With a half-arc underhand toss, I threw the yellow rose onto the middle of the table to announce myself. Several broad heads turned to look at me.

"Thought you were busy tonight," Torresi said loudly, above the music. Wearing a hard rubber smile, he stood up and shook my hand. "Sit and have a Martini with me and my boys. We wouldn't have a reason to celebrate if it wasn't for you anyway."

"Thanks," I said, pulling a chair out. There were three other men at the table, Vincent Reina and two others that I had never seen before and did not recognize. From the way they sat with their eyes glued, I assumed they answered to Torresi.

Reina wore the same wrinkled white shirt and a black, checkered jacket. Both were hopelessly too small for him, and it looked as if they were borrowed last minute from a smaller friend. The top button of his shirt was undone and his ample chin hung aggressively out over the collar. By necessity, his tie was loosened several inches to accommodate his fat neck. The jacket was too tight in the shoulders. It restricted his ability to move and when he stretched an arm out to reach for his drink the sleeve came far short of his wrist.

I grinned at him. "Hi'ya, Luke," I said to Reina.

He glared at me awkwardly, but didn't say anything. I shot him the gunner's salute and he glared harder.

"This is Marty Williamson and Albert Russo," Toressi said, indicating the two others with a casual wave.

"Jeez, it's good to meet you," Williamson said, leaning across the table to shake my hand without standing up.

"Marty's a Councilman," Torresi said. "A protégé of Big Bill. If you ever need a garbage license or a zoning variance in Cicero, he's the man to see."

"Swell," I said.

Russo was a hawk-faced man with deeply set eyes, thick, black eyebrows, yellowing skin, and a chipped front tooth. He merely nodded at me. He made no effort to shake my hand or show any sign that he knew who I was. His expression was one of displeasure, but I had no reason to think that it had anything to do with me. It seemed to be habitual and was accentuated by dark rings beneath his recessed eyes. He wore a well-tailored silk suit and his hair was carelessly combed straight back, held in place with too much grease. He was of medium build, with a bit of a slouch to his shoulders as he sat, leaning over an empty drink with his elbows on the table.

From somewhere behind me a waiter appeared with a Martini. He set it down in front of me on top of a lace napkin. I looked at it for a moment. It was perfect: clear and cold as crystal. With my thumb and forefinger balanced on either side of the rim and my little finger steadying the stem, I picked it up and took a small sip. Perfection indeed. I took another sip and allowed the civilized warmth to slide down into my chest. I replaced the cocktail on the lace, exhaled, and flicked the lemon twist away with my trigger-finger.

"It's a great band," Williamson shouted from across the table. "They came in from New York two nights ago, and they tear the place down! You won't hear anything like this at the Aragon Ballroom!" As if to underscore this point, trombones made their entrance and the entire brass section stood up. Dancers with white fringe hanging above their knees scurried frantically across the stage and a man in a top hat, seated behind a piano, waved a baton above his head.

The music was too loud to encourage casual conversation, so we sat without speaking for several minutes. The band played louder as the drummer increased the pace to a high-minded frenzy. I lit a cigarette and took another sip of the Martini, deploring the finite reality of an ounce of gin. Torresi made a gesture to someone behind me and, a few moments, later two waiters arrived with two Martini cocktails and two fresh lace napkins apiece. Without any appearance of motion, the empty glasses were cleared, the ashtrays replaced, and the waiters withdrew. They left the yellow rose as it was, centered in the middle of the table. We toasted each other with our fresh drinks and I noticed that Russo wore a large emerald ring on his little finger. It glittered wickedly as he finished his Martini in a single swallow and then chewed the lemon twist aggressively between his back teeth.

"The colored musicians go up to the roof to smoke reefer," Torresi said to me when the band took their break. My ears were ringing and his words seemed to echo. I took a long drag off a cigarette and held the smoke deep in my lungs while I crushed out the cigarette in an ashtray. After I finished that semi-destructive act, I exhaled rapidly.

"Probably like to look at the stars," I said.

"No stars tonight, it's a drenching rain. But you can't have them smoking reefer in the house, now can you?"

"No," I said. "You couldn't. Can't have illegal activity going on *in* the house."

"They all seem to do it – reefer and cocaine – to sleep with hallucinogenic dreams. Part of being colored, maybe."

"Or maybe just part of being a colored musician in a jazz world financially dominated by Italian and Irish gangsters."

Torresi laughed. "Maybe so. Did I mention Mr. Williamson is a Councilman? He's been one of Big Bill's boys."

Williamson grinned at me and nodded his head rapidly.

I nodded too. "Yeah, you mentioned it. I'll remember in case I ever need a variance."

"He's gracious enough to help us out from time to time. Plus, he loves colored music."

Williamson was still grinning, still nodding.

"Maybe he can help you with that problem you have with the special prosecutor," Toressi told me.

"Thought O'Farrell was your problem," I replied.

Torresi shrugged. "Our problem, your problem, what's the difference? We're all friends here, right? Friends help friends. Our problem is your problem, and vice versa. And we can help you with that other thing. Help us out, we'll make sure nobody – at least nobody official – bothers you while you're in our town."

I shrugged back and lit another cigarette. I dropped the match into the ashtray, and held the cigarette away from my face with my knuckles on the table before me. Smoke drifted silently, lazily up towards the bright track lights in the ceiling. Torresi made a gesture with his hand and, a moment later, four more Martinis arrived.

I took a sip of mine. Like the others, it was ice cold. "How can you help me with that other thing?" I asked seriously.

"You know, a little this, a little that. It's a big town, plenty of room, plenty of ways to disappear, plenty of cash to go around. Nobody has to bother you."

"Sort of like a variance, huh?"

Torresi grinned, but his heart wasn't in it. His lip quivered and the skin at his neck hung in loose creases as he pulled his head back from the table. "Didn't expect a public enemy desperado to have such a smart mouth."

I let the smoke ease from my nostrils and looked away without response. Williamson was eager to get into the conversation, and rapped his knuckle on the table several times, so we all looked at him. "I know O'Farrell," he said into the opening.

It was a stupid remark and nobody knew how to respond. Russo did not even look at him or acknowledge he had spoken in any way.

"He's a horse's ass," Williamson continued, "and he's floating in Irish green, probably sitting up there in his office right now as we speak."

Torresi nodded patiently. "Marty, why don't you go up to the roof and introduce yourself to the coloreds, it'll make 'em feel important." He looked at Reina.

"I take you, Mr. Williamson," Reina said, as if on cue.

"But won't the Irish mind?"

"Naw, not at all. They don't like us, but they want us to enjoy ourselves while we're here. They come to our joints, why shouldn't we come to theirs? Just don't smoke any of the funny stuff while you're up there. It'll make you stupid."

Williamson stood up, with just a hint of awareness showing at the corners of his narrow eyes. "Sure thing, but don't forget what I said about O'Farrell."

After they left, neither Torresi nor myself said anything for a good while. For all his participation in the conversation, Russo could have been sitting at another table. Leaning back in his chair with his legs out, he fidgeted minutely and absently fingered the bright ring he wore while he stared off at a forty-five degree angle, away from the center of the table where we sat. I couldn't tell what he was looking at or what he was thinking about.

Torresi allowed an unlit cigarette to hang from the side of his mouth. He played with a lighter without striking it. "Sorry about that," he said after a while. He put the lighter in his pocket and removed the cigarette from his mouth. "He's a bit dull, but he's been useful to us. And he doesn't even know who you are."

"Sure, surround yourself with morons, what do I care?"

"Yeah, but we really do need to do something about O'Farrell. You might worry too because he will know who you are, if the Irishman tells him you're in town."

I glanced over at Russo, who still gave no indication he was paying any attention to our conversation. "And it might square us with the Alvarini bump," I said, aware there was an edge to my voice, "if you still think I had a hand in that."

Torresi sighed. "Don't get sore. There's cash in it for you too."

"Never liked ultimatums."

"Never liked making them. This comes from above me, way above, if you catch my meaning. Let's take a drive and talk about it."

"Sorry." I stood up. "I came here to look for someone."

"The whores are a floor up."

"She's not a whore."

"She'd be the rare one, then."

I squinted at him and moved away from the table.

*

The band was still on break, but a solo pianist had decided we needed to hear one by Hoagy Carmichael. I stood at the bar near a big decorative jar of brandied cherries and placed a ten dollar bill on the counter, holding my hand over half of it. A barman quickly moved towards me. He wore a tuxedo and had a thick, dark mustache with a lot of wax in it. His eyes didn't seem to see anything in particular.

"What'll it be, sir?"

"A woman."

"You have to go upstairs for that," he replied without expression or judgment.

"No, I'm looking for a specific woman. I hear she finds her kicks down here, likes to dance."

"She have a name, this woman?"

"Elinore."

"That's funny. I know a woman named Elinore."

"Yeah, thought you might." I pushed the bill forward and lifted my hand off it.

"In fact, this Elinore is usually called Miss Rollings by most people because her man speaks with a thick Irish accent and most people wouldn't want to be on the wrong side of his very Irish temper."

"Let me be the one to worry about that. Just point your thick nose in her direction."

He stared at me for a moment and then his eyes led his nose off past my right shoulder. When I glanced down at the bar I realized the ten had disappeared and the barman was already shaking a Martini for someone else.

*

I saw her as soon as I turned around. She stood at the bar too, just four feet away from me, holding a glass of champagne to her cheek with her elbow propped against the back of her opposite hand. Her hair was jet-black and worn short with tight curls. It glistened under the chandelier light as though it was still wet. A light blue silk dress rippled easily at the lowest point of cleavage, clung neatly to her hips, and then stopped just north of her knees. She swayed to the music with her eyes closed and appeared to be mouthing the words to the song. I couldn't hear a voice, but her lips formed the words: "… the melody haunts my reverie, and I am once again with you …"

I moved towards her and then watched her for a while with my elbow on the bar, unable to suppress the ungainly smile I felt forming. She turned her head towards me, then away and quickly back again as she noticed me. Her curls bounced stylishly.

"What?" she asked abruptly, no longer working the lyrics.

"… and now my consolation is in the stardust of a song…" I continued for her softly, picking up where she left off.

"Hey, beat it. I already have a boyfriend."

"Sure you do."

"He's Irish and he owns this club."

I looked around and then over my shoulder. There was nobody there who meant anything to me. She just stared at me with those painted eyes, waiting without impatience. The piano continued its sweet ballad and the song lyrics carried on, though if only in my head.

"Yeah," I said, leaning closer towards her. "I know the Irishman."

"Well then," she said, but her defiance had lessened.

"So, where is he now?"

"He's busy, upstairs. Probably counting his money, he's very rich. But he has friends who are watching to make sure I have a good time, and to make sure nobody bothers me."

"Yeah? Where are they?"

"Who are you?"

"You know me. Don't you remember?"

"Sure, sure I do. I've known a hundred Joes like you." Her words were contemptuous, but her tone was softening. Her veil of confidence had slipped as she studied my face. I said nothing. The pianist played on, riffling through an improvised bridge between choruses. "Maybe, just maybe," she told me, relenting, "you do look familiar in a long-ago, far-away, not-sure-I-give-a-damn sort of fashion. Who are you and what do you want with me?"

"You knew me when I had fewer lines around my eyes."

With her nose crinkled slightly, she leaned closer to me so that the gap between us could be measured in inches. I sensed her breath on my face as she looked up at me. "Yeah," she said, "and less heartache in your soul. Where do I know you from?"

"The old neighborhood."

"I'm not from around here."

"Neither am I. We're both from Minneapolis."

"You must be thinking of somebody else, I'm from New York."

"You and every other kiddo with stars in her eyes."

"That's not me, Mister."

"Sure, sure it is. I know you. You came for a star."

"All the stars here have fallen already. Where do I know you from?"

With a quiet flourish of an ascending modal scale that finished off hanging in space, the song ended and the piano went silent. Our repartee continued in a near whisper now. "I told you: the old neighborhood, the Twin Cities, down on Hennepin Avenue. I used to run with your brother. We played sandlot ball and boosted jalopies together."

"My brother. You knew Colt?"

I nodded. Then it struck her and she knew who I was. Her eyes opened wide and she brought the champagne glass quickly up to her mouth to cover and swallowed twice in rapid succession. A thousand years worth of tormented dreams passed across her eyes, and flickered like so many disrupted movie stills. The past and the present came together in an instant, and with too much sudden clarity. She caught at her breath and leaned back against the bar suddenly, letting her hand drop down to her waist, still clutching the glass. I took it gently from her hand and set it on the wide counter behind her, pushing it back from the edge a good ways. Then I steadied her with a hand on her shoulder. She leaned into it.

"Remember?" I asked, knowing with certainty that she did.

She nodded, still leaning against my hand and the bar. "I remember. We thought … Colt thought the world of you."

"It was mutual. I looked up to him. Looked up to him like a …"

Elinore's eyes were sad and bright, shining in the glittering light of the room that was shrinking dramatically around us. "Like a big brother," she said quietly. "That's two of us."

I nodded.

"Were you there?"

I raised my chin, immediately understanding the question for what it was. "Yes, I was."

"Let's get out of here," she said as she pushed off from the bar with her hand on my forearm, pulling down on it slowly.

"What about your boyfriend's friends, the ones who are supposed to be watching to make sure you have a good time, and make sure nobody bothers you?"

She shrugged and shook her head. "Maybe I was kidding about that, maybe sometimes I like to go out on my own without any babysitters."

Her lips were large and wide, exuding a contrasting sense of undiminished innocence and fear. Hammers pounded in my gut and I sucked in my breath. After a moment, I nodded my head and gazed past the now empty table where Gino Torresi and Albert Russo had been sitting minutes ago.

Chapter Ten

In the dim light of the taxi, she leaned against me and I noticed that her perfume carried the scent of ripe plums. We headed out towards the West Madison district, away from the empty glamour of The Loop, with street shadows rippling over us as we accelerated. Silence rode with us for a long time. Only the street sounds and a low tune hummed by the driver kept us company in the darkness of the rear seat.

Elinore got a cigarette going and smoked absently without lifting her head from my shoulder. We crossed over Desplaines and then Halsted Street, moving with the flow of traffic, jockeying in the fast lane with the other late-nighters moving to unheard rhythms, gliding toward those sad two a.m. destinations that could never provide the kind of satisfaction anyone sought at that bleak hour. Time washed over us like so many unfinished heartbreak songs. When it seemed like neither of us would ever breathe again, I cracked the window an inch. Cool air rushed in and filled our lungs.

"We've come a long way from Hennepin Avenue," Elinore said finally, as she brought the cigarette back to her lips for a final drag, shielding it from the breeze with the cup of her hand.

"Yes, perhaps too far."

She exhaled smoke slowly in a blue stream that quickly dissipated in the rush of air that came through the window. "It seems like another life, a life that somebody else lived, so long ago, so far away. So distant in every way that matters."

"Is it really all that?"

"Yes. All that and more, much more. And you know it too, don't kid yourself."

"Isn't it painful to think so."

"I was a child last time I saw you." She lifted her head from my shoulder to look up at me in the dappled light of the back seat. "What do you think?"

"I think you're not a child anymore."

A smile spread slowly until her white teeth gleamed for just a brief moment. "No, I suppose not," she said as the smile faded.

"But it's not what you meant," I said.

She shook her head and looked away from me, towards the lights and the harsh angles that flashed past us on the street. A siren wailed from somewhere far ahead of us.

"You're beautiful," I said simply into the darkness.

"Utterly?"

"Yes, utterly," I told her, knowing it was easily true.

Elinore leaned back in the seat and then tilted her head onto my shoulder. Without having noticed the movement, I realized that her hand now tightly held onto my arm. She squeezed it more firmly each time the cab rocked sideways on the hard street. I didn't complain. I rolled the window back up. There was a large blanket of quiet around us again.

"When I was a twelve," she said after a while, "I was in love with you. I used to dream that we were married and lived in a beautiful mansion that we shared with Colt. He played baseball, you played the trumpet, and I was a dancer. We were rich and dressed in silk, surrounded by servants, and fine wines, and lots and lots of shiny, expensive, well-cut jewels. We had a big Packard and a driver who took us out on Sundays and showed us around the town. Every spring, we took a train to San Francisco for three weeks and stayed at the Fairmont Hotel. At night, we walked down the hill into the fog, holding hands, and listened for the steamers that we couldn't see blowing their horns out in the bay."

"A child's dream," I told her.

She nodded and spoke with little emotion in her voice. "It was a sentimental dream anyway. You never noticed me, not really anyway. I felt invisible when you came around. You didn't even say hello to me most of the time."

"You were a child and you were Colt's little sister."

"When you were in Joliet prison that first time, I wrote you letters."

"I never received them."

"I never sent them."

I was quiet.

"I know I'm acting like a silly girl now, but won't you just take my hand for a moment."

Slowly I reached over and squeezed her hand in mine. It was small, soft, and delicate in a way that I had not expected. I pulled it towards me and held it in my lap with both of my hands. Together we relished the tender darkness that we shared.

"Do you know where we're going?" Elinore asked me at last, breaking a long and gathering silence. The driver still hummed that familiar tune that I couldn't quite recognize.

"No," I replied.

"I know a place. It's quiet, dark enough that no one will notice us, and we can get a decent bottle of wine there. You can explain why you've found me now after all these years."

I nodded my assent and she spoke a few words to the driver. The cab slowed at the next corner and we turned left at Crawford Avenue. A few moments later we turned left again and accelerated down a slender avenue without many lights.

The cab let us out in the middle of a quiet residential neighborhood, in front of an old two-story brownstone that did not carry any commercial markings on the outside. It had double-width bay front windows that bent out over the street. A black wrought iron handrail led up to matching latticework around the door. We went up to the second floor where a small late-night supper club operated.

At a private table in what had once been a small back guest bedroom, we ordered pork chops, broiled tomatoes, and a bottle of white chianti. I sat so that I was facing the door. From the window we could see out over a small yard with a barren garden, partially illuminated by a streetlamp from the alley beyond. Strings of shadows lay across the leafless trees and nestled into a bank of long, brown, dead grass that ran along the side of an old carriage house. It looked like a still life oil painting from the late nineteenth century that had been done in dark colors – mostly grays and charcoals – with just a hint of yellow and beige.

Elinore leaned close to me in the dim candlelight, and looked at me from across a narrow table. In the light her face appeared artificially pale, and her eyes and lips were darker than they would otherwise have been. "Last summer – the last time I saw Colt – we talked about you."

"There could not have been much to say."

"He thought his time was running out, but he thought maybe there was just about hope for you. I don't know why, he must have sensed what would happen. He said, 'You can't buck the odds forever, at some point they'll catch up with you'. His eyes were so distant, even then. I remember wondering if maybe he was sick. Now, here we are, sitting together like this. It's been so long. I never expected to see you again. When did you arrive?"

"Four days ago."

She took a sip of her wine and considered my response, nodding slowly as her eyes focused. "I didn't sense you were here. Not that I should have, but in that old sentimental dream of mine, I would have, I would have sensed your presence nearby. How long will you stay?"

"I can't stay long."

"You can't stay anywhere long, can you?"

I shook my head. "Not for a little while."

"And maybe not ever – you're just that hot. What name are you using?"

I let my shoulders drop. "Duncan," I said and shrugged again.

She nodded as if in approval and took another sip of wine. I waited in silence for the next question.

"Are you fixed? Do you have a place to stay?"

"Yes."

"Is it comfortable? Safe?"

I nodded.

"I hate to think of you in some seedy, second-rate hotel, some place where the bugs and winos and the prostitutes are your only company."

"Sure, but I'm renting a room in a two-story house with elm trees in the front yard. It's clean living. There's a cat named Miss Charlotte who comes into my room late in the night and sleeps at the foot of my bed. In the morning, I wake to the sound of birds twittering in the branches outside my bedroom window. The landlady is a pious widow. She serves home-cooked meals every night and we eat together with her nine-year old son after she says a quiet grace with her head bowed, like we used to pray in Sunday school. There's nothing seedy about it – no wine, women, or song. A monk could live there." It was only partial invention.

Elinore smiled again, sadly, but with genuine warmth. When she spoke, her voice was soft and reed-like. "You're half kidding, but that sounds much, much better. Don't tell me where. But at least now I won't worry."

I remained silent, noncommittal, and then sat back in my chair as the waitress brought our pork chops. She served us without speaking, using a large wooden spoon and a salad fork, and then quickly left, stepping out into the hallway and then down the stairs. A soft vibration resonated within the room after she left, possibly from her footsteps or a generator in another part of the house. An electric light mounted on the wall over the door flickered briefly then remained steady. The room was warm. I wanted to take off my jacket, but with the shoulder holster and the .45 semi-automatic, I didn't dare. It was late and I realized that I was suddenly very tired.

"Why are you here?" Elinore asked. "Chicago can't be the best town for someone in your line of work."

"It's not a bad place for me, at least it should hold me alright for a few weeks."

"But why did you come?"

"I came for you."

Looking down at her plate, Elinore nodded as if that was the answer she expected from me. I picked up my fork. We ate without speaking for several minutes. The tired waitress came back to check on us and refilled our wine glasses. Moving without energy she stifled a yawn and backed away from our table and went out into the hallway. Once more the floor vibrated slightly and the light over the door flickered again, then held steady.

"Can you tell me about it now?" Elinore asked the question casually, but I knew what she meant. She was asking about her brother's death.

"No," I said. "Not tonight. I'm too tired and it's too late. This isn't something we just do like that. It's not easy to talk about."

"No?"

"No. I have something for you, but I didn't bring it with me. Next time."

"But you will tell me?"

"Yes."

"When?"

"Next time."

"You'll see me again," she said in her smallest voice. It was not a question and she did not ask what I had for her. I simply nodded in agreement.

Later, when the meal was over, I arranged my fork and knife on the empty plate so the waitress would know I was finished. Then I sat back in my chair and watched the small changes of expression that shaded her eyes as she looked back at me.

We finished the wine and then had black coffee that was served in true white china and came with a small plate of tiny almond cookies. After I paid the bill we walked three blocks to her apartment. Halfway there she took my arm and leaned against me as we walked. There was no traffic on the street and most of the lights in the houses we passed were out now. When we got to her building we stood together on the top step. The night air was cold and still.

"What about the Irishman?" I asked, looking down into her eyes.

Elinore pursed her lips. "Well," she said and then paused and tilted her head back to look at the sky that stretched quietly over us just beyond the ambient city lights. "He's not likely to be the understanding type."

"Are you really seeing him?" I asked.

She let out a slow breath and drew her shoulders in with resignation. Her eyes avoided mine. "A girl's got to eat," she said.

I felt her body sway gently away from me. The movement was subtle but unmistakable. "You don't have to explain."

"He's not such a bad fella, anyway."

"Nobody said he was."

"He knows how to have a good laugh, how to treat a lady, and he always sends roses, lots of roses. That's something these days."

"Of course." I put my hand on her upper arm, and caressed it through the jacket from the shoulder all the way down to the elbow as slowly and gently as I possibly could. "What I meant was: how easy is it going to be for me to see you again?"

"That's not quite what your words said."

"Let's pretend it's what I meant."

Elinore looked at me now. There was no hesitation in her eyes, and she half-smiled with her lips parted slightly. "Yes, let's pretend. He doesn't own me. I can see you again. We can pretend lots of things … only, we just need to be a little careful about it is all."

"I can be careful."

"What about the law?"

"What about the law?"

"There's a lot of people with badges who would like to find you, and I don't think they'd be too gentle about it. They'll shoot you if they get the chance."

I shook my head.

"Please don't let them shoot you down."

"Nobody ever has."

*

"I should go," I said.

"If you walk a few blocks in that direction, you'll come to some hotels or the Paradise Ballroom. You'll be able to catch a cab there … Good night."

With a small step forward, she moved against my body and leaned her head on my shoulder. Her arms hung limply down at her sides. I put my arms around her and pulled her towards me, holding her tightly with one hand on the back of her head.

"Do you want to kiss me?" she asked, lifting her head from my shoulder to look up at me. Both of her hands were lightly on my hips now and I could feel her weight against me.

"Maybe I won't tonight."

"They got my brother, Colt. Don't let them get you too, Mr. Duncan."

I left her on the steps and turned around towards the halos of the street lamps without looking back over my shoulder.

Chapter Eleven

Shadows floated darkly across the ceiling and wall above my head in changing patterns and at crooked angles, pushed by the headlights of occasional traffic and the slow arc of a one-quarter moon that dangled low in the sky and then disappeared completely as the morning began to break. At first light I was still awake, lying on my back, looking out the open window through the leafless branches of the trees. Elinore's ripe-plum scent lingered in my awareness and, like the bright torment of a rainbow, it haunted me with the promise of its ephemeral nature, as did so many other hard illusions in life.

Sleep had evaded me again, and then I dreamed I was dreaming and in that dream I lay awake in bed, unable to sleep for hours, as images of bullets and violent death, glittering riches, and quiet stolen moments sifted through that dream of a dream. There was Colt and his beautiful sister Elinore, and Colt's death scene played repeatedly for us all to watch, over and over in a vast mirror with gilt edges, until Elinore screamed and the mirror cracked apart and crumbled into a thousand brilliant shards. And then I awoke, startled and shivering. My eyelids were wet. Miss Charlotte was hunkered down at the foot of the bed, watching me with inscrutable bright eyes, as if she had seen the dreams I'd seen but was indifferent to them.

The early morning spring air was cold. The window was open and I pulled the blanket up to cover my chest. Yet, I was sweating heavily and the pillow was wet where my face had been. I couldn't tell how much of the dampness was caused by sweat, and how much was caused by my cold tears.

The sounds of small birds chirping and whistling calmly came in with the cold air. I lit a Chesterfield and thought about Colt while I smoked, taking the tobacco deep into my lungs.

*

As a youth, Colt Rollings had been one of those rare kids who effortlessly drew others to him. He had been my best friend since as far back as I could remember and I wasn't the only one around who would have made that claim. He was a large, raw kid with gangly elbows, a hooknose, embattled brown eyes, and thick ears that angled out from his head farther than they ever should have. He was generous to others and athletic in an all-around sort of way, and though he was not necessarily any smarter than the next guy, he knew how to take charge of a situation and inspire others to try just a little bit harder than they might otherwise have done. Half the kids down on Hennepin Avenue wanted to be like him and that included some of the older kids too. There were girls who wrote his name on their notebooks with different colored pencils and invited him to their birthday parties.

He was a good kid at heart. Most of us were getting into at least a little trouble back then – with small time stuff – and there was a lot going on in the neighborhood. There were just too many opportunities and bad examples for anyone to get through unaffected. It might have been bad luck or it might simply have been his destiny but, at age fourteen, he was picked up for taking a businessman's shiny, new, green Packard for a joyride over the bridge into St. Paul. The businessman was important to somebody in City Hall and it was decided to make an example of Colt. When he wouldn't say who he'd been riding with, they gave him six years. When I came forward, voluntarily, naively thinking it would help him out, they gave me five and a half. After that, six other teenagers, none of which had even been with us, confessed that they too had been in on the crime. By that time, the city prosecutor had had enough so it was just Colt and me who got sent out to the farm.

At the reformatory, Colt could throw a fastball past any batter who stood in against him. Later, at Joliet, he hurt his elbow trying to add a curveball to his repertoire, and he gave up pitching for good. We finished our last and hardest year in adjacent cells.

During daylight hours we did field work and at night, before curfew, we talked through the bars about how we'd own Hennepin Avenue when we got out. They released me six months before they let him go. I got a job working in an auto shop tinkering with engines, changing oil and replacing tires and fan belts. The day Colt walked into the garage and embraced me I knew something had changed inside him. I never knew what happened after I left Joliet, but something happened in that prison yard that had touched him too deeply for me to ever understand. I could never quite reach him again and there weren't any more girls writing his name on their notebook covers.

We worked straight jobs for almost six months after Colt got out.

Then he convinced me to help him process the occasional stolen car, using the garage after hours. By then my boss had entrusted me with a key and allowed me to do legit moonlighting work using the shop's lift. At the time I didn't give it too much thought. It was only later that I realized I should have seen it coming. When they arrested us for stealing cars, Colt seemed almost relieved to be heading back to Joliet.

It was another three years before I got out, and on this run he was waiting for me and he had a plan.

*

This time there was never even an attempt to play it straight. We were almost thirty. It was 1932 and the honest opportunities seemed to have passed us by. This time we got serious about it, and the new jobs required us to use guns for the first time. Along with Frank Walker, who had served time with us in Joliet, we drove down to Oklahoma and robbed six gas stations, four grocery stores, and two liquor stores in quick succession over a span of three days. It was easy money and there was no looking back.

Walker and Colt had scouted the jobs in advance, driving the back roads and studying county maps, while I was still sweating it out in Joliet. We never fired a single shot. Afterwards we split the money and went in two different directions. Walker headed for Missouri and then Arkansas, where he said he had part of a gang waiting for him. Colt and I drove on through to Texas.

Our plan was to keep a low profile for a few weeks until we knew whether anyone was looking for us. Then we were going to locate an arms dealer in Austin with whom Colt had traded postcards. The idea was to buy a couple of Thompson machine guns, a lot of ammo, and some bulletproof vests. Once we had had the merchandise, we were going to meet up with Walker and the rest of his gang in Kansas City.

We headed south and crossed the Texas state line late at night, with the moon low on the western horizon. On the seat between us was a bag of ham sandwiches that we had taken from the last grocery store, along with six cartons of Lucky Strikes, a gallon of milk, a jar of pickles, and all of their cash. We were driving a black, Model-A Ford with a special V8 engine that Colt had arranged at a shop in Chicago. It was almost three o'clock in the morning before we finally started talking about what we had done.

"You okay?" he asked after a silence of several hours. We had the windows up all the way against the dust in the air and it was hot.

"It doesn't quite work out the way you think it will," I said. "Not really, anyway, not the way you want it to. It doesn't quite work out that way."

"What doesn't work?"

I opened the jar of pickles and selected one. It was too sour. "The theory is that if you point a gun at someone they will do what you want them to and you won't have to shoot them. But what if they won't do what you want? And there you are standing with that gun and the notion that they are going to give you the money because you have the gun. But what if they won't? What if they won't give you that money? Maybe they're stubborn or heroic, or maybe they're just plain stupid. You see my point? It doesn't quite work out – the idea that you can rob someone at the point of a gun, but never actually have to shoot someone with it."

Colt nodded in the darkness and lit a cigarette. I could see his expression reflected in the light of the dashboard. The shadows it created on his face made him look thirty years older as he stared down the highway in front of us.

"Is that what you've been thinking about for the past five hours?" he asked.

"Yes."

"We don't have to go in strong."

"Yes we do, and you know it."

"There are other ways."

"Not for what we do."

He was silent for a while and I watched him as he smoked. His face was impassive. When the cigarette got short, he rolled his window down part of the way and tossed it out. "Okay," he said then. "Tell me what you're thinking."

"We go in like we do, but are you really going to use that shotgun if you have to?"

"This isn't about me."

"No. It's about me, you, and everyone else we move with."

"Okay," he said. "Give me one of those pickles." I held the jar over towards him, rested on his lap, while he fished one out of the brine.

"You know what I'm talking about. What does it mean to point a gun at someone?"

Colt bit into his pickle, crunching into it as he chewed. He did not seem to mind that it was really sour. "It means the whole world."

"Yes it does. To you, to them, to their family, to anyone they ever knew who cared for them."

"So?"

"So, what does it mean to point a gun at a man? Does it mean you're willing to use it?"

"It depends."

"On what?"

"On the situation." He put the rest of the pickle into his mouth and wiped his hand along his trousers as he chewed.

"Yeah, but you don't have much time to think about it in that moment."

Colt shook his head in the darkness of the Ford. "Mere seconds, if that."

"That's right. You have mere seconds, if that, to decide whether you're going to pull that trigger. There you are, pointing that gun, that shotgun or that pistol, and all you have are moments to decide whether or not to fire. What did that gas station attendant or that cashier at the liquor store do to deserve that—to deserve the fact that you only have mere seconds to decide whether or not to kill him?"

"They don't get shot if they don't do anything foolish."

"Do they know that?"

"We tell them."

"Yeah, but do they understand? And what if they do? Does that mean they deserve it if they do something foolish?"

"This is too abstract for me. We take down scores. It's what we do now."

"It's what we have decided to do. It's not what we have to do, or who we are. We could do something else."

"You're in a bit of shock. It think I felt the same way the after my first time. Threw up all over the back seat as we were getting away. Walker laughed at me, but later admitted he had thrown up too the first couple of times. It will pass. Anyway, we won't always be robbing stores."

"Because we'll start to rob banks with Walker's gang?"

Colt nodded. He lit another cigarette. This time he rolled his window down an inch to drop the ash out.

"We'll face the same dilemma. Do we shoot?"

"If we have to."

"Could you do that?"

"If I have to."

"I'm not really so sure you could."

"Best to worry about yourself."

"I'm not so sure I could."

"If you have to, you'll be able to."

I waited silently, with cruel ideas slipping into tight places. I'd thought about it before, but always distantly. Now it was real and very immediate.

"Maybe," I said eventually. "Maybe. It'd be tough to kill someone who didn't deserve it though. Could you shoot a man for doing his job? Could you shoot a man in front of his children?"

Colt didn't respond. He finished his cigarette and tossed it out the window. Afterwards, he rolled the window all the way back up and continued to stare out at the road before us. The thin, broken white lines darted past us in the dark.

"And what about the police? Are we going to shoot at them?"

"We are if we have to."

"Really?"

"I'm not going back to Joliet. Are you?"

"No," I said, looking out through the windshield towards the disappearing point that was the road before us. "I don't care to. But … shooting a police officer might be difficult. Not all of them are bad."

"Yes, but I ain't going back. I been there, and it ain't nice at all. Probably wouldn't even be Joliet next time anyway, probably be some place a whole lot worse. I ain't going back and if it's him or me, I'm going to bring that policeman down, if I have to. Remember the other side of it – he's got a gun too and he'll shoot you down like a dog if he has you in his sights."

I didn't argue with him and we drove on through the night. Shortly after dawn, and well past the Texas state line, we stopped for coffee and eggs. They came with fried hash and potatoes. After breakfast, when we came back out to the car, I offered to take a spell at the wheel and Colt got in the back seat, curled up and slept for five hours until we were near Austin.

We never talked again about what it meant to walk into a job with a gun. From that point on it was just something we had to do. We didn't talk about it. We just did it.

*

For breakfast, Mrs. Giacalone served up coffee, two scrambled eggs, a small beefsteak, and homemade oatmeal bread with current jam. I was hungry and ate everything that she put on the table. She did not ask about or comment on my late evening.

The sun was out and the birds in the trees were still twittering with excitement.

Chapter Twelve

There was blue sky with soft, white clouds overhead as I took a taxi down to Torresi's office. It was late morning, the time of morning when small children started to rebel in school and office workers started to daydream, by the time I arrived. There were several people standing on the sidewalk in front of the building. They were smoking cigarettes and enjoying the sunshine as it splashed down around them.

I walked through the garage, past a couple of mechanics that were racing a truck engine, trying to puzzle out some problem with the starter. I moved towards them, squeezed past a couple of large wooden crates, went up three concrete steps in the back and opened a heavy oak door with a large windowpane in the center. Torresi was sitting at his desk with a pencil behind his ear. There was an open bottle of Canadian whiskey at his elbow and an empty tumbler beside it. The air in the small room was stale with old smoke and axle grease.

"Whaddya know, whaddya say?" Torresi rasped when he looked up and saw me as I stepped into the room.

"Precious little," I replied.

"Naw, not you." His thick purple lips curved.

"Yep, precious little."

"Have a drink?" he offered, holding up the whiskey bottle for me to admire.

"No thanks. Little early for my tastes."

"It's past five o'clock somewhere."

"I'll wait till it's five o'clock somewhere within a couple thousand miles of here."

Torresi set the bottle down with a grunt and leaned back in his chair. His voice had sounded reasonably upbeat, although he looked anything but. A deep moat of dark smears encircled his eyes. A gray shadow of beard covered the lower portion of his face and a lock of his hair was hung down loose over his forehead. The warm clay that formed the skin on his sallow face sagged. He wore the same clothes that he'd worn the previous night, except now his tie was unknotted, and the ends hung straight down over his chest. The top three buttons on his shirt were undone and his jacket was heavily wrinkled, especially at the crease of the elbows. It was not simply that he looked dog-tired, which he did, but you could sense that his frustration and defeat ran deep.

"Looking over some financial papers for Alvarini's sister. She's alone now."

"Worked on it all night?"

He swatted his hand through the air. "Naw. Nothing like that. Been up all night, but that was other stuff. The usual rumpus we get around here. She sent this over by messenger a few hours ago, some problems with Lou's last will and testament that might require our attention … More of the usual."

"I imagine that the import business he ran didn't always allow for easy record keeping."

"Something like that. She'll be okay, but we'll have to help make sure Lou's old deals are honored, more or less. You know how it is." He leaned back in his chair and sighed slowly. His eyes were no longer just tired, they were sad. Little pin-pricks of humanity darted from them and then dispersed into the air. "Lou doted on her. Now she's got no one. She's got it rough, poor woman, not taking it well."

"No reason she should," I told him.

"No."

"Violent, sudden death is a fact of life. Doesn't mean we should accept it."

"Funny thing to say, given your line of work."

I smiled for him although it took some effort. My patience was thin. "Several schools of thought on that. A man can become used to the killing and the death or he can grow to know its putrid scent all too well and decide to abhor it."

"Philosopher, huh?"

I shrugged and moved over to a chair set against the side wall. "Are we doing business today?" I asked. The chair was heavier than I expected. I dragged it over to his desk and sat down.

"You see Reina or Russo out there anywhere?"

I shook my head. I got the pack of Chesterfields out of my front pocket and lit one. Tobacco smoke burned in my nostrils and filled my throat with a familiar and welcome harshness, letting me know I was alive. I took a second hit off the cigarette.

"Told them to meet us here at noon." Torresi looked at his watch and coughed. "Guess they got a few more minutes before they're late. Never can count on them, anyhow. Is it raining out there? How'd you make out with the broad?"

I shook my head again, stoic, allowing tobacco smoke to stream from my nostrils.

He grinned with his eyes though his lips barely moved. "It's okay," he assured me. "I don't kiss and tell either."

"What's the rumble with Reina and Russo today?"

"Right onto business? Sure, I understand. But no point in spilling it yet, I'll just have to go through it again when they get here. Let's save it for a few minutes. You want a cigar, coffee, soda? I can send a kid out for ice cream if you're hungry."

"No thanks." I took another long pull on the cigarette and crossed my legs. There was no hurry and I was content to wait.

*

Reina was the last to arrive. He came in about fifteen minutes past noon, with an angry, furtive glance in my direction, as though it were my fault he was late. His face was red and he smelled heavily of sweat and badly cooked Mediterranean peasant food. His jacket could have been something he'd found in a dumpster—after it had been run through a sewer and spit on by rats. I ignored him, which only made him madder. He mumbled epithets about the traffic.

When he was seated, Torresi addressed him: "You're late. You know I don't like to be kept, but we're not going to talk about that now, there's work to discuss. Tomorrow there is a funeral to attend. We'll respect that, of course. But the day after tomorrow we have important collections to make and, also, Alvarini's sister needs some help. Nothing we can do today or tomorrow, but we need to get on it first thing the day after tomorrow so that certain people don't get complacent about keeping up their payments, or start thinking their debts died along with the man they owed them to. Understand me? I want you guys to take Duncan with you, let him see how it's done. Let them see him, see his tough face and chin, but don't introduce him around – there's no need for that. They'll get the picture. Anybody asks about him, tell 'em to mind their own fucking business. Duncan, you go with them. Follow their lead, whatever it is. You got it? It's how Joe Batters wants it, and you know how he is about these things. He's a stickler for detail." The last sentence was said in a different tone, quieter, for my benefit.

I knew that "Joe Batters," the underworld nickname for Tony Accardo, was the real power in Chicago now that Capone was in prison. He and Paul Ricci, nicknamed "The Waiter" made all the decisions, controlled the torpedoes and the politicians. Frank Nitti was only a front man for the real leadership.

Reina nodded rapidly while Torresi talked. It occurred to me that his face was so red because his collar was too tight around his throat. He was sweating heavily and his collar was stained with a dark murky line. I dropped my cigarette on the floor and ground it with my heel.

"Duncan," Torresi said, turning his gaze on me and softening his voice just enough. "I don't necessarily intend you to do anything, but come prepared just the same. Are you carrying?"

I nodded slowly.

"Yeah, the .45? Good. But you won't need it."

"That's what they always say."

Torresi grinned and nodded in agreement. "They sure do."

*

After I left the garage, I walked two blocks to a cabstand and caught a ride to The Loop. The sun was shining hard and the wind blew like it meant business. On the sidewalks, girls held their hair and their skirts in place to limit the disruption of modesty caused by the breeze as it swirled down between the tall city buildings. Pedestrians of both sexes squinted against the dust and grit that filled the air.

I paid careful attention out of the back window so that I would spot any tails, if there were any. There didn't seem to be. I got out and pushed through the revolving doors of the Clark Street entrance of the Morrison Hotel and went right on through the Clark lobby to the Madison lobby. I paused briefly to look around. Nobody came through behind me except a group of four women carrying shopping bags, and they went straight to the elevators. It was an elegant lobby, done in Georgian style, with a 28-foot ceiling and a gray marble floor. At 46 stories, it was billed as the world's tallest hotel and it bustled with people who didn't notice me. I went out through the Madison Street exit and stepped into a waiting taxi.

Again, as far as I could tell nobody was behind me, but I continued to watch out the back window as we went down the street fast. This time

I took the cab to the Lincoln-Belmont district via Ashland Avenue, hooked around at the intersection with Belmont and Lincoln so that we came down Lincoln, and then quickly took the second left and went three blocks.

I got out there and walked two blocks back up towards Belmont, cut through an alley, and then another block toward Lincoln until I arrived at a run-down neighborhood tavern called Sullivan's. There was no traffic on the street or any movement behind me. I was confident that no one was tailing me.

I walked into the tavern. It was dark and nearly empty. There were a few old drunks sitting at the near end of the bar nursing beers – the afternoon liquid death. I walked past the length of the bar, nodding at the barman as I went by, and took a booth in the back. From there I was completely out of sight from anyone sitting at the bar and anyone walking through the door. I also had the advantage of being within sight of the top of the door, so any motion caused by anyone entering the tavern would catch my eye. It was a place I had picked with great care several years ago, both for the barman and for the spot. Mostly for the barman, who had been part of my crowd several years beforehand. We had bandaged wounds for each other and I trusted him.

I lit a cigarette and waited. After I had finished the first one and was lighting another, the barman appeared with a mug of beer. He set it before me, nodded smartly, and wiped his hands on his apron.

"It's good to be seeing you," he said with a fluid Irish accent. He was a bantam-sized bright boy with clear features and short, awkwardly clipped hair – he probably cut it himself. Developing lines around his eyes and mouth betrayed his age and the hardship of his life. Still, there was a quality about his almond eyes that left him with the presence of a bed well-made with yellow satin sheets.

"Good to be seen, as they say. How are you, Jimmy?"

"Right well. Is it a pick-up?"

I nodded and he disappeared immediately. I sipped at the beer. It was lukewarm and more than just a little sour. For twenty minutes I sat there smoking and occasionally taking small sips of the warm, sour beer. Part way through my third cigarette, Jimmy returned and slid into the booth, across the table from me. He pushed a medium sized metal briefcase across the table to me and I pulled it down onto the seat beside me, out of view.

"Thanks, Jimmy," I said.

"Been a long time," he said. "I was starting to wonder." His eyes held questions.

"No you weren't. If I was dead you'd have read about it in the papers. If I wasn't, you knew I'd show up sooner or later."

He nodded. "Ay, but that's not quite what I was wondering. I was wondering about the long period of time where I heard nothing and what that meant, and where you were, and what you were doing, and who you were doing it with ... And I'm sorry about Colt."

"Yes."

"He deserved better. Did it go like the papers said?"

"Not quite."

"No? Ugly business, that. How did it go?"

"Forget what the papers say. That old couple did right by him. He's dead and gone. Does anything else about it matter?"

"In the end? No. Damn lousy business, though. Glad you made it."

"How's your wife?"

I extended the pack of Chesterfields. Jimmy selected one and lit it before responding. His expression told me nothing. His almond eyes were impassive. "Good days and bad," he said after he exhaled. "More bad than good. Life's not worth much when you're sick like that. Most days she's in bed, sleeps some, stares at the ceiling a lot, cries through the night – or rather, whimpers, really. Her spine is shrinking, losing bone, they say. There's an operation that might help, but who can afford it? And no one really believes it would help much anyway, might even make things worse. I'd get it for her if she needed it, but they don't know even if she would survive. If the operation would help her, I'd find the money in a weekend. But they don't know, they just don't know. They say it could as easily leave her in a coma or paralyzed all the way down."

"Rotten choices, Jimmy," I said. I was surprised by the anger in my own voice. I had never met his wife. "Really rotten."

He nodded, though his face remained calm. "It is what it is," he said presently, sipping from a beer he had carried to the table. "What gets me is knowing it's coming and not being able to do anything about it, seeing her like that."

"That would get me too. It would get just about anybody."

"There just ain't nothing I can do. She can't have kids, we haven't even had relations in a year." Slow tears filled Jimmy's eyes and he leaned back in the booth with his chin tilted up slightly. I thought at first he might cry harder, but he did not. Instead he gazed at me, steadily, without shame, and then he brought the cigarette to his lips and pulled hard on it.

"I'm sorry," I told him. "What's your wife's name?"

"Helen."

"I wish there was something I could do."

He nodded as he exhaled a lungful of smoke. "Funny thing, confessing to you like this. You bear witness ... like a father confessor. Something about your place and our past together – you're a fugitive – oddly makes you safe. Even with the gun. You've seen things and spilled blood, you don't talk, you don't judge, you're outside it all, outside everything. Like no one else."

I mustered a smile. "Brother, a long time ago, for a short time, we knew each other pretty well and we counted on each other. You can call on that if you need to."

"I know. There isn't any thing you can do," he said and his voice choked off as he said it.

I sat there for a while with him in silence and we finished our cigarettes. I thought about what he had to face when each day was through. After we finished smoking, we drank a little of the warm and sour beer. We pushed the mug back and forth between us, taking turns sharing it.

"It isn't all that bad," he said finally. "I really do love her, you know." His eyes flashed hot suddenly, and then just as quickly cooled.

"That's something," I said. "It's a lot."

"Huh, hmmm," he replied. "I wasn't sure when I married her, but I'm sure now."

"It's a lot. I'm envious."

"You have other things."

"If you love her and she loves you, then I don't have half of what you have."

"No? I would never have thought that. Is there anything else I can get you?" he asked. "Anything else you need?"

"No. Thanks, Jimmy."

"I'll check back with you in five minutes," he said and slid out of the booth.

"Give me ten."

*

Once I was alone, I unlocked the box with a small key that I carried in my shoe. I pried the lid open and quickly inspected the contents: a Colt .45 caliber semi-automatic wrapped in oilcloth, 200 rounds of .45 caliber ammunition, two fake drivers' licenses, maps of the city and several nearby states, contact lists, and a claim ticket for a Model A Ford that I kept in storage at a garage that serviced it every month so to keep it ready to go if needed and an envelope containing $22,000 in one hundred dollar bills. It was my rainy day stash, my lifeline, my last chance when all hope was about to go, and it was all there, exactly as I had left it the last time.

I stared into it and all the fading dreams it represented. I had several more just like it spread around, a few in Chicago, and care packages in San Antonio, Kansas City, Saint Paul, and Reno. It was part of the cost of doing business – at least the business I had chosen – setting aside seventy-five per cent of the take, spreading it around where I could get my hands on it quickly if I needed it.

It was an expensive line of work and those of us who had chosen it accepted that there were high costs to be endured. Routinely, you paid double, triple, even quadruple rates for hotels, meals, and train tickets, hoping to buy discretion and privacy. You paid large sums for local police protection when you were in small rural towns, and for special mechanical services for the cars. There were gun dealers, mob bosses, and brothel madams. They all provided shelter, and they all held their hands out and took their cut. It was part of the simple cost of doing business and you paid without complaint. There were times when the money flowed out almost as quickly as it came in, but it was worth it for what it bought you in privacy and security.

There were plenty who didn't pay, but if you didn't pay, you didn't last. Each of my care packages cost me four to seven hundred dollars a year in storage fees, paid out in six-month installments. I didn't know if all the other thieves relied on them. I gathered most did not. But I maintained them and they were my saving grace, my trump card that allowed me to get just that little bit of sleep at night, knowing they were out there waiting for me if the day ever came.

I went through the briefcase carefully, with one eye on the room in front of me. I selected one of the drivers' licenses and put it in my wallet. I counted out $15,000, mostly in one-hundred dollar bills, and put the remainder of the cash back into the envelope and placed that back in the briefcase. Of the money I had taken out, I put $2,000 in my wallet, $2,000 into a regular white envelope, and $11,000 into a large manila envelope, which I then placed into the front interior pocket of my jacket, along with one of the local area road maps.

From the same pocket I removed a letter that I had written that morning and placed the letter in the case, on top of the envelope containing the remaining $7,000 so that it would be the first thing anyone would see if they opened the case. It was addressed to Jimmy. If anyone else opened the case, it wouldn't matter who it was addressed to. I closed the case and locked it. Then I lit a cigarette and smoked with my elbow resting on the briefcase while I quietly waited for him to come back.

*

Jimmy set a fresh beer on the table and slid into the booth across from me.

"Is it okay?"

I nodded. "This is for you." I handed him the white envelope with $2,000. It was far more than necessary, but there was his wife to consider. "Do you need to know?"

He shook his head. "It's better not to. Thanks for this." He put the envelope into a pocket without opening it. He didn't even seem curious to know how much I had given him.

I let my expression soften and stubbed out a cigarette. "If I die you should open the case immediately. If you don't hear from me within the next six months it probably means I'm at the bottom of the lake. You should open the case then, inside there's a letter addressed to you with instructions."

"If you're dead, I'll know about it. It will be in the papers."

"Maybe, but you never know. If you ever go six months without hearing from me – I mean not even a phone call or a postcard – then open the case. Even so, I may call you or write you with instructions to open the case."

His eyes narrowed with concern. "Supposing I do get a call or a letter, how will I really know it's you?"

"I'll ask about your wife."

Jimmy considered this for a moment and nodded his head. "You're the only one who ever does."

"No one else would know to."

"I suppose that's true."

*

It took me three hours to make two more stops around town – one in Uptown and the other back near the Loop. I kept up the precautions to ensure I wasn't tailed, but nobody was behind me. At each stop I went through a briefcase similar to the one I left with Jimmy, although the contents of both of the other two briefcases were more modest than the one Jimmy kept for me. It was just past five o'clock by the time I returned to my room and I had time for a short nap before dinner. I was exhausted. Without bothering to remove my jacket or tie, I lay across the bedspread with my head on the pillow and closed my eyes.

An imaginary cellist played low, moaning notes that carried me away.

Chapter Thirteen

Alvarini's funeral the next day was an early afternoon affair, busy with a lot of people and a lot of gaudy floral arrangements. It tired me to see it all.

Afterwards I returned to my room and lay on my bed. My sleep was dreamless and I awoke at exactly seven o'clock, mere seconds before Mrs. Giacalone knocked on my door to call me to dinner. She set a fine table. We ate thick, slow cooked country ribs with sauerkraut and canned tomato sauce, served over mashed potatoes. I was hungry and I ate a large serving. Tad ate well too, but excused himself soon after to play outside with some of the children in the neighborhood. Mrs. Giacalone did not initiate much conversation and I excused myself before coffee and dessert.

*

Later, I found Elinore standing at the bar of the Nightingale Club, near the large jar of brandied cherries, making small talk with one of the bouncers. She wore pearls around her neck and a clinging silk dress the color gin forms when you add a squeeze of grapefruit juice to it. Her make-up was black around the eyes, but bright and glossy everywhere else. A hand-worked silver clip held her hair back, and there was plenty of crème in it to help with both the hold and the shine.

When she saw me she managed to look pleased and nervous at the same time. "I wish I'd known," she said quickly so that the bouncer and I could both hear. "Sam," she said then to the bouncer, pulling me forward by the elbow, "this is my uncle. He's come to town recently, and I just don't know what he's going to say to my mother about seeing me like this." She winked for both of us and gave me an additional small curtsy.

"Not to worry, my dear," I said playing along. "We'd both have some explaining to do." I nodded to the bouncer and led him to believe my name was Duncan. He drifted away shortly and we found a table along the back.

It was still early and the band had not yet started. A drummer was playing a slow cadence with wire brushes. The lights were still up and waiting staff placed lace napkins and crystal ashtrays on the tables in the center of the room. Several large men, who I assumed were bouncers, had formed a semicircle around one end of the bar. Bluish smoke hovered over them as they chatted amongst themselves and prepared for the evening ahead. A smiling waiter in a tuxedo appeared beside our table. I ordered a Martini and Elinore asked for a White Lady.

"Cointreau and gin?" I asked.

I must have made a face because Elinore laughed out loud. "With lemon," she said, not at all defensively. "It has lemon too."

"With fresh lemon juice, I must suggest the lady is right," the waiter volunteered helpfully. His accent was middle European. "It is a delicate drink and very popular with the ladies."

"That's fine," I said. "Just bring us the drinks."

"Thank you … I don't have much time," Elinore told me after the waiter departed. Her eyes were pensive. "He's meeting me for dinner in a little while. I didn't know you were coming down here again tonight." She didn't have to say who "he" was.

I nodded and opened my jacket a little so I could remove the envelope. "I don't need much time," I told her. "I just wanted to bring this to you." I put the packet of $100 bills on the table.

"What is it?"

"Almost $18,000."

Her eyes grew big, but she did not speak. I watched her carefully.

"It's Colt's share, now yours."

"You don't owe me anything."

"Take it. I'd feel better."

She hesitated. Her eyes were anxious and sleepy together, but I knew she wanted the money.

"It's a lot of money," she demurred.

I smiled at her.

"It's not really all his share, is it? You've added some of yours to it."

"Just take it. I promised him."

I pushed it toward her so that it hung over the edge of the table. "Put it in your handbag before anyone notices."

She complied. A moment later our drinks arrived. We clinked our glasses together without a word of cheer. Elinore took a small sip from hers and set it down. I swallowed about half of mine and then watched the expression on her face.

"Now what?" she asked, still anxious. Her voice sounded funny, although I couldn't pinpoint anything specific.

"Now you finish your White Lady and then you go to your dinner with 'him'."

"Just like that?"

I nodded, still watching her carefully. "What else can you do? It's okay, it's just one of those things. I understand the way it is."

"What about us?"

"I can't leave you with much hope."

"Will I see you again?"

"I have business tomorrow, starting very early in the morning."

"When will I see you?"

"I'll call you in two or three days."

"Be very, very careful, Mr. Duncan."

I nodded. Elinore stood up without finishing her drink and walked away from the table, waving gaily at the bouncers as she made her way past them and left the room for the elevator that would take her up to the seventeenth floor.

I lit a cigarette and listened dumbly as the band went through their opening paces. There was something odd, something wrong, but I couldn't say what it was. Down on the farm, I'd known a guy – a regular guy we all thought – who slowly drifted away down his own lonely trail. At first, it had seemed like the usual crazy bug a guy can get when he's been inside for too long. After it was too late, we learned he'd been having long dreams filled with laudanum, right there in his cell at night. He drifted right off the precipice, crashing before anyone could do anything about it. Early one morning on a kitchen detail he'd used one of the mixing machines to plug himself into an electrical socket. He was so far into his dreams that he didn't even scream as the voltage ran through him.

I finished my cigarette, and then I left too, without finishing my drink either.

Chapter Fourteen

The next morning, I arrived at the garage shortly past dawn, having spent the night in a downtown hotel where I caught three hours of restless, shallow sleep. Reina was sitting with another man in a maroon V8-cylinder Imperial sedan parked in front of the garage. The engine was running. They were drinking coffee from a stainless steel thermos. I opened the rear passenger door and climbed in. With barely a grunt, Reina worked the clutch and the sedan lurched away from the curb.

No one offered me any coffee.

"Where's Torresi?" I asked after a couple of blocks.

"Hadda go outta town," Reina said without looking around. "He be back in mebbe three day. This here is Sal. He come with us. Remember, Mr. Torresi say you follow my lead."

"That's what he said to do," I acknowledged.

Sal turned halfway towards me and nodded without making eye contact. In profile, I could see he had thick Italian features: a large hawk nose, large brown eyes, heavy eyebrows, thick black hair, and a heavy growth of beard stubble on his chin – he presumably had arisen too early to shave that morning. He wore an expensive gold ring with a large diamond set in it, and a heavy gold watch that hadn't been cheap either. I could smell the oil in his hair.

The city was only just awakening. Delivery trucks and buses moved down the streets with their headlights on. There was a slight ambient haze in the air, which could have been the vestiges of sunlight filtered through fog and low hanging clouds. We drove through downtown where traffic was starting to get heavy, and then quite a way out onto Lake Street, without speaking among ourselves. At a relatively quiet intersection in the Oak Park District, we pulled into the driveway of a drugstore and another man climbed in and sat at the other end of the back seat. He was a lean, short fellow with hair the color and texture of old straw. The skin on his face was pale and freckled. It clung tightly to an oddly shaped skull that was a bit too flat in the front. Everything about his shape and posture spoke of poor nutrition and little self-care.

Sal made the introduction: "This here is Walt. He's riding with us today."

"Hey ya," Walt said as he settled in beside me. When he spoke, I could see that his teeth were misaligned and the top row bent inwards at an angle.

He was vaguely familiar to me, but I couldn't place him at first. Then an image of a scrawny yegg with thin arms and bad teeth pitching a tantrum in a prison yard some years ago came to me. This yegg was screaming loudly and attempting to launch a rock in my direction when one of the screws hit him behind the knees with a piece of leather that was wrapped around a steel pipe. He went down hard into the dust and I never saw him again after that, if it was the same poor kid. He didn't seem to recognize me.

We pulled back out onto Lake Street for a few more miles, without discussion, and then we found a road that looped around towards a highway. It carried us a while longer. When we hit Elmhurst, we turned south and headed towards Peoria or Bloomington, perhaps. I had no idea where we were headed, other than it was clear we were leaving Chicago for a long jaunt through the countryside.

"Three hours from here," Reina said to nobody in particular.

"I thought we were working around Chi-Town," I said casually. "Torresi said something about making collections."

Outside the car it was starting to rain.

"Mr. Torresi didn't say what collections," Reina replied. "We have a pick-up south of here."

"What kind of pick-up?"

Small raindrops hit the windshield at an angle and slid off in thin rivulets without the help of wipers.

Sal half turned to look at me over the back of his seat. His grin was ruthless. "Cash, and there'll be plenty of it. You'll get some of it too, so no bellyaching."

"A payoff?"

Sal grinned. "You might say. It's a bank – their payoff to us." He cackled deeply and turned around to look out the front windshield again where the spitting rain made it harder to see the road before us. There didn't seem to be any point to asking more questions. I didn't like it, but Torresi had said to follow their lead. Maybe they were being mysterious and intriguing for a reason, or maybe it was just for dramatic effect, but the full plan would be revealed when they were ready. I had to go along for now to find out. My cold seat was in the middle of a draft. I wished I had a cup of hot coffee, but I didn't say anything about that

96

either. I remained quiet – and wary.

The road south started wide, but after about forty minutes it narrowed to three lanes; after another twenty minutes it narrowed to two. Shortly after that, the road got bumpy. It had stopped raining and a brown Midwestern landscape rolled by. There were early scraps of green, more hints of it than anything real or solid. Still, sometimes a hint of something related to hope is better than nothing at all.

A lot of thoughts went through my mind and none of them were very pleasant. I thought of all the jobs that I had been on – especially those jobs that had gone wrong somewhere along the line, too many of them had. Arrogance and carelessness, which often spring from the same deep well, had been involved more often than not, along with greed and the urge to betray – those other two uniquely human traits that have scratched their signature so frequently on the panels of man's history. We were men with guns, living outside the delicate shadow of the law, running in a place rarely blessed by the female touch.

I cursed silently in my thoughts, but said nothing and revealed nothing to my companions. If any of them had bothered to look at my face, they would not have seen any of the dark, angry loathing that resided within me. It was a lousy situation I'd landed in, but not for the first time. Thinking of the Irishman's words, I started to see a way I might make this sorry mess work out.

When I could stand it no more, I found the pack of Chesterfields in my pocket and extracted one. I rolled it across my lower lip, whetting it slightly to improve the feel. As I glanced up, I noticed Walt's eyes on the near-full pack I still held in my left hand. Without looking at him directly, I extended the pack so that he could take one. He did, and then we lit up separately without a word of acknowledgement between us.

The smoke felt heavy and sharp in my lungs, and it reminded me of what it felt like to be alive and anticipate the next breath. When I finished smoking, I cracked the window down and tossed the butt out into the flat, bleak land that had become nothing more than a blur to me now. Immediately, I lit another one, but I took my time with this one, and smoked with less urgency, allowing the smoke to slowly ooze out of my nostrils and from between my partially closed lips, surrounding my face with a fog of gradually dissipating tobacco.

I thought more clearly about a job I had done the previous year and the part of it that reminded me of this one. Three had cased it and developed the plan, the other three were brought in at the last minute. Without adequate discussion or review, six men had gone into two banks; three men came out quickly, with all the money and took the only getaway car that seemed to function. The other car had developed a flat tire, probably caused by a burst of machine gun fire. Of the three that were left behind, one was killed immediately in the gunfire that came from the street when he left the bank to try and make it to the car with the hopelessly flat tire. Inside the bank Colt and myself had gone out a window in the back and hijacked a passing car that belonged to a rich merchant's daughter. She got us out of town and baited a nice ransom as consolation.

Before we could catch up to the other three, a sheriff's posse found them first. Two mornings on, they were camping in a field, near their car, which had a broken axle and a trunk full of stolen cash. The sheriff and his men shot them so full of holes that their girlfriends and mothers had a hard time identifying them. The six of us together, working from the original plan, would have gotten away clean with all that money. Better to survive and split 6 ways, than to split 3 ways and go out like that. But the men with guns didn't always see it that way. Arrogance and greed held too much sway.

I wondered what Reina's philosophy might be and how he would see things when it came time to think about dividing the spoils. We weren't well acquainted, but I hadn't seen much to instill confidence that his approach was likely to be a careful, thoughtful one. Whatever the real plan was, I figured Walt and I would only be told part of it. Sal was probably in on more of it, but he wasn't the creative force and would follow Reina's lead, regardless of where that led.

Torresi came into my thoughts and I wondered how much he knew – if he even knew anything at all. It didn't seem his style to spring a plan like this without some frank discussion. Anyway, I had formed the impression that he trusted me more than he trusted Reina. I would have to address it with him later. I'd keep an open mind, give him a chance to explain or trip himself up if there was cause for any tripping to be done.

*

A few minutes after half past nine o'clock in the morning, we stopped at a roadside café near Ashkum for eggs and steak. The sky promised more dark rain. I was the last one out of the car, but when I had my feet on the pavement I was ready for anything.

The café was long and narrow, with five booths lined along the front windows, angled at 90 degrees like a row of teeth. A long speckled counter ran the length of the diner, which was empty except for a cook and the waitress who waited without enthusiasm. Neither of them smiled at us as we came in. We headed towards the last booth in the back corner.

Each table was set with a black metal paper napkin holder, four coffee mugs, four tin spoons, a set of salt and pepper shakers, and a jar of sugar. The floor was stained a faded brown, and the walls were covered in peeling yellow paint with sparse blue dots. Instant familiarity, I thought. I had already spent a lifetime in ugly little places like this and it didn't do anything nice for my mood.

I got into the booth next to Walt, facing the length of the room. After we placed our orders and started on our coffee I addressed Reina: "This might be as good a time as any to clue me in on what we're really doing."

Reina looked at me over his coffee mug, and then shrugged. "Might be. Just remember, Mr. Torresi say you follow our lead. It's a heist, a bank job we been planning for two month time. Sal, tell him."

Sal nodded and set down his coffee. He crossed his fingers together and rubbed his knuckles. "It's a small town with two banks on opposite street corners, kitty-corner from each other, you know? We go in strong, right at the lunch hour, two into each bank, in and out quick and then back into the car for the ride back and the split-up."

I nodded and took a sip of coffee. Walt listened without expression.

"The take should be at least forty grand," Sal continued. "We kick ten upstairs, five to Reina for his legwork and planning, and then divide the rest six ways."

"Why not four?" I inquired quietly.

"Oh, fuck! Whaddya got break my balls for? We got two other guys on the job with us, one inside each bank." Sal's voice was quite a bit louder than it needed to be.

I nodded and sipped more coffee. "What about the tools of our trade?"

"Like what?" Reina demanded.

"Guns," I said. "Ammo, vests, to start with."

Sal put up a hand to take control of the discussion. His voice, when he spoke, was quieter. "We got four Thompson submachine guns in the trunk out there, all the ammo we could ever need."

"Sounds a little much, actually," I responded. "Vests?"

"We won't need 'em."

"Yeah? Nobody ever thinks they will, but sometimes they do."

"We won't," Sal said. "This is going to be quick – in and out – hard and fast. They won't know what hit 'em till we've gone."

I nodded.

"Sure, kid. Then why the four Thompsons?"

"To scare 'em. Shock 'em. Like I said, they won't know what's hit 'em."

I squinted at him.

"What about maps?"

"Which maps? Whaddaya talkin' about? We know our way home."

I stared hard.

"Maps of the bank, the floor plan. Maps of the city streets, so that we can find our way out. Maps of the area, in case we need to take a different route home."

"Come on. Don't be a wiseguy!" Reina exploded. "What you need those for? I know the way in."

"It's not the way in I'm worried about, it's the way out."

At precisely that moment, our eggs and steak arrived which effectively ended the discussion. We ate rapidly without talking. I focused on the food – it was lousy, but I knew it might be a while before we ate again. Walt quit eating first – he barely touched his meal. He leaned back to light a cigarette, one of my Chesterfields. He smoked and stared out the window with an angry scowl, while the rest of us finished eating.

*

We drove another four miles or so and pulled off the road into a picnic area that was deserted and heavily surrounded by trees. Highway sounds were faintly audible through the dense forest that separated us from the main road. Small birds jeered us from the trees. It was almost warm. The sky was gray, but it wasn't raining and there were thick brushstrokes of blue sky on the horizon to the south of us. We got out of the sedan and Reina opened the trunk to show us. He handed each of us an identical gray overcoat, black fedora, a Thompson submachine gun, and a canister of .45 ammo for the Thompson. Walt demanded a second canister and was given one, which he placed on his seat in the sedan. No one else asked for a second canister. There were two large, dark brown leather valises to carry the money.

"The identical clothing will help confuse the civilians," Sal explained, "make it harder for anyone to identify us later."

I nodded. It was the first sensible bit of tradecraft I had seen.

"How much time now?" Walt asked, looking at Reina.

Reina checked his watch, but Sal answered: "It's a thirty minute drive from here. We'll walk in at 12:20, during the lunch hour, when there will be few windows open and mebbe between guards. Means we stay here for nearly two hours."

Walt groaned in disgust. "Why the hell did we come out here so early, then?"

Reina and Sal both ignored him. I thought of a response: "Not a bad idea, kid, to get in position early. Gives us time to ensure we're ready, recover from any thing unexpected."

"Like what?" he demanded bitterly.

"Flat tire, oil leak, heavy traffic, getting lost. What else have you got?"

"Could have slept a couple more hours," he mumbled, but his heart wasn't in the argument.

Except for Sal, we all put our overcoats, hats, Thompsons, and canisters back into the trunk of the sedan and Reina closed it. Sal put his overcoat on and placed the rest of his gear on the front passenger seat. Nearby there were two faded tables for picnicking. We sat together at one of them and smoked.

"Let's go over the plan," I suggested after a while.

"We already did that at the diner," Reina snapped. "You follow our lead – Mr. Torresi say so."

I took a long pull off my cigarette and stared at him. "No, we didn't discuss any plan in the diner," I said presently. "All I know is that I've been told: we are robbing two banks, that those banks are kitty-korner to each other, that we're going in strong with two of us in each bank at the same time, and that we have an inside man in each bank. I also know you claim we'll be splitting forty grand six ways after kicking ten grand upstairs and giving five to you. That means that if all goes as you say, we'll be splitting twenty-five grand between the six of us. That comes out to about four grand apiece."

"Yeah? Not bad for a day's work."

"Maybe so. But it's not so much for what we have to do and what we have to risk."

"It's plenty."

"Yeah, like I said: maybe so. There are still plenty of questions hanging out in the air."

He let loose with a string of obscenities, then: "Like what for instance?"

"Let's start with the question of why I should go along with this. I didn't sign on for a bank robbery and I didn't hear Torresi authorize it. Why should I go along?"

Reina's neck and cheeks flashed red. He swore firmly, launching through a harsh barrage of Italian, mixed with obscenities that lasted for several minutes. The obscenities were the only part I understood. I smoked my cigarette and listened politely without understanding a word. When he finished, he turned toward Sal and made an angry gesture with the back of his open hand. His lips were so tight that grooved wrinkles appeared above and below his mouth and beneath his chin. Raising his hands up to his chest, Sal inhaled and then looked at me with nervous eyes.

"He says you have to come with us," Sal reported. "He says Mr. Torresi say so."

"That's not all he said."

"No. But there is no point in translating everything he said. He says Mr. Torresi did authorize it and you are ordered to come. He is very angry you question this, but if it will fix you, he'll skip the five grand bonus he was to take and share it four ways."

I brought the cigarette to my lips, slowly. "Sure thing," I said after I had exhaled. "But there are other questions."

"Go on."

"What banks are we hitting?"

"The two in Urbana."

"Going after some of that Urbana money, huh?"

Reina just grunted. Nobody else said anything. I grinned to myself. I hadn't expected anyone else to catch the humor. Probably the only people familiar with the financial history, outside of city limits of Urbana, were a few independent bank robbers with failed dreams and too much time on their hands. The previous year, when Illinois shut down the banks at the height of what the headlines were calling The Great Depression, the Urbana Association of Commerce issued "Urbana Money" to keep the local economies going for a month or so until the banks opened their doors again. I hoped they had real money back in play these days. I didn't relish going home with a duffel bag full of worthless paper coupons to divide.

"Anything else?" Sal asked.

"How will we be paired? What are the inside contacts going to do for us and how will we recognize them? Why are you so sure there is forty grand for the taking, and how can you be sure this isn't a set up? What happens if there is shooting? What's our getaway plan? It appears that nobody will be staying with the automobile, so who will drive if things are hot when we come out? Is there a back-up plan if the automobile is shot up? What is the escape route from town? What's the back-up escape route? What happens if we're separated? What happens if one of us is hit? You get my point? There are plenty of angles to discuss."

Walt chimed in now for the first time, nodding his flat chin at me. "He's got real points there."

Reina nodded without looking at either of us. "It is fair. We explain."

I lit another cigarette and waited. Reina looked at Sal and nodded. Sal frowned, then nodded back and fished a city street map out of his pocket.

"Take a look at this for a minute," Sal said. He spread the map out on the table and smoothed it with the flat of his hand. "This is Urbana. We'll come in from here." He traced the relevant street with the tip of his forefinger.

"We go in fast, with a screech?" Walt asked.

Reina shook his head with frustration. Sal was shaking his head too. "No," Sal said. "We go in casual. We park here, at the curb. Duncan and Reina cross the street and enter one bank here. Walt and I go up these stairs and enter the other bank here, through the side door. In each bank, we go to the nearest counter. The insider will be there. We'll know him because he'll have a pencil behind his ear. He'll cooperate; make sure we get the money fast and give us the big bills, not just the little ones. And he won't push an alarm."

"In each bank?" I asked.

"Yes, in each bank. Why?"

"What if we don't spot the pencil?"

"Then go to the first counter anyway. In your bank, you let Reina do the talking. He'll demand the money and he'll carry it. You watch his back. Make sure the security guards don't draw down. Be sure no eager customers get involved. Walt will do the same for me in our bank. Let me do the talking in there. Okay?"

Walt nodded. "Do you want me to shoot anyone?" he asked. There was no humor in his eyes as he said it.

Sal hesitated.

"No," I answered for him. "Don't shoot anyone unless you have to and even then don't. If we can get out without firing a shot, that's best. Means less chance we draw cops. Plus, if we start shooting, they're likely to shoot back – cops, guards, even civilians. We don't want to let anyone believe they have nothing to lose. If we're in and out clean there's less risk to us."

I looked at Reina. He just grunted and made an impatient motion toward the map with his hand as if to say continue. Sal leaned back over the map and put his finger on the spot where the car was to be parked. "We should be in and out in less than five minutes," he explained. "Maybe three or four minutes. The car will be parked about here, legally, so no need to worry about leaving it there. No one will notice it. Either Reina or I will drive us out, depending on who gets back to the car first. Whoever gets there first gets it started and ready to go. We follow this road here, through this part of town. It takes us south, but we can cut through here and around this way, to get back northward."

"If we're chased and on the run?" I asked.

"Always breaking balls," Sal said. "We still go this way. It's quick and the streets are good. It's as good a way out as any."

"Not if they're right behind us. We have no chance to lose them."

"Why we have Tommy guns." Reina's voice was harsh and loud. He seemed agitated.

I shrugged and looked back at the map. "What if there's shooting and we lose a tire or something else in town. Or what if that happens after we get out, like on the highway?"

"Then we improvise," Sal said.

"It's best to go in with two cars in case anything like that happens."

"We only have one car."

"And none stashed along the way home to change into, I suppose?"

Sal shook his head slowly. "We won't need it. This is going to be a piece of cake."

"And if anyone is shot or we have to split up?"

"Every man for himself. We regroup in Chicago, at the garage, for the split. You got a problem with that?"

I shook my head. I had a lot of problems with it, but I couldn't see any advantage to voicing them. I'd come to Chicago for a reason and I had to play this out a little further. "Go on," is all I said.

"That's it. Any other questions?"

I sighed and cleared my throat. "One: Exactly why are we so sure there will be forty thousand dollars?"

"Because," Reina said and paused. He took a last pull at his cigarette and dropped it at his feet, grinding it into the dirt, before he casually exhaled a long thin stream of bluish smoke in my direction. "Sal, explain."

"Because we have inside info that monthly payrolls came in last night to be paid out this afternoon. We're going to get there before any civilians do. You'll see. It'll be okay, everything will work out with this plan. We've spent a lot of time on it, and it's a sure thing."

Walt nodded eagerly, the straw on his head flopping with the motion. "I like a sure thing," he said.

"Kid," I told him, "the only thing that's for sure on this caper is that before the day is over, each of us will have had at least one unpleasant surprise."

*

I didn't like it, any of it, but I didn't see anything to do about it yet. I was still playing along. We were going to rob the Urbana banks together and then we would see what developed. We waited. There were still almost two hours to kill. Over the years I had noted this was the hardest part for men with guns. But the waiting was something I was good at. I had learned to channel those long awkward periods before the action started and to see the time not so much as hours to pass, but seconds to use.

I checked the .45 that I carried under my arm. I studied the street map, trying to memorize the general pattern of streets and alternate routes out in case we had to improvise quickly with heat behind us. I closed my eyes and envisioned the bank, imagined the customers, the clerks, the money. In my mind I pictured the scene and the action and rehearsed the steps I would take to ensure my own survival.

It was quiet there in the clearing. We were remote from the highway behind us and no other cars came through to the parking area where we sat. The sky darkened and lightened several times: clouds moved overhead and then away, beyond our line of sight as new ones came overhead. Time went by slowly and different melodies drifted through my mind. I hummed something tuneful I'd heard Bing Crosby sing, imagining the accompaniment of the soft a cappella backing voices that had carried him along. There wasn't much to do and the others quickly grew bored. We smoked cigarettes and drank water from a jug that had been in the back seat of the sedan.

Sal bragged about how he was a great pistol shot. Walt just laughed at him, goading him along. Waving a long-barrel .38 Sal decided to take shots at a tin can he found in the bushes. He set up the can on a picnic table and marked off 25 paces. On the fourth shot he hit it and knocked it into the air, off the table, with a hard clang. Grinning at the rest of us, he put the gun back in a pocket of his overcoat and studied his work. Reina walked over to get a close look at the can. He laughed when he stood over it and swore an oath loudly.

"You might want to conserve your rounds," I offered.

"Who's gonna need a .38, when there's a Tommy gun and more than enough ammo for it?"

"There's no such thing as enough ammo," I told him. "Remember the Alamo?"

Sal gave me a dumb look. Reina wasn't paying us any attention, and Walt just shrugged. None of them had ever heard of the Alamo. I didn't press it. I was starting to get the idea that the less ammo the others had, the better off I would be.

*

Time moved even slower. I lit another cigarette and studied the map some more.

"Don't I know you?" Walt asked me from across the table.

I looked up from the map, my eyes narrowed. "Yeah, kid. I think it was Joliet, a few years back."

He grinned, crookedly and his eyes became large. "Yeah it was. That was quite a joint, huh? I was inmate number five-four-six-eight."

"Five-five-nought-three."

"I would have seen you around in that old yard we had. Did we rumble?"

"Yeah, I think we had a confrontation."

"Hmmm. A disagreement?"

"Yes." I remembered now what it was, but I didn't say anything. At one time he had been furiously jealous with the impression I had been flirting with his prison "wife" on the laundry detail we shared. I hadn't been flirting with anyone, but there was no point reminding a man on the outside he had once pitched a violent tantrum over an imagined insult such as that.

"Probably both mad at the world, huh?"

"It was a tough place."

"Sure was. Those screws didn't cut a guy a break. At least they fed you plenty there."

I shrugged. "You want a cigarette?"

"Thanks," he said as he accepted the pack of Chesterfields from me.

"Keep it," I told him. "I've got another pack and this day is going to be long yet."

"What do you think about it all?" he asked, his voice quiet for the first time. Reina and Sal remained over by the other table, as if to continue their examination of the shot-up tin can, but they seemed to be whispering intently in Italian about something without looking back at us.

"Kid, I think you better have eyes in the back of your head, and you better use them carefully today."

Walt flicked a butt away off his thumb with his middle finger. "Aw. It's not like that," he protested mildly.

"How do you figure it's not?" I asked.

"It's just not that way. We're a crew now. We'll take down these two scores and lam it back together."

I formed a smile I knew evinced no warmth. "Maybe, kid. I'd feel better about it if we'd been part of the planning a little earlier on."

"For what? You still have to trust your partners."

"Yeah, but these guys aren't my partners, and, no offense intended, you aren't either, kid. I'd feel better if we had two cars, maybe three and vests to stop any stray lead that happens to get into the air."

"Ahhh," he waved a flat hand in the air. "It's bunk. I've been on plenty of jobs like this. With those Thompsons, nobody can stop us. I'm pure hell with one of those hot babies in my hands."

"Sure, kid."

"Stop calling me kid."

"No offense meant. Just watch yourself."

"Don't need you to tell me that. I know what I know, and I'm a man. I been around. I done jobs with Pretty Boy Floyd and Adam Richetti down in Oklahoma and I played straight poker with Vern Miller once or twice too."

I didn't believe him for a skinny minute, but I didn't see any reason to say so. I brought the cigarette up to my lips and watched him without speaking.

After a slight hesitation, Walt nodded, as if satisfied that I had not challenged him. "And I was in Kansas City last summer when the massacray happened."

He mispronounced the word "massacre" as many people did in the Midwest. Again, I didn't see any reason to correct him. My cigarette was getting short so I stubbed it out on the table in front of me. Shadows of light and dark continued to shift above us in the sky.

"We was still up drinking down on Eighteenth Street, been drinkin' and shootin' dice all night when the word came in they'd shot up Jelly Nash and those federal coppers at Union Station that mornin'. Some little nigger kid came in with his shine box yellin' there was bullet holes and dead bodies all over the place."

"Some excitement, huh?"

"Yeah. It was a big deal. But you know what the crazy thing of it was?"

"What's that?"

"We just kept on drinkin' and shootin' dice. That was the real pip of it. Everybody else went tearin' down to the station to see what there was of it. We just kept on playin'." After he spoke he stared off into space with his lips parted, breathing through his mouth.

I studied the inward slant of his front teeth. "Well, kid," I said at last, "there may be another pip of it today. Don't take your eye off your partner in that bank because he just don't care about you doing jobs with Pretty Boy or playing straight poker with Vern Miller." I shot him the gunner's salute and stood up.

It was time to go see what Urbana had in store for us. I didn't like it at all, but I was in a spot, and now I had to play it out.

Chapter Fifteen

As we entered the bank, Reina cursed fluently to himself in a mix of ancient Italian and broken English. He walked ahead of me with the barrel of the Thompson pointed straight up in the air. I carried mine pointed down, at a spot that floated about four feet ahead of me and I walked just a step behind Reina. Although I'd never carried a Thompson into a bank before, I knew from common sense and the experience of others that, if needed, you could swing it into play much faster from that angle. And I didn't expect much to go according to the plan we'd been shown.

Time and motion slowed together, as they always did when I entered a job, like a familiar old song, and the sensation gave comfort. Only I was aware of the melody and rhythm of the beat that accompanied me within my head. Once inside, Reina halted a few steps after he cleared the door. I watched him carefully. With his feet a stride apart and his shoulders bunched tightly in towards his neck he stood still. I came in behind him and stopped too. For a moment I wondered if it was a freeze up, but then Reina jumped forward into the middle of the marble-floored bank lobby and bellowed. His voice was near hoarse.

There were only six people in the lobby. Four of them were customers and one of them was a lady. All six turned to stare at us as Reina stomped towards the counter with his elbows out and the Thompson held practically aloft. He resumed swearing and talking to himself in Italian. The clerk at the nearest counter had a pencil behind his ear. The expression on his face was excited but not quite as frightened as it should have been. His lips were pulled tightly back over his teeth and the light of the chandeliers that hung low from the ceiling reflected upon his bald head.

A wide ray of sunlight came in through the side windows and played a bright alley down through the middle of the room. Reina crossed over that line of bright light and stood in the shadow on the other side, turning back and forth slowly, swiveling from the hips.

"Everyone down flat!" he shouted.

Everybody in the lobby dropped down, except the clerk with the pencil behind his ear. I switched the Thompson to my left hand, holding it aloft now for dramatic effect while I drew the .45 semi-auto with my right hand. If any shooting needed to be done, I wasn't going to do it with a submachine gun. With my thumb I depressed the safety on the pistol and ran my forefinger along the outside of the trigger guard. It felt smooth and natural, like an extension of my own hand. The cadence I kept in the back of my mind slowed further.

From the floor, the lady started to whimper loudly in waves of guttural moans that became progressively softer, but longer. She was middle aged and she wore a matching hat and dark blue dress that had been in style ten years before, with a powder blue wig and black high-heels that did not go well with her brown hose. She lay on her side and rocked backwards on her hip with her legs splayed widely. It was hard to look at. One of the men nearest her whispered fervently, although he quickly became quiet when Reina yelled again. Another man in a tan felt hat was crying and his feet twitched behind him as he curled on the hard, cold floor.

"Do as we say and we won't hurt you," Reina shouted. I could see the strain in his neck. "Move a bit and I'll plug you for sure!" He crossed over the rest of the lobby quickly, to the nearest counter and threw the valise onto it. Pushing the Thompson machine gun like a shovel, he motioned at the clerk with the pencil behind his ear. Another clerk was out of sight, having dropped to the floor at the command to do so. As soon as Reina barked it, I knew it was a beginner's mistake. There was probably a silent alarm that could be easily triggered from down there and maybe even a gun that the clerk could reach for. If it had been my operation I would have kept him within my sight, brought him out from behind the counter so that he could not cause mischief. But it wasn't my operation and now it was too late.

"Fill it with the large bills first," Reina said, poking the Thompson towards the valise. "Move it, fast!"

"The safe is back here," the clerk said. His voice was a monotone.

"Fill it."

"I'm moving, but I have to step back this way."

"Faster!"

I gazed about the lobby, looking for signs of movement. There were none, other than the rocking of the lady's hip and the twitching feet of the man in the felt hat. The only sound was the lady's whimpering and the velvety thumping of the clerk placing stacks of paper-bound cash into the leather valise. I turned to look away, out the window, momentarily scanning the street. There was nothing unusual there and no sound of sirens mounting in the distance. I crossed to look out the window fronting the side entrance. There was nothing there either.

"Faster," Reina shouted again at the clerk.

I turned back just in time to see the clerk close and latch the valise and push it across the counter. His head was bobbing anxiously and I could see large mats of sweat forming in his shirt beneath his armpits, spreading down toward the suspenders he wore. His Adam's apple swelled noticeably when he gave a dry swallow.

"Hey," Reina said loudly with his head half turned my way. "Are we clear?"

There was still no movement on the street. "So far," I replied, keeping him within my peripheral vision.

"Let's scram. I follow you out." He grabbed the valise with his left hand and lurched back from the counter. The machine gun was in his right hand, pointed towards the ceiling again, and he gestured towards me with his right elbow, urging me on. The look on his face was bright with excitement and his thick neck strained against the white collar of his shirt.

I was turning back toward the door when I heard the first shots. They came from across the street and carried the unmistakable rapid pattern of a Thompson submachine gun. There were two short bursts, a pause, and then two more and then time slowed further. I turned halfway around, just in time to see Reina shoot the clerk in the chest with a burst from his Thompson.

The man went down hard and the pencil flew out from behind his ear. That was perhaps Reina's fatal mistake. He should have shot me first, if he could have. As it was, the barrel of the Thompson I held in my left hand was part way through the door and there was no way I could swing it around in time. With my head turned looking back over my shoulder, I could see Reina swiveling towards me after shooting the clerk. The leather valise full of cash waited at his feet as he operated the machine gun smartly with both hands. He seemed to be moving in slow motion, relishing the moment even, as if he thought he had all day, confident I would not be able to bring my Thompson around in time. There was a sickly grin on his face as he glared at me in a moment of false triumph.

I shot him two times through the back of my overcoat with the .45 held underneath my left arm. He never knew it was coming. The heavy dum-dum slugs caught him in the chest and throat, and knocked him backwards with a red spray that splattered the cream marble counter behind him. I'd had him covered the entire time.

I stepped back into the lobby just long enough to grab the valise. I looked momentarily at Reina's dying body. He was convulsing and gasping for air, with only a few seconds left before he slipped away off the mortal ledge into the wide abyss of death. He was trying to say something, but couldn't find the wind.

I had only seconds before he crossed over, but I got it in: "You're an amateur. Amateurs die alone in this business."

I didn't give him a second look as I left the bank with my fedora pulled down low and tight over my forehead. Behind me I could hear the lady still whimpering softly on the floor and the sound of the first siren far in the distance.

*

Sal was in the Imperial sedan with the engine running. He held his Thompson out the window with his left hand, his arm hanging out over the outside of the car and the stock of the machine gun jammed into the crevice of his elbow. Sirens, more than one, were louder, closer now.

The V8 revved aggressively. Sal was studying the road behind him with his neck turned far to the left, straining to catch sight of the first police cruiser when it appeared. His leather valise was already sitting on the floorboard behind the driver's seat. He didn't even see me as I came up on the right from behind and opened the passenger door and set my leather valise on the floor. I prodded him once with the barrel of my .45 as I climbed in slowly and pulled my door shut behind me. He turned around fast and his eyes became wide and dilated.

"What!"

He had been expecting Reina and not me.

"Doesn't look like you were planning to wait for Walt," I said evenly.

"What?" He was struggling to understand what had happened. His mind hadn't quite connected the dots – that my appearance meant Reina was probably dead.

"Or the inside man?"

"Hey now!"

"Now you're going to tell me that Walt and the inside man both bought it in a shoot-out with a security guard – or perhaps they killed each other?"

He was stunned and tried to find the words, nodding his head rapidly. The sirens rapidly drew nearer. We had only moments to get out of there.

"Except there wasn't any shootout with a security guard."

"No, he shot at us—"

"Forget about it. I only heard one gun firing and it was the sound of that chatterbox you're holding out the window. Go ahead and drop it away from the automobile."

"What?"

"You heard me," I said a little louder. "Drop it away from the automobile!"

I pushed the hot end of the .45 against his neck. He recoiled and then quickly complied. I heard the Thompson clatter to the pavement. Instinctively he brought both hands up near his face and held them there, palms out in a gesture of surrender. The sirens were only blocks away now and a uniformed guard had emerged from the bank where I had left Reina. He was holding a large revolver and looking for somebody to shoot at.

"Drive!" I commanded. An instant later the guard saw us, shouted something, and brought the pistol up to point it in our direction. We were about thirty yards away from him. His first shot sailed by without hitting anything, but his second shot took out the rear passenger window. Shattered glass confetti filled the air and dissolved quickly.

By then Sal had grabbed the steering wheel with one hand and engaged the engine with the other. We lurched forward with a squeal of rubber and accelerated down the street. I heard more shots fired in our direction, but none hit their target. After we'd gone five blocks and the firing had stopped I told Sal to stop the car for a moment. He came to a quick halt without pulling over towards the curb.

"What?" he yelled frantically. His face was slick with perspiration. I could smell the sudden stench of his dry-mouth breath.

"Get out," I told him calmly.

For a moment my words didn't seem to register. "Here?" he asked dumbly.

"Yes, here. Get out now. Move quickly."

"What are you gonna do?" he asked in a pleading voice.

"Get out."

113

He got out of the car and closed the door behind him. The breeze tipped his hat off and blew it onto the street behind him. He didn't seem to notice. I moved over into the driver's seat.

"What are you gonna do?" he asked again, standing in the road with trembling legs and his hands in the air. He was sweating heavily and his eyes dripped with self-pity and fear.

"Sal, you're supposed to look out for your partners. It's part of the code. Walt may not have been much, but when you ride in with a man you're supposed to ride out with him."

"Don't leave me like this," he pleaded.

"Where's your .38?"

He tentatively patted a bulge over the left breast pocket of his jacket.

"Guess you better use it now. These small town cops ain't gonna be too gentle with an Italian gangster from the big city. Especially not one who shot up their bank and took their Urbana money."

"Only have a couple shells left."

"Tough luck for you, boyo."

Sirens drew closer. I hit the accelerator and drove as fast as the Imperial would go for three blocks and then turned left on two wheels. I looked over my shoulder and gathered one last image of Sal, for just the briefest of moments. He was crouched by a row of hedges with his pistol drawn as a police car pulled up short. Then I was out of sight, but I heard the volley of shots. There were a lot more than two of them. Then a period of silence and another four shots rang out in the distance, evenly and calmly, spaced about two seconds apart.

I kept driving fast. A few blocks later I thought I heard the sound of one last final shot. It could have been my imagination filling in the scene I expected, or it could have been real. I couldn't tell. I went through a stop sign without stopping, took a hard right and then, two blocks later, a hard left. There was no other traffic on the road. It was the southern route out of town – not the direction I wanted to go, but the quickest way to put distance between myself and the sirens that were now converging on the banks and the dead bodies that were left there.

I slowed down, still going fast, but not so much above the speed limit as to attract attention. Quick glances over my shoulder reassured me that nobody was coming after me ... yet. As soon as I was able to, I looped around eastward and took a series of connecting roads that gradually led me north until I hit upon a secluded picnic spot. It was shielded from the main road by a copse of large elm trees and heavy underbrush.

With rapid movements, I put the two leather valises into the trunk, along with the fedora and overcoat I had been wearing. Then I rolled all the windows down so that the rear passenger window the guard had shot out would not be conspicuous. I swept the broken glass off the back seat and floor with an old newspaper. Then I took a drink from a jar of water that was on the seat, gulping quickly and not caring that some of the water ran down my cheeks and onto my neck and collar.

Out on the highway again I pointed the car north and accelerated that big V8 hard, I needed to do the 160 miles back to Chicago as fast as I could. There was no point in being clever now. I was reasonably confident that nobody had had a chance to take careful notice of the automobile. I doubted there would be an organized pursuit or that they would have had time to set up roadblocks towards the north. Even if they did, as a lone driver I stood a fair chance of getting through unnoticed. More than likely they would be looking for a car with multiple passengers. All the same, I drove with the .45 resting flat on my lap and a spare magazine tucked beneath it just in case.

Chapter Sixteen

After driving up into Wisconsin a ways and doubling back on myself a couple of times to be sure, I entered Chicago under the cover of darkness. Law enforcement wouldn't be expecting me there, but I didn't want some eager flatfoot matching the car to any description he might have heard on an all-points bulletin.

I ditched the Imperial pretty far up Lincoln, leaving it in an alley just off the main street, and then walked twenty minutes to Sullivan's tavern with one of the leather valises. One was enough to carry all the cash from the two banks, but it was heavy in the kind of way that left me feeling hopeful about what I would find when I started counting.

I walked fast, but not too fast. The air was cold and the temperature was dropping as cars rushed past me, taking people off to warm homes where dinner presumably awaited. My stomach was tight and I remembered I hadn't eaten anything since the eggs and steak in Ashkum.

Sullivan's was even darker then it had been the other day and it was just as empty. The same few old rumdrums occupied stools at the near end of the bar. I couldn't even be sure they weren't nursing the same beers. I headed for my booth in the back and waited for Jimmy, who appeared almost right behind me with a mug of beer. The foam was still expanding and it slopped over the edge as he set the mug on the table before me. A sour odor wafted up from it.

"Back so soon," he said with his gentle Irish brogue. It wasn't a question and he just smiled at me with those almond eyes, as he stood there with his hands on his hips. His hair was a bit mussed and there were dark circles under his eyes. He didn't look as together as he usually did and I wondered how his wife was faring. "It's only been two days."

"Have any food fit for a man to eat?"

"You didn't come here to eat."

"No, but I'm damn hungry all the same."

"Long day of it, huh?"

"Long enough."

"They've been shouting about things on the radio since just after lunchtime."

I shrugged and took a long pull at the beer. It was warm and even more sour than it smelled.

"I'll bring you bread and cabbage and veal soup."

"That would be nice."

"And then, if you'll give me a few minutes, I'll bring your briefcase."

"Thanks, Jimmy," I said.

Netted under a thin wire mesh above me a light bulb glowed dimly. I lit a Chesterfield and waited quietly under the crosshatched shadows. When the food arrived I was hungrier than I realized. I ate half a loaf of rye bread with butter and the entire bowl of soup. The meal was simple, but surprisingly good given the quality of the beer.

"Lady in the back can really cook some, huh?" Jimmy said when he returned with the briefcase. "She's from Hungry or Poland, one of those countries anyway."

I nodded. He didn't sit down; he just cleared the bowl and plates, then wiped the table and quickly left. He didn't ask if I wanted more food or another beer. He didn't ask about Urbana or either of the dead Italians I had left there. I counted the money quickly. It was just under $65,000, all of it mine now, and the largest score I'd ever taken down – easy money some would have said, but I considered it something else. It had been anything but easy and the real trouble still lay ahead.

I put $15,000 in my pocket, $1,500 in a small pile of hundred dollar bills that I left on the table, and the rest went into the briefcase.

When Jimmy came to collect it, his eyes registered the tip I'd left him.

"It ain't for you, brother," I said climbing out of the booth. "It's for the lady you got at home who has to put up with your smiling Irish eyes every day."

He just grinned and nodded as I walked past him and left the tavern to go in search of a taxi willing to take me on a tour of the wilder side of town.

*

I found Torresi in the second place I looked for him. He was in an area known to the locals as The Patch near West Side. He was in the Pioneer restaurant on West Grand eating a late supper of steak and beer with some coochie-coo I had never seen before and the look on his face suggested he knew nothing about what had happened down in Urbana. The woman was a tall platinum blonde in a green dress. They had a table just large enough for two.

I pulled a chair around from another table and sat down between them, looking back and forth for a moment. Then I tossed a fat envelope containing $10,000 in old fifties and hundreds onto Torresi's lap. It landed neatly in the basket formed by a white napkin and settled slowly while he stared at it.

"What's this?" he asked. The expression he wore was more puzzled than angry or upset.

"Urbana money," I said. I turned toward his companion. "Miss, could you give us five minutes, please?"

She hesitated and looked at Torresi, who nodded once. She stood up slowly and walked away from the table. I pulled my chair up closer to the table and leaned an elbow across the space she had just vacated.

"What is this, really?" Torresi asked again. He hadn't touched the envelope. His shoulders were straight back as far as they could go.

"Ten grand, your share of the score."

"What score?"

"Reina said you were in for ten grand."

"I have no fuckin' idea what the fuck you're talkin' about. Where's Reina?"

"You don't know?"

"No fuckin' idea, pal." The expression on his face grew angry.

I unclenched my teeth and took my elbow off the table, straightening up. "You don't know where he is?"

Torresi shook his head. His eyes held the challenge in mine.

"Okay, I'll tell you where he is: down at the morgue in Urbana, Illinois. He was shot up in one of their banks today, two slugs from a government model .45 semi-automatic pistol. In fact, this very model here." I tapped the spot under my jacket that floated my shoulder holster.

Torresi's expression slid into a white fury, but his lips remained tightly pressed together.

"Remember, I was to meet him. When I did, he said you authorized it," I continued, "and you were to get ten thousand as your cut. There it is, all of it. Go on and count it."

From half-slit eyes he just looked at me without moving. "Are we gonna have a problem?" he asked instead.

I nodded slowly. "Maybe so, unless you can convince me. Go ahead, count it."

He picked up the envelope and flipped through it quickly. "Yeah," he said quietly. "Looks like about ten thousand. Now, tell me, what's the rumpus?"

I told him, quickly, but accurately, and with the important details. It took me maybe three minutes to describe the events of the day. Torresi listened without interruption, without comment, and even without change of expression. His face was impassive. When I finished I leaned back in the chair and lit a Chesterfield.

"Is that everything?" Torresi asked quietly.

"Those are the facts of what happened today," I said.

"You left out one detail."

I nodded. I had told him everything, except for the final count of the haul that was contained in the two leather valises. "Go ahead, ask it."

"How much?"

I grinned and took a large pull off the cigarette. I was in no hurry to answer the question. "A hell of a lot less than what the radio broadcasters are claiming," I said after I exhaled. "But the exact amount is none of your fucking business."

Torresi considered this for a moment and then smiled slowly. He picked up the envelope and held it up near his face. I wasn't sure if he was trying to study it or smell it. Then he extended his arm towards me and dropped it in my lap. "Keep it," he said. "I got no claim."

I let it sit in my lap, but made no effort to pick it up. "You sure about that?"

He nodded slowly, still with a half smile. "I didn't authorize the job, it didn't take place in our territory. I had nothing to do with it. I got no particular claim over you beyond any individual agreements we may come to for work you might do for me. It's your score. It's your money, keep it."

"But I am in your territory now, and I do need your protection to stay here."

"Not ten grand's worth."

I thought about this. "Perhaps two?"

"Six."

"Three."

Torresi stared at me hard for a solid ten count, and then the smile blossomed forward again. "Sure, per quarter," he said, laughing afterwards. I counted out three thousand dollars, which I handed over to him, and placed the remainder of the envelope in the front right pocket of my jacket. He put the bills into his wallet. We were both smiling now, but there was still business to discuss.

"Do I have to worry about any accounting for Reina or Sal?"

"They put the snatch on you."

I nodded.

"And it was to be a one-way ride."

I nodded again.

"You had to defend yourself."

"So you're okay with it?" I asked.

Torresi nodded.

There was another question I had to ask: "Do I need to be concerned about anyone else in the Outfit? Reina and Sal had friends maybe, friends who might revenge?"

"Who could love either of those two mugs?" Torresi asked, dismissing my concern.

"I need your reassurance."

"There's other things we need to talk about."

"That's not reassurance."

"No. But it is what it is. I tell you what, give me some time to ask around. I'll put the word out – make sure. Meet me tomorrow night and I'll let you know. I think it will be fine. Nitti will back me, Ricca and Accardo will too. But I just need to be sure."

"It's good to be sure about a thing like this."

"I'll let you know tomorrow, and we can talk about our other business, the O'Farrell business. We still got that hanging out there."

"When and where?"

"You know the Hy-Ho club?"

"Yeah."

"Say eight o'clock?"

"Okay. But I'm going to be very careful until I've heard your assurance."

Torresi lifted his chin in the direction of the hostess' stand. "See the guy over there, just came in?"

I turned and found myself looking at a tall, slender, glamorous boy in an obviously expensive, tailored blue pinstripe suit and black overcoat, twirling a white fedora in his hand. He was accompanied by an equally tall, though significantly more curvaceous, platinum blonde with a mink stole wrapped around her neck. "Who, Hollywood?" I asked.

"Yeah, just keep the chuckles coming. That's McGurn, Machine Gun Jack McGurn. You don't want to let him hear you calling him Hollywood. He's the one took out Bugs Moran's North Side gang back in '29, on Saint Valentine's Day."

It was a message, but I sloughed it off, lighting another Chesterfield. "Just another cheap torpedo to me."

He nodded. "So you'll meet me tomorrow night?"

"Yep. At the Hy-Ho Club, eight o'clock. See ya there."

It had been a lot longer than five minutes, but the coochie-coo was nowhere to be seen. I suspected she had taken a flyer and gone off in a huff.

Chapter Seventeen

My next stop was the Nightingale Club. Heading there caused me to think about Elinore and I wondered if she would be there.

The sentimental thug was on side-door duty again. His eyes were a little bloodshot and he wore a thick five-o'clock shadow, without enough cologne to hide the odor of stale gin and Angostura bitters. I doubted there had been a bath or a shave in his life the past few days and I wondered why he was trampling down that path, but I didn't ask. He climbed slowly off a high, bar stool when I came in through the door and his eyebrows went up as he recognized me.

"Jeez," he said in a loud voice that tailed off at the end. "You're all over the radio tonight. Some brouhaha down in Urbana."

"You should be working, not listening to that contraption."

I offered him a cigarette and he took one. For a moment, we stood there lighting up and then smoking in silence. He was a thoughtful type, though I didn't have any real evidence that the thoughts he had meant anything to anyone. Maybe if they did, even just a little, he wouldn't be making it so tight with the pink gin. I smiled at him without actually thinking it would help any.

"Whenever you're ready," he said after awhile, looking wistfully at the half of his cigarette he had not yet smoked.

"In a minute," I replied. "I'll finish my cigarette."

"Sure," he said, barely concealing his pleasure. "We can stand here awhile. Got all night." He took another hit off it and looked at the glowing tip again to see how much was left.

"What are you hearing? Are they using my name?"

"Naw, they don't know who it was. Some are blaming it on Dillinger, I guess. It's what they usually do. But we all sort of know that he's lamming it up in upper Wisconsin these days, so it probably had to have been you. Anyway, they found that wop you left behind, sort of clinched it for those of us around here in the know. A couple of forty-five size holes in him, right?" He allowed himself a sloppy wink.

"He had it coming," I said quietly.

The thug nodded seriously and brought the cigarette up to his lips. His eyes squinted as he took a draw on it and he held the smoke in his lungs for a bit. "They always do. No one's crying for him up here."

"You hear the take?"

"Maybe a hundred grand they're saying, maybe more."

"They lie."

"They always do."

"They surely do."

"Anyway, we all know banks are the real crooks."

I nodded absently and shuffled my feet in a circle. I didn't buy into the story that banks deserved to be robbed. I was no Robin Hood sticking up the rich for the poor, and neither were Dillinger, Floyd, the Barkers, Karpis, or any of the others. That folktale was popular in the daily rags. They sold millions of copies by printing stories of foreclosures and self-pitying drivel like Bonnie Parker's "*Story of Suicide Sal.*" I'd inadvertently memorized the last few lines and they floated through my mind, like the refrain of a song that you don't like but hear too often:

> Some day they will go down together,
> And they will bury them side-by-side.
> To a few it means grief,
> To the law it's relief,
> But it's death to Bonnie and Clyde.

I smiled privately, drew on my cigarette, and reflected. They may go down together, but they'll die alone, they all do. It was no skin off my teeth and it certainly didn't hurt my business any to have that little bit of nonsense floated out there, but I wasn't going to lean too heavily on any nostalgic excuse to justify what I did. As far as I knew, the banks I took down had never done anything wrong to anyone; I was robbing them to steal their money and put it in my own pocket.

What was it about this world that gave people the urge to let guys like me off the hook? Why was it that grown women became misty-eyed and filled with blue sentimentality over the mawkish words of Bonnie Parker prophesizing her own well-deserved death? How many men had she murdered for nothing more than a bag of groceries? When I came out of my reverie I realized that the thug's cigarette was burnt down to his fingers and he was staring at me as if he were counting time in his head.

"Come on," he said. "I'll take you up to see the man."

The Irishman was beaming. His tuxedo was immaculate and, as always, he looked the part of the successful American entertainment host, ready and set to bring glamorous leisure to the wealthy people of Chicago. As long as you didn't inhale, there wasn't a whiff of sin about him. He shook my hand heartily, slapped me on the back, and grinned like a piper.

"Absolutely clever, Laddie," he proclaimed loudly. "Lure the foolhardy Italian off on a distant bank robbery and leave him there with bullet holes."

I shrugged modestly.

"We must have a drop. A bit of the Irish stuff, perhaps?"

"Why not."

"You don't need ice?"

I knew there wasn't any. "No," I said. "Neat, like it was meant to be."

"Excellent."

The Irishman stood at his dry sink and poured out two large whiskeys into the fine crystal tumblers that were lined up there. Again, I noticed the weight in my hand as I brought the drink up to my mouth. The smooth heat slid down my throat and warmed my chest, leaving me with a sudden sense of clarity and a revisiting of the dry, thoroughly mundane memory that one day in the near future I, and everyone else I knew would be dead, and utterly forgotten by everyone shortly thereafter. I chased that with another swallow and watched the Irishman as he adjusted his tie and then the cufflinks on his right wrist with his left hand.

"To fatalism," I said, and then drank without waiting for his response.

He took a small sip and paused. "Another toast," he said then, holding up his glass in a formal manner. "To the many talents you bring to our table and the beginning of a swell business relationship."

I raised my glass several inches in acknowledgement of his words. "Swell," I said and took another drink of the whiskey.

"Shall we sit?" he said, gesturing towards the same chair I'd sat in last time with the back of his hand.

I sat down and shifted the whiskey to my other hand. In the sickly soft yellow light of the room, the colors of my clothing seemed to warp and blend. Blues became orange, browns and whites became washed out pale spaces of ugliness. Brightness and vividness ceased to exist under the pale gloom of the chandeliers. Maybe that's why the Irishman always wore black. It left him intact and in command, as if all his power came from some deep and awful place that required him to undermine the very existence of others.

I gazed about and studied the intricate molding of the dark walnut veneer that covered every inch of the room's walls, from crack to seam. The vast desk still offered nothing more than a simple crystal vase with a single yellow rose. I guessed he had it changed every day as a matter of principle, still, it didn't look quite right in that light. It was certainly yellow. I knew that intellectually. But it didn't look yellow. It was changed by the dingy contained light in the room, corrupted from a thing of natural beauty to something else, something that you instinctively wanted to pull back from in a way that was hard to think about in mere words. Human aspects of the room were entirely absent and, when I gazed into his vacant eyes as I sat there drinking his expensive whiskey, I had to stifle a shudder.

"You must forgive me," he said at length. "I had been concerned, Laddie, that your three days were drawing to a close. I should have known better than to worry meself on that account."

"Perhaps you would have sent Eugene?"

"Perhaps." He smiled and nodded vaguely without committing himself.

It was not clarified whether he might have sent Eugene after me or after Reina. I had another swallow of the whiskey. The advancing warmth in my chest mirrored the creeping sensation of my own fatalism.

"There is the small matter of my fee," I told him.

"That there is, there surely is, Laddie, and you shall have it. I believe the sum of two thousand dollars was mentioned as recompense for the elimination of Mr. Reina."

I nodded once.

"And a weekly retainer of three hundred," he continued.

I shook my head. "Just the two thousand. I'll do contract work, but I won't be yours for a retainer."

He smiled gently and kindly, except without using his eyes or emitting a drop of warmth. "I reckon with a hundred grand of Urbana money in your coat, the three hundred is a bit irrelevant."

"You shouldn't believe everything you hear on the radio."

"No, I suppose not."

"Radios are for drama."

"Indeed. Still, must have been a bit of excitement down there? Quite a lot of shooting, I suppose. Lot of bullets in the air, no?"

Without responding I took a swallow of whiskey and receded into the chair. I let my eyes fall down towards the floor as I thought for a moment about Urbana and the five men I'd left behind: four shot dead with .45 slugs before we even got out of the banks, another still unharmed and walking when I left him there in the street, but already just as dead as the other four. I thought about the money that would have been theirs. It was an ugly business and I cursed myself for being a part of it.

Like a bad, bad dream I saw each of the five as they must be now, laid out cold and discolored in a county morgue with paper tags stringed to their toes. When they were first born, would their mothers have predicted such an end? With a bit of a start I reoriented to current time and place. The walls were closing in and the putrid yellow light of the room seemed to be gathering in effect. When I looked over at him, the Irishman was frowning up at the ceiling. My eyes followed his upwards, but found no answers there to any of the questions I might have asked. With my right hand only I got a Chesterfield between my lips and then located my matches.

"Mind if I smoke?" I asked before striking the lighter.

"By all means," he replied. "How can you trust a man who doesn't smoke?"

"Reckon you shouldn't," I said as I exhaled.

"Where shall you keep your newly acquired funds?"

"Pardon me?"

"What I mean to ask is where will you keep the newly acquired assets from your recent banking activities? Obviously you can't put them into another bank for security."

"Ahh," I responded. "That point is not quite so obvious to me. There are plenty of places a man like me can bank his money."

"Certainly, Laddie, this issue is not a new one to you and you've thought through all the possibilities, and no doubt you have your own method that you use. I'm simply wondering what it is and whether it is adequate for your purposes. Is it truly secure and does it maximize the investment potential?"

I nodded and took my time responding to his question. Cigarette smoke filled my lungs a couple of times before I spoke again. "Yes, well. It is an issue that we face in our line of work. Cash sums can't easily be stored with a state bank without having to complete certain paperwork … and there are risks and complexities to that. But don't assume it can't be done."

His eyes were wide and skeptical. "Are you telling me that you save your money in a bank, a formal government-backed financial institution? That seems rather preposterous."

I didn't see any benefit to telling him the truth on this matter. Instead I grinned at him and waved him off.

"At what rate of return?"

"First," I said. "It would be none of your business. Second, don't assume there aren't multiple options for a guy like me and that I wouldn't diversify for a wide range of reasons. Third, if you have a proposal to make, I suggest you make it straight away."

"Well said, Laddie. You are correct with your first two points, as to your third, my proposal is this: if you will trust me with some of your profits, I will guarantee their security and will return to you two points per week. And at any point after a minimum of three months time, I will return all or part of your principal to you upon request."

"You'll put the money out on the street?"

"That is the common parlance."

"At what per cent interest?"

"Now that would be my business."

"But you'll make a sizeable profit over and above my two points?"

"Of course, we're both businessmen. And there is the added benefit that we will, in the process, clean the money you turn over to us and we'll take the large bills, the ones that might raise eyebrows were you to spend them in certain places."

I nodded. "And if I'm caught and put in prison?"

"Then the money will be there for you, to support whatever needs you may have, legal or otherwise."

"And if I'm killed? You keep the money?"

"Leave me written instructions. If you're killed, I'll bequeath the money as you like, minus a twenty percent processing fee. That's less than an estate lawyer would run you, not to mention any taxes, in a more traditional arrangement."

"True. Except this involves quite a bit of trust on my part and very little on yours."

He nodded very slowly before responding. "It's the business we've chosen for ourselves. I will give you my word and my handshake."

"And if you're bumped or convicted?"

He smiled wanly. "Well now, Laddie. We'll just both have to hope that doesn't happen."

"How large a stake can you absorb now?"

"What do you think?"

"How much?"

"Any amount you care to invest. Maybe start with fifty thousand?"

It was my turn to smile towards him and play along with this game of false trust. "Told you not to believe everything you hear on the radio. I might give you ten."

"We can start there," he replied. He chewed his lip pensively then said, "And then, as you grow more confident, as you realize the benefits of my services, perhaps you'll put more in over time."

I nodded and finished my whiskey. The Irishman stood up quickly with his own empty glass and crossed over to the dry sink. "Another drop?" he asked holding the bottle forward.

"Half a finger," I said. I stood up myself and walked towards him with the idea in my mind that I wasn't going to sit down again. We didn't have that much to talk about.

"Just that extra little measure to set up the evening." He poured an overly generous amount into my glass and then his own.

"Cheers," I said, without any.

We drank. And then we stood there in silence for a moment next to the dry sink.

"I've got your two thousand over here." The Irishman set his glass down and stepped behind his desk. I set my glass next to his and followed him across the room. Without sitting down he opened the top center drawer and found an envelope that held several inches of very green cash. He rifled through the bills with the edge of his thumb quickly, a skill he had apparently mastered through regular practice. I could see him counting silently to himself. When he reached the desired amount he thumbed it out of the envelope as one might fan a deck of cards. With his other hand he peeled that off and thumped it once on the desktop to square the bills together. The envelope disappeared back into the drawer.

"Here ye be, Laddie," he said, extending the money towards me. "This is for your work on Mr. Reina."

I took the bills without counting them, folded them in half, and sunk them into my front right pocket as if they meant little to me, which they did.

The Irishman grinned again. "That's money well earned and your manners are gracious, passing up the very human urge to count it."

I smiled at him, shaking my head. "I had no such urge – you wouldn't cheat me."

"That I would not." He seemed pleased with himself and my response to our transaction. "And what about our other transaction?" He referred to his prior offer to serve as my investment bank.

I removed an envelope from my front jacket pocket. It held ten thousand in large bills that I was not going to enjoy changing. "Here's ten," I said, handing the envelope to the Irishman.

He smiled and put the envelope in the left breast pocket of his tuxedo, without counting it, and made a slight bow.

"I should leave now," I said.

He nodded pleasantly. "We'll have other business to discuss soon. There's plenty more water in the well that came from. But another day, yes? Come back in seven days and I'll have your two hundred. Or, if you prefer, I can roll it over into the principal."

I nodded firmly and tapped him the gunner's salute. "I'll let you know."

"Tell me something," he said, as I was turning away. "When you shot him, did he see you before you did it? Did he know it was coming? Did you see the look in his eyes in that last moment?"

I took two steps towards the door, cutting slowly through the yellow gloom, and then stopped for a moment without turning to look back at him. Suddenly I was very tired. I considered the tone of his question for a short moment, and then I walked on without responding to his question and pulled the door closed tightly behind me. Out in the hallway, I resisted the urge to go back in and shoot the old Irish ghoul. I took the elevator down to the ground floor, also resisting the urge to press the button for the Nightingale Club where I might find Elinore. I was just too damn tired from a single day that seemed more like three.

*

The house on Prairie Avenue was mostly dark when I arrived. Mrs. Giacalone sat in the kitchen with a cup of tea, reading her Bible in the dim light of a small lamp at the kitchen table. Miss Charlotte was curled on her lap when I came in. As soon as the cat saw me, she hopped off and did a slow, languorous stretch with both front paws well out in front of her. With her tail in the air, she pressed her chest almost to the floor, then rose up slowly and moved forward like a wave briefly raising her back. Moving quiet as a whisper, she then glided towards me and rubbed the length of her body against my ankles in a long smooth motion that made me feel very much appreciated. I reached down and reciprocated, running the backs of my knuckles across her muzzle, and down along her neck and side. She leaned in towards me and purred, and then just as quickly she disappeared into the enveloping shadows of the house.

"You might have called," Mrs. Giacalone said, closing her Bible carefully on a pressed leather bookmark. She lifted her chin to look up at me more carefully in the stark light and brushed the lock of hair off her forehead as she did so.

"I told you before I left that I would be away for a night, maybe two."

I was surprised, but not angry that she would confront me.

She sighed quietly. "With all the commotion on the radio, I was worried."

"You needn't have been."

"You heard what happened down in Urbana?"

"Mrs. Giacalone, I took the train to Milwaukee, for business."

She looked at me with disapproving eyes, holding the lie there, floating it gently in the space between us. Yet there was something else in her face: a thin veil of relief. She didn't really want to know, even if she had her suspicions. "Yes, of course, you were selling insurance today."

I stood next to her chair and put a hand gently on her shoulder, rubbing it quietly in a slow, absent circle. "Yes," I said. "I don't want you to worry."

"It's this world we live in."

"Well, it's the only one we've got."

"We make do. We have our blessings."

"Yes."

"I'm glad you're here with us."

"Me too."

She looked up at me with eyes that were, all of a sudden, large and grateful. "Are you hungry? I can heat up some stew and potatoes." She placed her hand on top of mine. Her touch was so light that I wasn't sure it was even there.

"No thank you, Mrs. Giacalone. I'm not hungry and I'm very tired now." I pulled my hand away gently and went up the stairs to my room.

Chapter Eighteen

A blustering rain swept across Garfield Park. Five days had passed since the Urbana adventure. I stood at the west entrance, just off the main path in a spot that was sheltered from the brunt of the wind. My collar was up and I had an umbrella, but I still got wet. Few people were moving about. It was late afternoon and I was waiting for Elinore.

She arrived ten minutes late with a red umbrella held slanted against the water that was coming down at an angle. Her hair was moist and several thin, dark wisps stuck to her cheek and neck, giving her the look of a small, vulnerable child as she tottered against the gale. Black make-up around her eyes melted with the rain, and dripped down her cheeks.

As she moved in closer to me, I could see that her eyes were puffy and red beneath the dark make-up. Perhaps she had been crying along the way, coming to meet me. She kissed me briefly on the mouth – a soft, more than friendly kiss that almost lingered in a shadow-like way. As her face drew away from mine I caught the faint, orchestral scent of laudanum.

"Over here," I said, taking her arm with one hand and holding my umbrella so that it overlapped hers. We dashed to a small, covered grandstand that had two park benches. Several little birds skirted about. They were not happy we were there to share their refuge from the downpour. "We can sit here."

She was out of breath just a little and the way she looked at me tightened the knot in my stomach.

When she spoke her words were urgent, but her tone was flat. "I'm relieved you're safe. I was so scared when I started to hear the reports."

"You have to ignore what you hear on the radio. They usually get it wrong."

"It was in the papers also."

"Ignore those too, they're written to sell advertising."

"I thought they'd shot you, that you were one of the dead men the law killed down there in those banks."

I snorted. "The law didn't kill anyone in those banks."

I wasn't surprised the police would claim credit for the three men in the banks. They were welcome to it – it didn't hurt me any to have that off my sheet. But it didn't leave me feeling too good about the men who were in charge of enforcing the law. I'd seen the corruption before from men with a public charge to enforce the laws, in small towns and big ones, in courts and in prisons. They weren't all bad, but there was still enough corruption so that you couldn't always be sure who the real bad guys were and it put a bitter taste in the back of your mouth any time the subject came up.

"According to the radio, the police shot three men robbing the banks and another man several blocks away. I thought you were dead."

With an arm around her shoulder I brushed my cheek against hers and whispered. "It's okay, I'm not hurt." I rubbed her shoulder, rocking her body gently against me, trying to soothe her. We sat there like that, rocking gently together, before either of us spoke again.

"I was so scared. You didn't tell me you were going on a job."

"No. I couldn't do that."

Elinore absorbed this for a moment. Her eyes worked hard to focus. "I guess you can't, can you? You never can." Tears welled in her eyes and she quickly turned away, pulling her shoulder out of my grasp. There was now a distance between us that seemed wider than mere inches.

I shook my head, even though I knew she could not see my response to her question. "Take this," I said then, handing her my handkerchief. She took it, still without looking at me, and dabbed at her eyes. When she was finished, she passed it back to me. It was smudged variously with the black, blue, and red she wore on her porcelain face, a face that needed none of the presumed enhancement offered by any of the beauty products that she wore.

"Let me see your purse."

"What?" Her eyes, when she turned back towards me, were slow, quiet shutters filmed with the mists of fear, sadness, and induced languor.

I took the purse out of her hands, sliding the strap off her shoulder. She did not resist. The oily, brown bottle, with its label peeling off from moisture, was on top. It was nearly empty. I took the stopper out and sniffed once. "Why are you using this stuff?" I asked as I replaced the stopper.

The expression that slowly spread down her face, started from her eyebrows and worked down to her chin, had not even a hint of anger, just dry, hard pain. "It makes me gay."

"No, it doesn't," I said. "Don't ever believe that, kid. It never makes anyone gay."

She reached for the bottle and I let her take it out of my hand. "Only use it once in a while, anyway, when I really, really need it bad. But sometimes I get so blue."

"Who gave it to you?"

"The doctor."

I watched her eyes, hoping to discourage the lie without saying anything.

"I take it for female trouble," she said.

"How long?"

"Since about a month after Colt died."

I calculated in my mind. Colt had died in early February, so she hadn't been using that for long – a little over two months. There was still time to turn it around.

"And each bottle only lasts half as long as it used to."

Elinore nodded dumbly. She removed the stopper and took a quick, defiant swig from the little brown bottle, then quickly placed it back in her purse.

"It's the pattern. Before you know it, the bottle will only last a third as long, then a quarter. That's the way it goes."

She shook her head. "I don't use it every day. It's the only thing that makes me gay."

"It's killing you. Slowly for now, without your knowing, but it is and will do so quicker and quicker. Eventually it's like sliding off a ledge and you can't help yourself anymore."

"Take me home now?"

The rain had slowed and the little birds that had been there first were carping at us to leave their sanctuary now. "Come on," I told her quietly. "The walk will do you good."

*

I knew where she lived, but I'd never been inside. It was a corner studio apartment walk-up on the third floor, with a small foyer. Once inside the foyer, a set of double French doors opened into a relatively large living space that included the living room, dining room, and bedroom as one unit. A small open kitchen was off to the right, covered by a large sliding door that was open part way. There were two more doors. I assumed one was a closet and the other a bathroom. The furniture was simple, but tasteful. The colors were earth tones, mostly off-whites and browns, and the patterns were all solids and stripes. None of it was inexpensive. The walls held several charcoal drawings of horse and pasture scenes.

The only bright color in the room was a large vase of fresh yellow flowers on a corner table beside the sofa. I knew where they had come from and it made me feel sick to think about. I stood in the middle of the room and turned around slowly.

"Cocktails?" she asked. Using her toe she pushed the sliding door so that it was open all the way.

"Do you have whiskey?"

"Two whiskey cocktails coming up."

I watched as she muddled the sugar, Angostura bitters, and branch water in two glasses with the back of a tarnished silver spoon. Then she poured out a large amount of whiskey, stirred once, and handed one of the glasses to me. She tossed the spoon onto the counter with a small, hollow clang.

"I can chip some ice."

"No thank you, this is fine."

"Here's mud in your eye," she said, clinking her glass against mine. We drank and our eyes held each other over the tops of our glasses. The drink was strong, laced with more of the sweet-bitterness than one usually received in a whiskey cocktail. I moved my glass in a slow circle to swirl the mixture around.

Elinore leaned towards me. "Will you tell me about my brother now?"

I swallowed more of the bourbon and nodded. "Yes. Let's sit on the couch and look out at the rain."

Lightning flared outside, flashing in the atmosphere above the city.

Chapter Nineteen

I'd spent most of the fall of 1933, through the holidays and into the New Year at a small cabin near Reno, Nevada on the northeast shore of Lake Tahoe, off the slopes of the Sierras. It was a simple place and people minded their own business.

Colt wouldn't stay there for long, but he came through at regular intervals as he moved back and forth between Reno and San Francisco, where he had a girl. The Union Pacific had a train that made the two hundred-mile trip every day at a regular time. He liked the life in the bigger city and could only stand the peace and quiet of the cabin in small doses – a few days every other week or so – and then he would be off again.

I was content there. I liked the sun, the desert, the sagebrush, and even the vastness that surrounded me when I looked off towards the horizon. I liked the quiet that you found at night when you took a rowboat out onto the lake. Sometimes I dropped a line in, but I never made much effort to catch anything. I simply liked the peace I found as I floated out there, with nothing particular to do past listen to the water drip off the oars.

When we had first arrived, coming through in the dead of night, we'd had no intention to stay for more than a cup of hot coffee and a stack of flapjacks. I had been taken with the way the stars looked in the crisp night air, hanging over the ridge of the Sierras, dangling and bouncing brightly there. A diner waitress flirted with Colt and suggested a hotel she was pretty sure would take us in at that late hour. So we decided to stay for a few days. Colt disappeared with the waitress and I caught up on my sleep.

On the third day Colt showed up again, without the waitress. Instead, there was another fellow with him. He introduced me to Curly Graham. I'd heard of Graham and knew his reputation in the underworld. He owned and operated a glitzy joint – the Bank Club. When the Nevada State Legislature had legalized gambling in 1931, Graham had been ready with influence, muscle, and plenty of smooth cash. He'd had the Bank Club up and running from Day One. He was a lanky fellow with long hair and he wore dusty cowboy clothing, including boots and a wide-brim leather Stetson. When displeased, he was also a killer. A couple years back he had emptied a six-shooter into one of his own faro dealers, a man named McCracken. When Graham's pal, the sheriff, arrived on the scene at the Haymarket Club, another of Graham's casinos, the killing was promptly ruled justifiable homicide on the spot.

That was the kind of guy Colt liked to deal with. Still, even with the casinos and legal prostitution in the Stockade, Reno's red-light district, there wasn't quite enough excitement for Colt in Reno. When he was in San Francisco he did occasional work for Joe Parente, who smuggled rum and other spirits but made a point to avoid violence. Colt was okay with that too. He went along as muscle when the shipments came in and escorted the convoys out to the distribution points. It was quiet, dull business and Colt could only stand a little bit of it at a time.

There were a lot of big-time bank robbers and other criminals around Reno. When Colt was in town we'd bump into them when we hung around the Haymarket or one of the other clubs. Mostly they were friendly, although a few were just cautious and you couldn't really tell what they were thinking.

Along the way, we met up with an ex-con named Gordon who had come out from Oklahoma after serving a six-year hitch in McAllister for armed robbery. He'd been in with Doc Barker and after he got out he'd hoped to join up with the Barkers and Karpis, but they didn't have need for another man. Curly Graham introduced him to us as one of the top jug markers in the business, said he'd worked with Harvey Bailey and Eddie Bentz before being sent up. I liked him okay and Colt seemed sure that he knew how to do his job, so we invited him in with us one night after playing cards until three a.m.

It was at one of those late-night sessions that we decided to take down a string of small-town banks across Iowa, Illinois, Indiana, and Ohio. Gordon was a heavy-set farm boy who carried a lot of weight around the middle and in the shoulders. He was from Ohio and knew the Midwest states, said he knew the banks and the roads too. On a map he drew up a route through those states with eight banks on it, saying at least four of them would be ripe targets at any given time. He convinced us he knew how to case them and plan the routes in and out. He was already familiar with most of the roads in that part of the country. Somehow, at the time, the idea didn't seem half bad.

One Sunday afternoon in early January, while we were stone-cold sober, we decided to rob every bank along that route that seemed promising. Gordon would go first, in his car, to mark the banks and the roads. Like every other jug marker in the business, he had ways to obtain bank floor plans and learn about their safes. He also would observe employee and customer patterns, and would drive the roads himself to study the routes. Colt and I would follow two weeks later and meet up with Gordon at the shore of Lake Michigan in Indiana, a small beachfront community at the northeastern tip of Michigan City. Gordon had been there before and knew of a cottage we could rent. He promised it would serve as a good base to work from.

The day we left Reno the sun was shining and snow glistened along the peaks of the Sierras. We had a fast car, a dark blue Essex Terraplane, with a full tank and a trunk full of guns, ammo, vests, two hand grenades, maps and first aid supplies. As we drove out of town, Colt was happily whistling the melody line from an old piano rag. I didn't know which one and I didn't ask.

*

We drove straight through without stopping other than to fill the gas tank or eat a quick meal. After the first few hours there wasn't much left to talk about so mostly we rode in silence. I smoked a little and tried to keep my thoughts clear. An hour from the Indiana shore, Colt spoke the first words that either of us had uttered in almost eight hours. I was driving and he had been sleeping in a curled position on the back seat.

"Can't sleep," he said. His voice came from just over my right shoulder as he sat up in the back seat.

"We're almost there," I replied.

"What do you think of this?"

"You have doubts?"

"Maybe. Nothing particular. I reckon not. It's the life we chose."

"You missing the skirt in San Francisco already?"

He chuckled and then yawned slowly. "Naw. We're quits anyway, see."

"What then?"

"What do you mean?"

"Something's eating at you."

He seemed to consider this for a moment. "Why are we doing this? Why are we robbing more banks?"

"Because we're bank robbers. It's what we do." I was grinning to myself

as I spoke the words.

"Doesn't make much sense. We hardly know this guy, Gordon, and you would just as soon retire from this business as walk into another bank."

"Somebody has to go along to make sure you don't screw it up."

"You could have stayed in Reno."

"Too dull."

"Not for you. You liked the quiet, out there in that little rowboat, pretending to fish. Did you even use a hook on that line? You never caught so much as a minnow, did you?"

I shrugged. "What's got you unsettled?"

"Nothing much that I can say." He was quiet for a while and we listened to the hum of the car wheels. "Just got that bad feeling running through me, like somebody is stepping over my grave."

"You sleep any back there?"

"Naw."

"It's almost dawn. We always have our worst, blackest thoughts just before sunrise. It's natural. Especially if you haven't slept much."

"Reckon so. You think Gordon will be ready when we get there? Think he knows what he's doing?"

I moved my shoulders again in the dark, knowing Colt could sense the movement sitting behind me as he was. "Hard to say. He used to work with Bentz, who's as good as there ever was. We'll know a bit when we talk with him, see the plans he's got for us. We'll know more after we walk into that first bank ... we'll know even more when we walk out of it."

"Gimme a cigarette."

I found my pack of Chesterfields on the seat next to me and held it back, over my shoulder so that he could extract one.

"Thanks," he said after he lit up. He didn't usually smoke too much. For him it was a nervous gesture.

We drove without speaking for a while. Behind me I could hear the faint, solitary sounds of his smoking: the draw on the cigarette, the exhalation, the wind rushing in each time he cracked the window a notch to flick the ashes.

Slivers of red-orange light were appearing along the horizon ahead of us and the sky just above those slivers was gradually becoming a lighter shade of blue and purple. Colt rolled his window down farther than usual for as long as it took to toss the cigarette butt out. The inside of the car whistled with cold air and then it was quiet again. My ears felt singed by the harsh air.

"I reckon you're right about that," he said finally. "Just black thoughts in the middle of the night ... don't mean nothing. Too much time to sit around and

140

worry about little things, things that don't matter or mean much anyway. Once we get moving, everything will be fine."

"Sure it will," I replied.

"You remember my sister, Elinore?"

I just nodded without turning around, already knowing where he was going with this.

"I know you used to be sweet on her back when we were kids on Hennepin Avenue. If anything happens to me I want you to look her up in Chicago, give her my share if it amounts to anything."

"There's no use in talking that way now."

"Promise you will."

"Of course, I promise," I said, with the splendid dawn rising up before us now, causing me to squint into the brilliant sunlight. I noticed that my heart was suddenly beating faster.

*

Our first stop was for coffee and breakfast. We arrived at the cottage on Lake Shore Drive just after eight o'clock in the morning. From where we parked, we could sense the lake idling there on the other side of the dunes. It was unusually warm for late January. Seagulls called out from above us as they glided by, toing and froing over the shoreline. Otherwise it was quiet and there were no signs of other people around at that hour of the morning. In the winter there were not many people around town anyway – it was too cold to go in the water or spend much time on the beach.

Gordon had done his work. He had detailed maps, hand-sketched floor plans, and pages of hand-scrawled notes. The house was a roomy two-story brick structure that cost us $100 a month, and Gordon had paid four months in advance to the Long Beach Reality Company. They were happy to have any business at that time of the year.

Standing on the back porch, I looked out over the vast expanse of water and heard the waves lap at the beach. The colors of the water were dark browns and greens and the sky was gray all the way out to the horizon. That night we grilled steaks and toasted rye bread on a small outdoor grill and sat on the steps that led down to the dunes, eating our steaks and drinking cold bottles of Hamms beer. The air was brisk but with a heavy sweater on it felt good for a while. We ate quickly, making only small talk, before moving inside to the kitchen table to discuss our plans.

141

"Where do we start?" Colt asked. He stood up to retrieve three bottles of beer from the icebox. He opened them at the table and switched on a small electric lamp before he sat down again.

Gordon cleared his throat. He coughed once and then drank some Hamms, and swallowed several times. He set the bottle on the table. "Make sure our plans are good," he said. "Any idiot can walk into a bank with a gun and grab the cash – it's getting away that is the tricky part."

"No argument there, and so?" Colt asked.

Gordon nodded and seemed pleased to review the plans that we had already discussed several times before in Reno. "So, first, we focus on small-time banks. We can get in and out of those without getting caught up in traffic congestion. There's fewer cops, and then plenty of nearby countryside to get lost in."

Colt grinned and nodded. "But less money perhaps."

"True, but less risk. All the money in the world won't do you any good if you're in stir or filled with lead."

"Yeah, so we knock over banks in hick towns."

"Yes," Gordon responded. "And we need at least two more guys."

"Two, are you sure?"

"Yes, we talked about this before. Two inside: one to skim the cashier's cages and one to go after the vault. Two outside or just inside at the windows: to cover exits, keep a look-out and keep people from going in. And then one to stay with the car and keep the engine running. That will be my job. It would be best if we could find a sixth man, another man to go inside to help with crowd control, if we need it."

"We've done banks with three before, it's how Floyd does it." Colt spoke evenly, not trying to start an argument.

"Had some close scrapes too," I added. "If we can find the right two to join in, I'm for it. No need to be greedy about the split-up."

Colt remained impassive and drank down his beer. "Fine with me too," he said after. He set the empty bottle on the counter behind him and leaned back in his chair, with his elbow on the chair-back and one toe on the floor to balance everything. The house itself creaked with age and wind.

Gordon nodded. "Okay, and we got the right car. That Essex can go plenty fast. We need at least two machine guns, one inside the bank, one with me in the car."

"We gonna shoot people?" Colt's chair rocked forward and then back, ever so slightly.

"Not to shoot people, to scare the hell out of 'em if necessary, to blast out the

142

windows of the cars and store fronts real good so that nobody will come out to bother us."

"We got 'em," Colt said. "Two of 'em, Thompsons. Plus shotguns and pistols, .38 revolvers and .45 semi-autos. This is where it gets fun." He grinned hard.

"And you brought vests?"

"Surely did. Plus two kegs of roofing nails to throw down in the road if there's heat behind us. We even have grenades."

"Medical supplies?"

Colt shrugged casually. "Sure, just in case."

Gordon nodded thoughtfully and a smile slowly formed on his face. "Well, damn," he said quietly. "We're almost ready."

"Just got to find two more hands," I reminded us all. I finished my beer and lit a cigarette.

"Yeah, and I want to drive the routes again just to be sure of those roads I've marked. Maybe try to go in two weeks?"

I nodded and Colt slapped the table top with the palm of his hand.

We sat there for a moment without speaking. My mind turned several things around. Finally I spoke: "We have to find the right two. It's important."

"There are reliable guys out there."

"They have to be more than reliable. We need them to be level-headed too."

"Sure, that's what I meant."

"No, I mean level-headed in a situation, not the kind who overreact or get mean if they don't have to. We need to have an understanding among us."

"What kind of an understanding?"

"We're robbing banks for the money, not doing this to shoot people who don't need to be shot."

"No doubt of it. But if things get hot—"

"We don't shoot unless we have to, and even then we have to be cool about it. We have to treat people in the banks – I mean the civilians – without cruelty. They're just people in the wrong place and we need to remember that."

Colt was frowning and his chair came forward. "But if we need hostages?"

"If we need them, I mean really need them, we take them. But we treat them with courtesy. We treat the women, especially, with courtesy and respect. We don't hit them, or scare them any more than we have to."

"It's wise anyway, no sense riling up the men any more than we need to."

"That's right, but even more than that, we just don't do it. You wouldn't want your mother or your sister or your lady-friend treated badly. We have to agree on that."

"I can agree on it," Gordon said."

I looked over at Colt and he smiled. "Of course, it goes without saying."

"And we have to be careful about who we choose for the other two. They have to abide by our rules."

Gordon nodded. "No hurting the women or children ... unless we have to."

I gave him a dark look but I didn't say anything more. My cigarette had burned down and I stubbed it out before pushing back from the table. A gust of wind shook the house. The windows and shutters rattled as if haunted.

*

It wasn't hard to find two guys. Through our contacts in St. Paul we recruited Maxwell Tenney and his partner William Durant, who preferred to be called Bo. They had served time at Lansing with Karpis, who recommended them to Gordon through Harry Sawyer, and had pulled two postal jobs in Milwaukee. Sawyer promised they were levelheaded when it counted.

They were hiding out in Chicago and came up and joined us in Long Beach just eight days later. When they arrived, they brought with them an arsenal of firearms and ammunition, a fast car, and a fifteen hundred dollar stake to contribute.

The next day, Colt and I went down to Chicago for two days and met with James Murray. Murray was a middle-aged bullyboy with a thick neck, soft features, and a crooked scar that ran across the side of his head over his left ear. As a young man he had worked in the Chicago court system and then served as a precinct captain in the "old bloody 19th Ward." At the start of Prohibition he had invested in near beer breweries around Chicago and southern Wisconsin that manufactured more potent alcohol than was legally allowed and distributed it to the O'Donnells and other smaller Chicago gangs. In the mid-twenties he had served a five-year stint in Leavenworth for the Rondout train robbery. He had helped plan the operation and had fenced the bonds. The Newton brothers, who had committed the actual robbery, were still in jail with little hope of getting out any time soon.

Murray agreed to help launder the money from our planned bank robberies and to sell any securities and bonds we obtained. I didn't like him. I figured he had traded information for an early release; let the Newton brothers take the long fall. But as long as we didn't give him anything to work with we'd be okay, and we were going to need somebody to help clean the money afterward. That was the toughest part about this business – finding the right people to *work with.*

*

The evening before we headed out, Colt and I took a walk down through the dunes together. It was just the two of us, away from the others, watching the dusk settle away from the lake.

"How you feeling about this?" I asked him.

We stood near the water with our hands in our pockets and our collars turned up. There was a smell close to juniper in the air.

"I'm feeling okay. I like Gordon. I think he's a good one, knows what he's doing. The other two seem okay too. Karpis vouched for them, so they'll be fine. What do you think?"

"Yeah," I said slowly, "I agree about Gordon. I have no reason to doubt Tenney or Durant, but remember we don't know them. Not personally, anyway. Until they prove themselves, let's be careful."

"Sure. And even after they prove themselves, we'll be careful. We always are. You worried about how they'll do?"

"I have no reason to. They've made all the right noises, spouted all the right lines."

"Promises are one thing, keeping them's another."

It was what I was thinking and I nodded.

"It'll be okay," Colt assured. "We'll watch them. If they don't work out, don't follow our way, we'll stop them well enough from spoiling things."

"We surely will. Unless someone else does it for us first."

"What about the plan?" He squinted at me in the fading light. The faint juniper smell had disappeared.

"It's ambitious – five banks in nine days, but Gordon may be right. Hit them hard, hit them fast and get out before anyone has time to organize anything against us. With cars, supplies, and hideouts organized and set up in advance it might just work. He's done the homework, I like his routes and his bank layouts."

Colt pulled his collar tight across the back of his neck and stepped closer to me. "Gordon can drive, I've seen him. He's reliable and he's cool. We won't need much from the other two, not with you and I on point inside the banks. We just need Tenney and Durant to cover the door, run a little crowd control. I know Bo, at least, can shoot and he seems steady enough."

I nodded, and thought of all the things that could still go wrong. "What

145

about after?"

"You're always thinking ahead. You know I don't do that so well."

"You have to have a plan."

Colt grinned at me in the flickering twilight. "Yeah. I've thought about it. I think it's time to retire, at least for a while. You gonna argue with that?"

"No sir, not me."

"I've been thinking about it ever since we left Reno."

"So what?"

"We finish this, we'll have the stake we need, start over somewhere."

"How are we going to start over, they'll always be looking for us?"

"You know what I mean."

"Where you thinking of?"

"You liked Reno," Colt said, grinning. "Bet we can find you another rowboat."

"It's too close to the action, maybe not a good choice for the long-run. There'd always be those temptations."

"You afraid I won't be able to stay out of it?"

"Could be."

Colt leaned back on his heels, thoughtfully. Sand crunched beneath his weight as he shifted about. "How about Mexico?"

"You speak the language, do you?"

He shrugged and looked out over the water. "Could learn. The weather's warm."

"Seems kind of complicated."

"Texas? We liked San Antonio okay that time."

"Maybe. I was thinking about going north. North of the Sierras – maybe Oregon or Washington state."

"We going alone?"

"Well, we can't bring Gordon."

"No. I guess not. And he wouldn't ask, after all. What about Elinore? You know she's in Chicago now."

I smiled, standing there under the stars, thinking about a retirement with Colt and Elinore somewhere quiet. "Yeah," I responded. "That might be nice. Would she come?"

He nodded, and then said: "Are you still in love with her?"

"Me? I never was."

"Sure you weren't. Everybody on Hennepin got that wrong."

I stared at him. It was hard to read his expression in the waning light.

"It was in every look you ever gave her, every question you ever asked

146

about her. There was always that look or that tone."

"It was a long time ago."

"Not for you. You don't let go of things like that. I know you better than that."

I shrugged and turned to look out over the water. The last few spoonfuls of light played across the small waves that rolled in and lapped at the shore. If you didn't think about the realities too hard, it might have been easy to imagine living in an idyllic world.

"We could be happy together, the three of us, up there in the Northwest, away from it all."

I turned back towards him. "What would we do with ourselves?"

"Just be, just be."

I shook my head. "It would never work out."

"It could."

"I guess it's pretty to think so, anyway."

Chapter Twenty

We took down the first three banks without a hitch.

At the fourth bank they were waiting for us when we tried to leave with the money. If they'd held their fire until we were all out, standing exposed and spread out on the concrete steps between the front columns, it would have been a duck shoot for them. Instead, they opened up as soon as Tenney pushed open the main door. He caught a shotgun blast in the chest that knocked him back into Durant's arms. Durant caught him and held him for a moment amid the splintering of glass, as an entire police division opened up from across the street. Then he went down too, riddled with bullets from the volley of small arms fire.

Colt and I both made low on the floor and crawled back towards the teller's cage as lead flew over us. From somewhere on the street a machine gun opened up and there were more shots from small arms. There was also the sound of shattered glass falling from window casings and then an explosion that was probably one of grenades. It shook the building and interrupted the firing from the street. That would have been Gordon.

During the lull we heard the sound of men shouting and calling for help. From somewhere above us an alarm now rang loudly. Tenney and Durant lay tangled together in a bloody heap where they fell. They were dead and it was too late to do anything for them. Colt looked at me, and I nodded. He reared up on one knee and calmly fired half a magazine of machinegun bullets. Then he dropped and rolled away from me towards the side exit.

I had the small leather suitcase that held all the money we had just collected. I pushed it hard, and slid it across the floor towards Colt and then rolled towards him myself. He gave the suitcase another shove towards the side door twenty feet away, and waved me past him. As I crawled by he emptied the magazine out towards the street. While he attached a new magazine, I came up on a knee, just as he had, and fired all eight shots, two at a time, adjusting my aim slightly between each pair. I had sighted two targets and they both went down as I fired. I couldn't be sure whether I had hit them or they had taken cover. Ducking down again, I ejected the empty magazine with my right thumb and slammed a new one in with my left hand. I heard the metallic clang of the empty magazine as it hit the marble floor and bounced away from me. For a moment nobody was shooting at us *and I could smell the cordite.*

"Now," Colt yelled.

He reared up again and fired about fifteen shots, moving the barrel of his machinegun in an arc that covered the entire front of the bank. The windows of storefronts and cars on the other side of the street shattered under the strafing. The racket in the tight stone room was incredible.

I grabbed the suitcase and jumped through the side door, running at a low crouch. A uniformed officer was just coming around the corner as I reached the pavement. I fired twice from about thirty yards away. His face twisted and he fumbled a rifle, his arm swinging awkwardly like they do when a bone is shattered. Colt came out behind me, cursing. He worked a new magazine onto the machinegun as he moved, and we sprinted down the street together and around the corner, away from where the shooting was.

"I counted seven," *Colt yelled as we spun around the corner and out of the line of fire. There was a hoarse urgency to his voice that had never been there before.* "And we must have got at least three or four of them, right? Where's Gordon?"

We were following our back-up plan. After dropping us at the front of the bank, Gordon had taken the car around to a wide alley on the side of the building opposite to where we had just come out. If there was shooting and it looked like we were in trouble he was to take the car all the way down that alley, turn right and pick us up on the street behind and a block down from the bank, where we now stood.

"He'll be along," *I said loudly. My ears rang from the shots.* "We'll have to make a stand here until he comes. Set up the Thompson over there. Sight it along that line."

Colt moved immediately to the spot where I pointed and dropped to one knee again in a shooter's stance with his back towards me. His hat was tilted low over his forehead. He aimed the machinegun in the direction I had indicated, towards the street corner that we had just rounded. From his position he could also shift aim and cover the street that we were on now. I ranged about fifteen feet down the street from him and set the suitcase against a fire hydrant, kneeling beside it with my .45 extended out towards the alley from where Gordon should appear.

For almost ten seconds there was no sound from the street. It was one of those moments where all you could hear was your own heartbeat, and it shook like thunder. Then we heard more shots coming from the other side of the bank and there was a screech of tires.

"It's Gordon," *I said. The Essex Terraplane appeared from the alley, barely*

150

braking as it reached the street and made a hard right. At the same time, a police car came down the street from the opposite direction behind me, siren blaring.

I turned to look over my shoulder. An officer leaned out the back window firing a single shot rifle. I could see the expression on his face. His eyes were bunched together beneath slanted eyebrows. He fired three times. The second shot caught Colt in the side and spun him around. I pivoted around the hydrant and emptied my .45 at the windshield of the automobile. At that range I must have hit the driver at least a couple times. The car went off the road to the left and hit a telephone pole straight on.

For a moment, the sidewalk was a vibrating plank. Then Gordon was past me with the Essex, pulling up beside Colt. I quickly crossed the distance and tossed the suitcase of cash and securities through the front passenger window and holstered my .45. Colt had crawled across the sidewalk concrete. He got the back door open by himself and pushed the Thompson in, onto the floor. I got behind him and lifted him by the belt and helped him onto the seat, climbing in behind him.

"Go, go, go!" I yelled at Gordon as I pulled the door shut behind me and we lurched away from the curb.

*

The silence behind us was eerie. There were no sirens and no pursuit. Within a minute we were out on the highway, making good time on our escape route.

Gordon had the Essex up to eighty as we got out into the Ohio countryside, past the sidewalks and rows of city buildings. Beside me Colt was writhing horribly, lying half on his side with one foot jammed up hard against the back of the front seat. The scent of perspiration, fear, and pain was heavy in the air. His shirt and the seat between us were heavily soaked with blood. It ran down onto the floorboard. I realized I was covered in blood too, though I did not think I had been hit anywhere.

"What's happening, why aren't they behind us?" Gordon asked urgently as we hit a straight away, running fast through winter fields that would hold corn in a few months time.

I looked out the rear window. The highway sloped gently upward behind us, through wide fields now flooded with orange twilight that allowed me to view the road for a mile or two in that direction. Nothing moved along it.

"I don't know," I replied to Gordon. "Maybe we hit too many of them, took *the fight out. Maybe they're organizing pursuit still. We must have taken out at least two or three of their cruisers there on the street. They may need time to find others."*

"I didn't hear anything before it all started."

"Could have been a silent alarm, or somebody spotted us going in."

"They didn't give us a chance to surrender."

"No. They never do."

"Tenney and Durant?"

"Dead."

"You're certain?"

"They caught it immediately as we were coming out. You heard the opening barrage."

He nodded. "I rolled a grenade under a Ford with police markings. Must have killed at least a few of them, probably wrecked two of the autos they had out there."

"So, they took it as bad as we did. Let's stop and spread tacks just in case."

Gordon braked hard without pulling over. I took a 25-pound keg of roofing nails from the front seat, next to Gordon's elbow, and hopped out of the car. Working quickly, I spread the nails evenly across the road in a stripe that was about three feet wide. Even though I knew that they were there, and I stood just above them, they were hard to notice. Then we were moving again. Gordon accelerated the Essex up to eighty again on the long, straight highway. As we crested a small rise I looked behind us, down past the long shadows that pointed away from where we were heading. There was still no movement, only the lonely thought of what we had done and what we had left behind.

"If they do come, those nails will fix them for sure," Gordon said. His voice was hard.

*

I struggled the heavy vest off and got Colt bandaged up as best I could. I gave him a shot of morphine to cut the pain and keep him from going into shock. As we rolled along I wrapped two blankets around him.

After thirty minutes, Gordon slowed the Essex down to sixty so we would not attract any unnecessary attention. We changed directions, going from east to north and then east again. The roads we took were smaller and did not take us near any cities. They kept us away from lights and traffic, and past quiet, barren fields that were partially covered in patches of hard melting snow. An Indian summer was upon the area and the temperature had been twenty degrees warmer than usual for the past two days. It was a minor fortune, which ensured that there was no ice and that our traction on the road was firm and steady.

*

An hour later, a hundred road miles from the ambush in Ohio, we stopped at a secluded spot that was off the state highway, a quarter mile down a winding, gravel road. There, in a crumbling old barn that no farmer had used in twenty years, we'd left a back-up car, a Ford Model A sedan.

We transferred all our possessions to it, put the suitcase of money and most of the guns into the trunk, along with a five-gallon can of gasoline and four quarts of oil. In the front seat we had another 25-pound keg of roofing nails, two gallons of drinking water, and a fresh first-aid kit waiting. To that, we added a bag of groceries that Tenney had purchased the evening before: ten ham sandwiches wrapped in wax paper, a dozen apples, three cans of sardines, a tin of soda crackers, and oatmeal cookies with raisins.

I removed the license plates from the Essex and carried them a short distance out into the bare forest where I concealed them beneath a thicket of underbrush and dead tree branches. For a moment I stood there, in the quiet evening, wishing I could undo everything. The forest remained still and mysteriously deep around me.

When I came back, Gordon was standing by the Essex. He had the rear passenger door open and was holding a water jug in his hand, staring down at the twisted body in the backseat. Colt had lost a lot of blood and lay on his side with his eyes closed. His breathing was short and awkward. The effort for mere survival was evident.

I leaned into the automobile and placed my hand on Colt's neck. I felt for his pulse and then allowed my hand to rest on his cheek for a moment. I whispered his name several times. He did not respond or give any indication that he could hear me.

Gordon spoke through clenched teeth: "I can't get him to drink."

"He's out now," I said, "not unconscious, exactly, but he doesn't even know we're here."

Gordon brought the bottle up to his own lips and had a long drink. Afterwards, he wiped his mouth across the sleeve of his wrist and extended

153

the bottle to me. I took it and drank.

"How bad is it?" Gordon asked.

"Bad," I replied.

The bullet had gone in through the right side, under Colt's arm in a spot that was not protected by the vest, and had come out of his back. It might have rattled around a bit on the way. I didn't know what organs it might have hit, but I was pretty sure it had broken up his rib cage and caught part of his lung. There was a gurgling sound as he breathed and he had already coughed up tiny red bubbles that broke along his chin.

"What can we do?"

"He needs a doctor."

"Will he survive until we get to Chicago?"

I didn't know and I said so.

"We could find a hospital in one of the towns up ahead, maybe leave him there. They would care for him."

I thought about this and then slowly shook my head. "No. I don't think so. He wouldn't want that. They might save him, maybe, but just long enough to put him in the chair, or stir for life. I believe he would rather take his chances with us making it to Chicago."

"He might die first."

"He might."

"Or he might die anyway."

I nodded.

Gordon nodded too, stoic about it. "I agree. It's best. Let's go."

Chapter Twenty-One

We drove through the evening, into the dark. Colt lapsed in and out of consciousness. When he was out completely, he was quiet. Otherwise he groaned in demented pain and talked gibberish at us in a low tone.

At one point, we pulled over into a deserted roadside parking spot. I got out of the car and went around to sit in the back seat with him. Colt curled instinctively to make room for me on the end and I lifted his head onto my lap. His eyes were open and he looked at me, blinking patiently. I soaked a clean bandage in water and dabbed it on his lips. He responded by tilting his head back and moving his lips in a short rhythm. I repeated this several times. I was unsure how much water to give him with a likely chest wound. I whispered soothing words to him and held his head for some time more, stroking his head. He found the strength to squeeze my hand for just a moment. Gordon waited quietly in the front seat, staring straight ahead without speaking or moving as we sat there for about ten minutes.

Before we left the parking area, I gave Colt another shot of morphine. This put him out. We got back on the highway and continued toward Chicago.

*

Shortly before two a.m. we got a flat tire. Gordon pulled off the road partway to work on changing it. He had the car jacked up and the bad wheel off when Colt started to let out a series of shrill yelps. I was out of the auto, rolling the new tire around to Gordon.

"Take it," I said, pushing the tire toward him.

"I'll let the jack down."

"No, keep working. I'll check him, but I can do it without getting into the car. We need to make time."

I got the rear passenger door open and knelt there beside Colt's head. He looked at me from upside-down eyes that didn't appear to see me. He was no longer yelping, but groaned savagely and made harsh guttural sounds from the back of his throat, as if he were trying to speak but had forgotten how. His lips were dried and cracked. I dabbed more water on them, only to be pushed away with a sudden vigor I was unprepared for. He rolled and tossed on the seat in gray agony and I caught the acrid scent that told me he had lost

155

control.

I looked at my watch, counting the hours since our last stop. It was too soon to give him any more morphine. I whispered to him but he did not respond, did not seem aware of me, and he continued to groan and talk another language no one on this earth would ever understand. Rocking sideways, I spoke louder myself, moving closer to his ear, holding his head still between my hands, trying to soothe him.

After a few moments the automobile settled abruptly and jerked forward an inch. The new tire was on and we were ready to go. Gordon came around to stand beside me. He held the jack in one hand and the tire iron in the other, swaying against his leg.

"We're ready," he told me. "Any time."

I shook my head. "He's dying. Let's get him out and flat so he will be comfortable. We'll sit with him."

I straightened up and we stood there together, surveying the area. The road ran along a narrow unpaved shoulder that was flanked by a soft decline into a ditch. On the other side it dipped back up towards a long field that receded into the darkness. There was no shelter in sight. Dark silhouettes of trees stood off in the distance, shaped against the opaque darkness of the cloud-covered sky. The ground was cold but dry.

"I'll get a few blankets," Gordon said.

"No," I said then, changing my mind. "It's too cold. We have to find him a roof."

"We passed a house a mile back, not too far from the road."

"Any lights?"

"No. But it's late."

"I don't like it."

"Me neither. Hard to know what we'll find there."

"But he needs a bed, a warm place."

In the darkness Gordon looked down at his feet, shuffled them slowly, and then nodded.

We climbed back into the Essex and made a Y-turn there on the road to head the car back the way we came. In the back seat, Colt reacted to the motion of the car and the bumps in the road with a series of high-pitched groans, a disturbing sound that didn't seem human. It got worse when we hit the uneven turn-off for the farmhouse. It took us two horrible minutes to make it all the way down the gravel lane.

When we reached the house, we knocked on the door with our pistols drawn, but held behind our backs. It was several minutes before a porch light came on. The man who opened the door appeared to be in his late fifties, with eyes that had nothing left to see. He was lean, and had white stubble on his chin and very short hair serrated across his skull.

A middle-aged woman peered over his shoulder. She had thick gray-black hair bunched up in a mess from her pillow, and sagging skin under her eyes from a life of bare, hardscrabble existence and privation. They each wore flannel nightclothes and he held a shotgun ineffectively by the barrel, pointed towards the ceiling.

I leaned in towards him so he could see my face in the dispersion of porch light and brought my hand around to hold the .45 in front of my chest. It wasn't aimed towards them or even held in a manner that suggested I had any intention of firing it. But it was there and they could see it. As he oriented towards me he handed me the shotgun and I took it from him gently.

"Evening, sir, ma'am."

"We heard the gravel crunching as you drove in."

"Sorry to wake you. We mean you no harm. Our friend is hurt and he needs a warm place to lie for a little while."

"What's wrong with him." The man's voice was low and deep.

"He's been shot, sir."

"Shot?"

"We robbed a bank in Ohio and we have to avoid the law."

"Heard about it on the radio."

"We won't hurt you or your family. Can we bring him in, just for a few hours?"

"Is he bleeding bad?"

The lady pushed forward, with her chin, past her husband. Her expression was no longer sleepy. "Harry, tell these boys to bring him in right away. I'll get the other bed ready."

Harry came out of the house and walked down to the Essex with us. Together he and I draped two blankets together to form a stretcher. We wrapped it around Colt, rocking his body back and then forward onto it, and carried him into the house like that. Gordon stood off to the side, still holding his pistol awkwardly. We maneuvered our way into the house and the lady led us down a narrow hallway to a back bedroom. The wood floors were bare and unfinished.

In the bedroom she had the sheets on the bed already folded back and helped guide the makeshift stretcher into position as we lowered it. Colt started to writhe and jerk as soon as he was on the bed. I held his head up to drag a pillow beneath it. A line of red foam dripped from his mouth suddenly and

157

seeped onto the pillow. He clutched at the air and turned his head toward me. His eyes were closed tightly. A horrible odor was released into the air. I averted my eyes.

"Ester, you go back to our bedroom," Harry told his wife with no determination.

I looked up at her. She stared at her husband through tightened eyes for a moment. "I'll do no such thing," she replied. Her voice was weary. "This boy's dying. I'll get some water heating and some towels. Meanwhile you get him undressed. The least we can do is help provide him some comfort."

"Ester—"

"Never mind that, I don't care what he's done. He's still one of God's own and he's dying. It's our duty."

Gordon and I got half of Colt's clothing off. Harry stood at the foot of the bed, watching us blankly. We were still fussing with Colt's belt when Ester came back in with a stack of towels and a bottle of rubbing alcohol. She shooed us back from the bed to take over. With gnarled hands she quickly had him undressed and removed the bandages I had fashioned over the jagged, ugly wound. Blood and tissue seeped out. She covered it quickly to slow the release. It was not the first time she had tended to an injured man. I had our first aid kit and spread it out on the bed. She picked through it for what she needed.

"Fetch the water," she told Gordon.

"Yes, ma'am."

"You hold his arm here, and take this bandage, like so."

I followed her directions. When Gordon came back with the water he stood beside me and balanced the pot carefully on the bed near Colt's shoulder. Ester told us what to do. Harry moved to the foot of the bed to hold Colt's legs still while she soaked the towels in the hot water and then started to wipe at the blood that covered his torso. I swabbed him with a dry towel, working behind her as she washed him. The smell of the alcohol, when she opened the bottle and poured it out onto a cloth, was a relief. Her movements were quick and expert, and soon we had him re-bandaged and bundled within another blanket.

"I'm sorry we're ruining your bed, your linens."

"Never mind about that."

"We'll pay you two hundred dollars."

"No you won't, not that bank's money. We won't take it. I'm a Christian lady."

Colt groaned loudly and moved sideways on the bed. The blanket opened and fell off his shoulder as a curled fist rose from within it.

Harry sucked in a breath slowly. "*This boy's hurtin'*," he said.

"*I'll get my Bible*," Ester replied.

"*We have morphine*," I said. *I held up a glass vial.*

Ester peered up at me with eyes that did not soften. "*How much you give him already?*"

"*A couple of shots.*"

"*How recent?*"

I estimated.

She nodded. "*Might as well give him another one now. No reason not to. I'll get my Bible from the other room.*"

*

Soon Colt became quiet. We stood there around the bed without motion. After a while Ester said a short prayer. The way she spoke, the prayer sounded like one single long word with hundreds of syllables. Then she told Harry they should move out to sit in the front room. Gordon went out with them. I scraped a chair close up to the bed and sat, leaning towards Colt with the worn Bible on the bed between us. Cracked from age and use, the corners of the dark leather cover curled down to embrace the pages.

"*Colt, can you hear me? I'm here with you, brother.*"

There was no reply, but he rolled his face towards me in response to the sound of my voice. His lids were dusty and they trembled faintly. I opened the book and turned the thin, fragile pages of King James' version and my eyes found the middle of a passage at random. It was Matthew 25. Presently I realized that my lips were moving and there were sounds of a voice reciting slowly, pronouncing the words carefully, with softness:

"*Then he will say to those on his left, 'Depart from me, you who are cursed, into the eternal fire prepared for the devil and his angels. For I was hungry and you gave me nothing to eat, I was thirsty and you gave me nothing to drink, I was a stranger and you did not invite me in, I needed clothes and you did not clothe me, I was sick and in prison and you did not look after me.' They also will answer, 'Lord, when did we see you hungry or thirsty or a stranger or needing clothes or sick or in prison, and did not help you?' He will reply, 'I tell you the truth, whatever you did not do for one of the least among you, you did not do for me.'*"

There was a shifting noise that brought me to a stop. When I looked up, Colt had turned toward the light, facing me now. His eyes were human again, sentient. Tremors rippling down his jawbone and it seemed he was trying to say something, though was having trouble forming the words. I closed the unfamiliar book gently and bent towards him, my elbows on the bed, with my chin inches above his. When he managed to speak he said just the one word. It jangled through the haze of pain and blood loss and morphine like a bell: "Elinore."

His eyes watched me with a heavy inevitability, a final charge of clarity. There seemed to be a phrase in his eyes and its meaning came through to me clearly and I nodded.

After he saw me respond, he seemed to nod too, with a half smile that I'd never forget. It had been a question, and one that I had answered.

Then he closed his eyes and remained quiet, breathing, waiting with patience. I sat there with him, right there, quiet too and without the urge to read from the book again. Maybe an hour later, in that remote hour of the morning with the dawn still off, he silently died. I heard his final breath and sat there with him for another long while before I stood up.

In the corner of the room stood a simple cherry wood dresser which was as high as the middle of my chest. On top of it I placed six hundred dollars in thin fifties, folded beneath a small ceramic figurine: an angel with a tilted, painted face that gazed down over the room with sorrow.

Chapter Twenty-Two

When I finished the telling, Elinore took my hand and held it against her cheek. She was a fiddlehead curled on the sofa beside me with her head in my lap, her knees impossibly near her chest, and her stocking-covered feet tucked in. I had pulled a small comforter over her and smoothed it across her legs to cover her all the way up to her shoulders. The expression on her face was hidden from me, but I could feel the warm moisture of tears forming against my hand.

We sat together like that for a very long time listening to the rain beat steadily against the window. Ten minutes went by and then fifteen, twenty … The rain continued its rhythmic tattoo and still we did not speak. It was a comfortable silence.

Shadows in the room stretched and shimmered as the angle of light changed and darker clouds moved by and pushed lighter clouds before them. As I looked down over her I studied the slender vulnerable neck and the line of tiny hairs that ridged her cheek and jaw, becoming first more apparent as the light moved over her, and then disappearing altogether as the light faded past a certain point.

I was tempted to lean over and kiss her on the cheek and then probably the mouth, knowing where that would have to lead. But there was an impulse conflicting with desire, a feeling of responsibility that restrained me. I was eight years older than her and it was a strange and confusing mix of emotions that I had long carried since Hennepin Avenue and which were now magnified somehow by the death of her brother. With Colt gone, I was all she had left in the world and there were the inviolable promises, spoken and unspoken, I had made to him. She needed me to take care of her, to protect her, not to seduce her.

Instead of a kiss, I brushed my finger tips along the base of her neck in slow, gentle strokes that gradually moved lower, down over her face, brushing the hair back away from her eyes, caressing the side of her face, down her cheek, past her lips, to the point of her chin. I wiped at my eyes with the back of my left hand. Still we sat there quietly, without moving now, and gradually the light around us faded into a monochrome dusk.

"What happened to Gordon?" Elinore asked finally.

"He headed out West. I don't know where. With his share he can disappear for awhile."

"You could disappear too."

"I plan to."

"Then why did you come here?"

I did not respond. The rain beat on.

After a minute passed Elinore sighed. "I'd like to visit that old couple some day, thank them for their kindness."

"They were kind."

"Do you feel responsible?" Her voice sounded as though she were far away. She neither sat nor turned her head towards me. Instead, she took my hand and brought it back to the spot on her neck. She started those fingers in motion again and curled tighter.

"I didn't keep him alive."

"That would have been a tall order."

"It was the only order that mattered."

"You're not responsible."

"Yes. I am."

"How can you be?"

I did not answer right away. There were many responses that I considered. Some included discussion of childhood relationships and decisions that were made, actions taken long ago. Others focused on recent events, conversations that had taken place late at night all the way from Nevada to Ohio. I thought about the risks Colt and I had taken and the lives we had wasted and I didn't want to answer her question.

When my mind had run through the possible answers I could offer and had gone down the different paths that each might have elicited, I said simply: "'Whatever you did not do for one of the least among you, you did not do for me.'"

"Is that from the Bible?"

"Mathew 25."

"You read it to him that night."

"No. Not to him, to me. I wasn't reading to him. I was reading to myself."

"He would never blame you."

"I placed him there, directed him to that spot on the street where he was hit."

She paused before responding, and during that moment I stopped stroking her neck. "That's not the whole story," she said.

"When did the whole story ever matter when it comes to those things that we each hold deep inside, alone and private, that tear at our souls?"

"It does matter. You were partners, loyal to each other. You were each doing what you thought was your job at that moment."

"Yes."

"And so?"

"Yes, and so," I said, and paused. Then it all came out in a rush: "So that doesn't help. It doesn't matter at this point, doesn't change what I did or didn't do, or what he did, or what happened. We shouldn't have been there. We could have quit it all well before that. There was enough money. I should have anticipated what happened. I should have placed him somewhere else, somewhere with more cover. And I should have saved him afterwards."

"How could you have saved him? He was shot through the chest, he was dying."

"He was choking on his blood. I should have done something different. I should have saved him."

"What? How?"

"I don't know, but something. We might have found a hospital."

"You know he wouldn't have chosen that."

"No. I don't know that. I thought it at the time, but now I don't know."

"Yes, you do. You did the best you could have."

I shook my head, fighting back the emotion.

Elinore sat up, guiding the comforter off her shoulders, folding it casually onto the end of the sofa in one fluid motion. The room was dark now with only the ambient light from the street for illumination, but our eyes, like our thumping hearts, had adapted to the darkness. She positioned her feet on the floor and looked at me. Then she leant towards me for a moment before settling against the back of the couch, still holding my hand tightly in her own. Her eyes were hidden in large, shining shadows that seemed to reflect starlight from an infinite well of tears.

She shook her head slowly. "No. You mustn't say that, you mustn't ever look at it that way."

"It's the only way I can look at it."

"I know, it's who you are."

We were quiet for a long time. Then: "Did you and Colt really talk about going to the Northwest some day?"

"Yes."

"And you really talked about bringing me?"

"Yes."

"I wish we could have."

"So do I."

"Maybe we still could."

"Yes, maybe."

"I'd like that."

"So would I."

"What would we do?"

"Like Colt said: 'Just be.'"

*

"Did he really say my name?"

I looked at her, knowing what she meant. "Yes," I told her.

Her face lightened as it dawned on her: "That's why you're here, in Chicago."

I held her gaze for a moment and then looked away, searching across the room. "Where are you getting the laudanum from?"

"I don't want to talk about that."

"You can get help."

Her lips tightened and I felt her pull away.

"There's a sanitarium in Topeka, Kansas – Menninger's. I can take you there. I'll wait with you until you're ready to leave." I was speaking too fast and I knew it. Her eyes dimmed and she did not respond. The room held the quiet around us, pulling from within. I could feel the pulse in my fingertips. Eventually I spoke into that vacuum. "Why not?"

"Who wants to be looked at that way?"

"That's nonsense. They can help you. Who gives you the laudanum?"

"It doesn't matter."

I turned my eyes towards her again. "The Irishman?" With the way the words sounded we both knew it was not a question.

Elinore shook her head, adamant.

"If not from the Irishman, then someone close to him."

"Eugene gives it to me. He said it would help me feel less blue."

"But the Irishman knows about it, of course."

Again she shook her head.

"Don't kid yourself," I said, standing up into the shadows of the room. "Robinson doesn't do anything the Irishman doesn't know about and approve."

"Where are you going?" She hunched her shoulders like a sleepy kitten.

"I have to meet a guy."

"Why not stay?"

"Because I have to meet a guy."

"You don't have an appointment now, not at this hour."

"Yes," I told her. "I do."

She started to choke up. "I wish you'd stay."

"I can't."

"You could come back later."

"Probably not a good idea."

"What if we never make love?"

I leaned over and kissed her cheek. She tried to hold my arms, pull me in towards her, but I pulled back and straightened up. I ran the back of my hand across her hair. "Think about coming to Topeka with me."

Before I left the apartment I looked back over my shoulder at the hardest sight I'd ever seen: the dark outline of her folded, tiny body framed by faint light from the window behind her. She was bent forward, with her forehead in the crook of one arm, weeping uncontrollably.

More than anything I wanted to rush back to her and console her.

Instead, I closed the door softly behind me and headed down the stairs, out into the wet city night, where lake effect fog was moving in low and silent. I walked quickly away.

Chapter Twenty-Three

Four days later it was still raining and still blustering much of the time. Early May was a lot like April had been. The Hy-Ho Club on South Cicero Avenue was partly owned by Tough Tony Capezio. It was filled with all sorts of the city's night-running troubled: drinkers, rounders, gamblers, musicians, whores, spendthrifts, criminals, a few big shots, the merely petty, a couple of boxers, and the full range of low class wannabes.

Dull smoke filled the air, mixing with the scent of garlic and beer. A man in a bowler hat shouted obscenities at a dark skinned woman who wore a bright lavender evening gown. Flicking her sequins at him, she pouted and rolled her eyes over to gawk at me as I walked by. I stared back; then I looked away.

"I bet he knows," she said, grabbing my elbow and pulling my eyes back to her. She grinned uneven teeth at me in a way that wasn't completely unpleasant.

"Certainly not," the man shouted, resuming his string of epithets, and I slid away deeper into the sordid room.

Elbows chipped away at me. A carnival arcade of noise and light swarmed around me and I blinked hard against it as I moved. My eyes roved until I spotted Torresi sitting at a round table with three other men in a back corner.

"There he is!" Torresi boomed. He stood as I approached the table. His large purple lips were laughing as he reached for me.

"It ain't the Nightingale Club," I said, shaking his meaty hand.

"Hey! Careful, I own this joint," one of the guys seated at the table said loudly. A hooknose hung over his crooked grin. His sideburns were shaved close. "This fuckin' guy!"

"Duncan, this is Tony Capezio." Torresi laughed as he said it, pointing with a jerk of his thumb.

"Hi'ya."

"And this here's Mr. Frank Nitti."

Nitti stood to nod. "Good to meet you," he said.

The skin on his face sank on the bone. His eyes were shadowed, strange and paranoid; haunted by too many deaths, unrealized dreams, and perhaps the fear of his own downfall, which the odds suggested could be sooner rather than later. He seemed to fidget his way into a low mood as I watched him.

"And you remember Albert Russo."

I nodded. Russo nodded back at me this time, though I had the sense he didn't want to. His eyes were still dark and cruel, revealing little more than a general loathing for humanity. He wore the same wrinkled silk suit as he had when I met him the previous time at the Nightingale Club. His rough yellow flesh and the shrinking down slouch were the same too, as if he no longer quite filled out his own skin.

Nitti stood, moved his chair around and pushed it under the table, squaring it carefully – as if that mattered. In some small way, maybe it did to him. Using the sides of his fingers he concentrated on the act. Then he stood behind the chair with his hands holding the back of it tightly. Swollen knuckles sprouted and the chair itself wavered a bit from the pressure of his grip. "Thanks for taking care of that rat," he said looking at me. He didn't wait for me to respond. "If you'll excuse me, I have another engagement."

Capezio also stood up and made his excuses. He winked at me to let me know he wasn't really sore about my unfavorable comparison to the Irishman's club. After they left, I scooted my chair around to sit closer to Torresi. Russo stayed put, but slouched further down inside his skin: his elbow was on the table and his chin hovered just over it. His harsh eyes were narrow slits that looked at the center of the table and didn't seem interested in much. Pale light shined off his hair grease.

"What was that about?" I asked.

"You want a drink?" Torresi poured champagne into a flute and pushed it towards me.

"Thanks."

I did not drink from it. He shoved the dark bottle back into a silver ice bucket, dribbling small condensation drops across the table and then the floor as he stretched his reach.

"He was referring to Reina. Reina was the rat."

"Sure he was."

"You doubt it?"

"I knew Reina was a rat from the first moment I met him."

"Yeah, I guess we all did at that. He was a low-life and he got what he had coming."

"Just because he's a low-life, doesn't mean he betrayed you – or that he's the only one doing so."

"No, you're right about that. It doesn't have to mean that. You got another name?"

I shook my head.

"A theory? Maybe you have a theory?"

"Same one I always have – the obvious answer isn't always the only one, or the right one."

Torresi glanced at Russo quickly then back at me. His eyes blinked darkly and he pursed his lips. "Reina took a contract on you from the Irishman. He was gonna kill you one way or the other. Thought he would pick up some bank cash in the process, leave you behind with a few extra holes. It would have been a double score for him."

"Not such a good plan."

"It was, in a general sort of way."

"Bank heists rarely go according to any general sort of way. He should have taken the bank first and hit me after."

"You know more about that than I do."

I nodded without meaning and tried the champagne. It was dry and cold as ice. The bubbles tickled my throat as I swallowed rapidly twice.

"Amateurs often get it wrong – taking down a bank is not as simple as all that. Why would the Irishman want to hit me and if he did, why not use one of his own gunmen? Why make it fancy? That Robinson looks like he would probably enjoy the assignment."

I set the glass down. Torresi immediately poured more champagne. "Have some more," Torresi said, handing me the flute again. Now it dripped condensation right onto my lap. "He would enjoy it. He'd enjoy an assignment on his elderly mother. But it wasn't just you. Reina was working for the Irishman across a number of fronts. He set up Alvarini, set up our convoy that night we went up into Wisconsin, passed them other information about our operation, gave over a full list of all the police captains, judges, aldermen we have in our pockets. Figures and dates too. He gave up everything he could."

"Too bad somebody trusted him with all that info."

Torresi remained even-tempered. "Nobody did. He must have pilfered my office at the garage and just took it a few days ago."

"Nice security you have then."

Torresi muttered under his breath and then nodded, conceding the point. "Maybe we did trust him too much – or maybe not."

A part of this was personal to me. I didn't let go of that part so easily.

"Why would he come at me? Why would the Irishman want me out of the way?"

Russo snorted but didn't emerge from his slouch.

Torresi shot him a warning look that was ignored. "It's a good question," he said.

"What do you hear, what does the street say? It doesn't quite make sense to me, yet."

"Well, I do hear things."

"What kind of things?"

"You know, things that ain't so good."

"You're going to tell me it has to do with a girl."

Torresi's eyes feigned exhaustion. "Don't everything?"

"Maybe in some kind of funny, sad, complicated, impossible way. But where does she fit in here?"

"The Irishman's kind of sweet on a particular lady-friend you've been hanging around. Dame with the big eyes, tight curls, does a little hosting at the Nightingale."

"She does more than that," Russo exclaimed, pushing back on his elbows. We both ignored him in unison.

I shook my head. "That doesn't make for a hit."

"Green jealousy might."

"She's practically a sister to me."

"Yeah, yeah – your dead partner's sister. Don't kid yourself, no else is kidded."

I had to give him credit: Torresi seemed to know everything there was to know in the city. "Still doesn't add up to a hit. Why not warn me off her, try it easy first?"

"It adds if he's scared of you, thinks you're working for us, worries you might get ideas about taking her the old fashioned way. Maybe he didn't want to tip his mitt about her."

"He made a show of accusing me of shooting one of his gunners in Wisconsin. Waved Paddy's splintered machinegun in my face, tried to shame me over expensive coffee in a fancy little china cup."

Torresi paused. "He served you his coffee?"

"Sure."

"The Egyptian stuff?"

I smiled, nodding once, with the taste lingering in my mouth at the memory.

"Well, I'll be damned. It's supposed to only be for special people. I guess you rate. I've only heard about it. How was it?"

"It was swell."

"Was it sweet?"

"If you wanted it to be."

"Did the girl serve it, the one with the green eyes, wears flannel suits but you can still tell she's really got it?"

"Sounds about right."

"Hot damn!"

"Yeah."

"That might be it. He didn't care about Paddy, but can't have other talent shooting down his men. He can't let that go – unless he can recruit you."

"But I didn't admit it; he doesn't know for sure it was me."

"Who knows what Reina told him … Did he try to recruit you?"

I thought about this and shrugged.

"What did you say?"

"I'm here ain't I?"

"So was Reina, and some of the facts fit you as well as they did Reina: Alvarini, Wisconsin, Urbana. They all could have been you."

"I didn't have any lists of alderman or police captains."

"It coulda' been you burgled my office."

"I wouldn't have known where to look, wouldn't even have suspected you'd keep that info there, even if I wanted it – which I didn't."

"No. Maybe that's why you don't have those extra holes yet."

I nodded and thought about the Irishman, who now had ten thousand of my money. I had no doubt that my death would enrich him by that same amount. "Okay," I said. "So maybe I have to watch my back a little more carefully, sleep a little less soundly. Even if we leave me out of it for now, how are you so sure that Reina is the one?"

Torresi grinned. "The Irishman's not the only one with informants. We've got several on the spot, right there inside the Nightingale Club, watching everything that goes on over there. Reina came in too often, spent too much time upstairs. A couple of our guys followed him the week before Urbana. They saw him having lunch with Robinson at a downtown deli last week. Envelopes were exchanged."

"Don't tell me – he even ate corned beef."

"Wiseacre."

"It could fit. Though it's tough to know for sure what he gave them and how much damage there is, no?"

"Perhaps. We started to suspect him a month ago."

"And you were careful?"

"Very."

"Usually suspected rats don't last so long in the Outfit."

Torresi shook his head with sincerity. "Don't misunderstand me. It's true they don't, but we had to be sure and we saw an opportunity."

"Nice you tied him to me so neatly."

"No, don't get sore about that. We had no reason to think he'd go after you. If anything, we thought he might slip up, let you learn something."

"You were trusting my abilities?"

"Yeah, sure. Something like that. You don't have to like it."

"What else? What other smart plays did you make?"

"The list we let him have was only a partial list … some of our fish are on there, but also a couple-a extra names."

"You passed bogus names intentionally?"

He nodded.

"Anyone interesting?"

"O'Farrell's name might have been on there."

I picked up my flute and gestured an unspoken toast. Torresi raised his flute. "Neat," I said, after we both swallowed bubbles.

"We really have to do something about him, and soon too, within the next month. Now we're hoping the Irishman is thinking the same way, himself. He might just be."

"If he thinks you've got O'Farrell in your pocket, then he'll have to be plenty worried for himself. Seems natural he might expect that he'll be a target of the special prosecutor. Newspapers been fingering you as the target, but they've been known to get it wrong before. The Irishman will have to do something, he can't risk it." The more I thought about it, the more I liked it.

Torresi nodded. "Yeah, probably, but we can't count on it and we can't wait. It's a nice trick if it works, but it's not Plan A."

"I still say we set up a machine gun nest across the street from his hotel. When he comes out, blast him," Russo exclaimed suddenly.

"You know we can't do that. There's too many guards and they vary his routine."

"We can hit him that way."

"He uses different entrances."

"So we're patient. We wait until he uses the one we've got covered."

"Too risky. We need more finesse to the operation." Torresi looked at me. "Are you in or not?"

I sat quietly for a long moment, turning it around in my thoughts. "Why would I do it? It's not my line."

"We'll make it worth your while."

"Enlighten me."

He mentioned a pleasant five-figure number.

"Nice, but I can get that other ways, easier ways."

"There's more."

"I'm still listening."

"Keys to the city."

"Huh?"

"So to speak."

"Spell it out."

"We have an understanding. I'm offering you a lifetime pass in Chi-town. Any time you're here, any thing you need: protection, shelter, medical, support, dames, connections, even loans you need 'em."

"A lifetime pass?"

Torresi nodded.

It was an interesting offer. I drank the last of my champagne. Nobody moved to refill it. The bottle was empty.

"It's a pretty damn good deal for someone in your line," he assured me and I almost believed him.

"I need a few days to consider it."

"Don't disappoint me."

"Three days."

"Yeah, sure. But no more."

We sat there for a moment. Russo looked to be dozing – his angry slits had narrowed. Torresi pushed an envelope towards me.

"What's this?" I asked.

"It's from Nitti. His thanks for taking care of the rat."

I looked in the envelope and realized it was the same three thousand I had given Torresi the night before – red-hot bank loot.

"Is this the going rate for pest extermination?"

"More or less, yeah."

"It's not much for such an ugly job."

"It is what it is. You were helping yourself too, remember."

"Anything else?" I asked, inching my chair back.

"Yeah, just a moment." Torresi tapped the table with his wide palm. Russo's slits widened and his chin moved almost a quarter inch. "Check on the car, Russo. I'll be out in a few minutes."

Like a dripping hulk emerging from deep water, Russo slowly rose. It seemed like he was expanding within his yellow skin. Through the floating, green smoke of the room, I watched him lumber into the crowd and disappear.

I put a cigarette in my mouth. Torresi leaned in close to me and spoke in a voice that was barely above a whisper. "Listen, what's really going on with you and the dame?"

"How is that your business?"

"Word is you're a bit too sweet on her – another man's girl. Can be dangerous in this town. I don't like it. The Outfit don't like it. It doesn't lead anywhere good for any of us. It complicates things."

"I'm just looking out for the kid."

"Yeah? That's what you call it?"

"It's what I call it."

"Why not spend some time down in the Levee instead. We got some nice houses there you could visit."

"I don't go with whores."

"Might help keep things simple."

"Things are simple enough."

"Don't underestimate the Irishman. He'll play you along like a song and then cut your fuckin' heart out."

I lit the Chesterfield and added to the smoke already in the air.

"Word is, she might be playin' you too."

I brought the cigarette up to my lips again.

"Don't bat an eye. I just hate to see it that's all."

Torresi pressed a fist against the table and stood up. He turned without saying so much as "good-evening." Across the room a drummer struck up a rhythm on the hi-hat, hitting a syncopated foot-pedal bass.

Chapter Twenty-Four

They picked me up on South Cicero, outside the Hy-Ho as I was trying to wave down a cab.

The black Cadillac had just arrived at the curb in front of me when I felt the sharp jab in my lower back, above my right kidney. It could have been any number of harmless items found in a hardware store or a kitchen, but odds didn't favor that.

A voice behind me with an Irish accent said, "In case ya wonder, me boyo, it's a snub-nose .38."

The rear passenger door of the Caddie opened and I climbed in. I was cooperative. The snub-nose got in right behind me.

Another man was waiting for me – his cold eyes came up like pale searchlights.

"Easy," Eugene Robinson reassured. "The ride's not one-way. The Irishman wants to see you and it's urgent, so we didn't have time to make an appointment."

I looked at my watch. "Now suits me just fine."

We rode in silence. I sat awkwardly between the two men in the back seat, without quite enough elbowroom to be comfortable. As we glided beneath streetlights the snub-nose twinkled intermittently. It was nickel-plated. Although it was no longer pointed directly at me, it wasn't in a holster either. Time and memory and fear all wrinkled and flexed and flowed around and through me like water. It formed a hard brick-like surface I kept butting up against, then liquefied and flowed again, refusing to be grasped or tamed. Torresi's warning about green jealousy echoed around in my thoughts. What hadn't seemed likely twenty minutes ago suddenly seemed plausible. I tried to concentrate on the various scenarios and my options. Coherent thought evaded me and I knew time was closing in. I could feel the sweat drip down the small of my back.

After we turned onto Madison, Robinson gave the driver directions, "We'll go around to the side, past the loading dock and enter through that way. You'll leave the car running." He then said to me, "Probably only take ten minutes, then Tom will drop you wherever. The Irishman has a few questions, and maybe a job for you."

"Any hints?"

"Uh-uh. You'll find out soon enough. Relax, it's just the work we chose."

"Did we make the same choice?"

"We both do the work."

"Like your work do you?"

He spoke without looking at me. "It suits me okay. You got complaints?"

"Not me."

"That's just fine then. We both like our work. It's good to be satisfied."

We got out of the car and went into the building through a side-alley door that was normally reserved for deliveries. The guy with the snub-nose followed in behind me and went as far as the elevator, then disappeared without ever providing me a good look at his face.

*

The Irishman was coming around from behind his desk as we entered. He wore the usual immaculate tuxedo like it was his very own skin. The human qualities in his features had been carefully arranged so as to provide a front suggesting something akin to good cheer. I pretended a grin myself.

"Cheers! And what can I say?" he said to me, apologetically, with a wink. "Sometimes, in this business, things come up in a hurry. I do hope my emissaries were polite at least. I'm glad you've come. Whiskey?"

The mahogany-encased room pulled me in and enveloped me with its dull yellow light and uncirculated air.

"No thank you," I said as I pulled a cigarette from my front pocket.

"I'll get right to the point then."

I lit my cigarette and flicked the match towards an ashtray as I exhaled. The smoke improved the air quality in the room.

"That would be good," I replied when I was ready.

He gestured toward the chair I'd taken last time with his left hand cupped open. "Let's sit first, Laddie. This will be quick, but no reason not to be comfortable. Eugene, would you mind joining us as we discuss this matter that you already know about?"

It was a rhetorical question. Eugene didn't bother to answer it. He was already moving towards a chair and we all knew having delivered me at gunpoint, he wasn't likely to leave me there unguarded. I leaned back in my chair, slowly and thoroughly, and took another slow drag on the cigarette, letting them notice the lack of haste or urgency in my movements. I watched their eyes and, with the soft focus of my vision, their hands too.

The Irishman took a large and showy breath before he began speaking. "I'm preparing for a large funeral. It's for a very important man, a man who will command a great many wreathes and floral arrangements from across the city. Politicians, policemen, businessmen, and journalists will all be there for the send-off. It will be grand. Everything must be ready and perfect for this man because he will be hailed as one of the leaders of our city, with many mourners."

"Anyone I know?"

"Indeed, I believe so: Walter O'Farrell is his name."

"Didn't know he'd died. Lead poisoning?"

"You remain impassive?"

Robinson's eyes studied me while revealing nothing. "Lot of people looking to see him go. How did he get hit?" I finally asked.

"He hasn't. Yet."

"Yet?"

"You haven't killed him yet."

"Yet?" I said again. The line was as clear as I could be, but he wasn't getting it.

"You're going to kill him for me, before the end of next week."

I took a moment with that one, bringing the cigarette to my lips and holding the smoke for a 5-count, before I stretched toward the ashtray.

"I rob banks. It's what I'm good at."

"You can shoot too, you're good at that."

"Only when the target is shooting at me. Not in cold blood. Not murder."

"It's a fine distinction, don't you think, Eugene?"

Robinson's expressionless face made a movement that might have passed as a nod in certain circles. I didn't know which circles those were though, and I didn't ask.

The Irishman continued. "Whether you shoot policemen, acting as agents of our society, who are trying to stop you from robbing a particular bank, or whether you shoot a prosecutor, also acting as an agent of our society, who is trying to stop you from robbing all banks, in general there seems to be a thin distinction within any moral code. No?"

I thought about this. He had an actual point, and one that I'd struggled with before. "A bank is a tactical combat situation. You have a gun, the police have guns. Often they outnumber you. They can choose to try to stop you or they can take cover and let you take a flyer. If I shoot a man in self-defense I may not have to kill him, I may wound him or drive him back for cover. Yes, it's a fine moral distinction because theoretically that cop is an innocent man enforcing the laws of society – an agent of our society, as you put it. He may have a family, children, parents who depend upon him and he's just doing a job. But if I go to stop a special prosecutor, I'm shooting an unarmed man who made no choice to face me and I don't have the option to merely wound him or drive him away. It's different."

"Only in the shades of it."

"Maybe so. But maybe those shades matter. I've never murdered a man in cold blood."

"Do you fear you could not do it?"

"It's ugly business." I squirmed within my own hypocrisy.

"Yes, but it's business nonetheless and I need you for this one. We will give you good support and we will pay you well."

"How well?"

He named a figure. It was more than the Italians were offering, but he didn't mention the keys to any city. His offer was made all the more compelling by what he didn't say but I knew to be his intention: that a refusal would mean I would not make it home alive.

While I sat there with the offer, spoken and unspoken parts weighed together, the Irishman stood without fanfare and squinted ironically. "I'll pour that whiskey now, for you and I. Robinson never has one."

When he turned from the dry sink, he had a crystal glass in each hand. He passed one to me. He held onto the other as he returned to his seat. Holding the glass up to the infected yellow light for inspection, he spoke slowly.

"I came to this country in 1889 on a steamer. I was just a wee lad at the time and my parents decided the very long trip across the Atlantic would provide opportunities for our family that would never exist in the home country."

The Irishman paused to drink some whiskey. I took a pull from my glass too and looked straight ahead at Robinson. His expression registered nothing. I looked down into my lap and waited.

"My mother, well, she died somewhere during the passage and my sister died shortly after we arrived at dock. I recall that you could see the Statue of Liberty from a porthole, but she didn't have the strength to walk toward it, or even sit up for it if we carried her. She never saw it. But my parents were right – for those who survived, there were opportunities in this land. It was an enchanting fairytale … for those who survived."

For just an instant, there was an unexpected distant Irish landscape in his eyes as he spoke. It faded quickly as his developed nature won out. Fatigue washed over me as I realized how far removed a man could become from his own soul.

"I've not been back to the old country since I left," the Irishman continued. "Never had the chance, never the urge, the desire. I never wanted to take on the responsibility it would have incurred, bringing the hope of America along to so many back there who didn't have the strength to leave. Kill this man for me. Ensure that we all survive, that the opportunities remain for us, that the fairytale does not end. You'll work with Eugene to do this. He'll help you and we will all continue to profit in this city."

It wasn't a question, so I made no response. Instead I sipped the whiskey and allowed my cigarette to burn out a long ash.

*

Robinson escorted me down in the elevator, back to the delivery entrance. Once outside the building, we stood on the loading bay, with a swathe of the Milky Way balanced above us on the tips of the city's tallest buildings. The air was heavy with moisture. Muted street sounds bordered my awareness. I couldn't see Robinson's eyes for the shadows that hung over us like low banners. He handed me an 8 by 11 manila envelope, which felt thick and solid as I hefted it on my palm.

His voice was abrupt. "There's photographs in there of O'Farrell and the key people around him: his bodyguards, confidants. Also, you'll find information: addresses, daily schedules, notes on the people that work with him and around him, that sort of thing. My suggestion is that you should follow him. Learn his habits, learn to recognize the people around him, identify when he's most vulnerable."

"And then?"

"Get started on it right away. We'll talk again in three or four days.

I'll get you whatever support you need: weapons, explosives, cash, inside info, back-up. Whatever you need. Bring a list. You've planned other operations, this isn't so different."

"I've stalked banks before, never a man."

"Its not really so difficult, you'll see."

"To kill a man?"

"You've killed before."

"I never liked it. It doesn't go down like the newspapers paint it."

The corners of Robinson's lips, all that I could see of his face, pulled back wanly. "With practice, it gets easier. You get used to it. Like stepping on a bug."

"No. Only if there's something wrong with you to begin with, something missing in the soul. No. For most it gets harder, each time – harder to the point where sleeping and dreaming and feeling like an actual member of the human race come to be just about impossible. You don't get that do you? You're one of the others."

Robinson ignored this and reached for a silver cigarette case. He opened it slowly and with much deliberation. Then he lit one without offering the case to me.

"Let me ask you a question," he said, pausing only momentarily. "The girl – the addict – you know who she belongs to, and yet you don't stay away from her."

"I didn't hear a question."

"Are you sleeping with her, how is she? With all that laudanum in her system—"

"First of all, I don't know that she belongs to anyone. I don't think of other people that way. Moreover, whether I'm sleeping with her or not, never mind how she is and never mind the laudanum, would never be a question I would answer to you. It's exactly none of your business."

"Your best speech yet."

I half-saluted with the manila envelope. "Thanks for this."

He waited until I was half-turned before speaking again. "Don't cross that thin line. You're treading it on tiptoes, arms flailing for balance. If O'Farrell is not dead within two weeks, I'd hate to think about what could happen to the girl. It would sure be easy for one like that to over do it with the laudanum."

At the edge of the loading bay I halted in my turn and looked back at him. I glanced over my shoulder; my hat brim now protected my eyes from an overhanging streetlight while I watched him sink deeper into the subterranean shadows behind me. "Something like that happened, I'd probably lose all inhibitions about killing a man. I might become one of *the others* myself."

"I'll keep it in mind," Robinson replied and then he disappeared. I couldn't even hear his footsteps as they receded.

Chapter Twenty-Five

O'Farrell's red brick apartment waited emptily in a cozy nook off the lake some twenty minutes from city center. Pulled curtains and an old flyer sticking from his mailbox tipped me that nobody had been around for at least a week. It took me the better part of four days to learn that he and his two sons were stashed in the Hotel La Salle. The boys appeared to be about eight and nine years old – energetic, but obedient to their father.

The next morning I picked O'Farrell up as he came out the eastside doors at 7:23 a.m. Two large men escorted him. They came out first, looked around, and glanced up and down the street. When O'Farrell emerged, he stepped out gingerly, with his head down and his hands cupped to his cheeks. All three of the men wore gray suits and gray hats. For all I knew they wore gray right on through to their underclothes. A plain Ford pulled up close to the curb and they quickly crossed to it. As the Ford pulled out into traffic I looked at my watch. He had been standing on the sidewalk for less than seven seconds before being whisked away.

A thought formed in my mind: you could get him with a machine gun or a rifle if you were set for him, maybe. But it wouldn't be pretty. And that was if he came out the same door, which I doubted he would do every time.

I took a leisurely breakfast and read just about every word of the *Tribune*. Then I hailed a taxi down to the state building and waited to see if he would come out for lunch. He didn't.

When it was eight o'clock in the evening and most of the lights in the state building were out I decided I'd missed him altogether, again. Maybe he was still working, or maybe he had snuck out a side exit. Or maybe he'd never been in the building in the first place.

*

On my way home I stopped at a pool hall to use the telephone. The joint was wedged in a city block between a tavern and leather goods store. I fed coins into a long rectangular box while small clay balls clicked

183

across green felt around me.

Torresi answered on one ring. "Speak to me," he said curtly.

I pulled the folding booth door shut. "You know who this is?"

"Uh huh."

"I've decided to take the job."

"Of course you have, never any doubt."

"I may need help."

"We may be able to give it. What do you need?"

"I need information."

There was a pause on the other end that might have been Torresi drinking from a glass. "What kind of information?" he asked.

"The kind that's hard to come by. Ever been in the state building?"

"Yeah …"

"Know where his office is?"

"Probably up high."

"Probably. Know how high?"

"No, but I got a guy who knows a guy who probably does, and if he don't know, he knows a guy."

"I need to know, plus the layout, staff schedules, building security, all that."

"Give me a few days … maybe three. Swing by Saturday afternoon, say about three."

"Make it four. Your office?"

"Yep."

"See ya."

I hung up and then dialed for an operator again. I gave her a number that had been in the manila envelope that Robinson gave me. There were two short rings and a lady with a syrup voice answered. She seemed to like her job and happily took the number of the booth where I sat with the promise that someone would call back within an hour. I stood waiting outside the booth and watched the hustlers play one another for little green bills that they folded length-wise and left at the heads of the tables. Ten minutes later the phone startled me when it rang.

I reached in to pick it up. "Yeah? That was quick."

Robinson's stark voice replied, "Tell me about it."

"I've got a plan, but I'll need back-up, and possibly a diversion."

"We can do that. Can you meet tomorrow?"

"Tomorrow is too soon. Better make it four days on. By then I'll have a better idea of what I'm going to do, and how, and what I need from you."

"You want to meet on Sunday?"

"Sure, why not? Don't tell me it interferes with your church plans."

He ignored my dig. "Where?"

"The Hy-Ho Club."

He played it straight. "We'll pick you up out front."

"Never mind that, I'll come straight away to the Nightingale. Monday evening."

"Monday is better. Go to the main bar. Have a drink, relax a little, enjoy the music. I'll send someone down to find you there around seven o'clock and we'll talk then."

After I hung up I got a bottle of Hamms beer and sat on a tall stool watching the games of nine-ball and the little folded bills changing hands after each round. A Darwinian process played out: one by one the players with lesser skills faded away and disappeared, broke and disillusioned of their empty billiard dreams.

One of the pock-faced losers bummed a cigarette from me before ambling off into the chilled night.

Chapter Twenty-Six

For over a week I cooled my heels while the silver rains continued and wetted down the entire city, loosening the dirt and swirling it around the streets.

I drank coffee, read newspapers, rolled string around the floor for Miss Charlotte to chase, and let Tad beat me at checkers in the afternoons when he returned from school. Mrs. Giacalone hovered in the periphery, in the kitchen mainly, where she could ensure a steady supply of hot food as each day wore on. We didn't speak much, but there was no mistaking the presence of her eyes and the prayers she whispered in the quiet moments of recess that filled the day while Tad was away at school. I tried not to look at her too often or too directly. Occasionally, I went to meet Elinore here or there, always discreetly.

*

On a Saturday afternoon the sun came out for a while, poking sharp lines of light through gaps in the mist and the fast-moving black clouds which were over the choppy lake. The effect magnified the intensity of the colors where the points landed, greening the greens, reddening the reds, and more than anything showing up the disheartening swirls of dust particles that rotated in the glowing air over the concrete city.

Down on Clark Street, the awning over the garage had been rolled back, but it was starting to rain again, forcefully, as I arrived. Large drops splattered down like eggs around the panes of sunlight that still lay along the sidewalk and street surfaces. I paused to think about it before going in. There was nothing to lose, not really, anyway. My umbrella flexed in the wind as I pulled it down to slide through the partially open door that was propped with a stop. The garage was empty. I went on through to the back and opened that door without knocking. It was quiet enough to hear the tick of a clock.

Torresi was at his desk with half a cigar hanging from his mouth. The other half rested in a loose pile of ash, filling the obsidian ashtray and forming a trail back to the edge of the desk where his left wrist rested at an angle. He smoked absently with his non-dominant hand.

The expression under his eyelids was absurdly obscured behind a cloud of cigar puff that hung around him stubbornly. He showed no evidence that he minded.

"What you got?" he barked at me with theatrical hardness. His eyes did not glance up.

"You mind if I sit first?"

"Hell no, you help yourself. Is it raining again? I thought maybe we were finished with that for a few days. I must be waterlogged down to my spleen. Whiskey? Just came in from Canada last night, new shipment, good stuff." A bottle of Seagram's was on the desk, closer to my reach than to his, though the cap was partially unscrewed.

I waved that off.

"I'll have to hit him at work."

"Right to the point. Why make it so hard on yourself?"

I shook my head and found a Chesterfield. It wasn't too damp to light it. "It's the only way I can see it."

"You can't get him at home?"

"Not a chance. He's not at home anymore. They have a multi-room suite on the eighth floor of the Hotel LaSalle, with armed guards in the hallway day and night. It's no scene for us."

Torresi's cheeks stretched and his nose crinkled into a bright red mass of veins and skin folds. He looked up at me. "They? He have any family with him? Thought he came in from D.C. Why would he bring family for a rum assignment like this? Must be something wrong with him. Doesn't he see the news reels about crime in Chicago?"

"He's a widower. Lost his wife to the hot fever six months ago. A man can't leave children behind after something like that, not even a man with his ambitions. He's out here with two boys and a matron who looks after them through the days and nights alike. But they're careful. They never leave the apartment, not even to play outside. The food is checked and tasted in the kitchen before they send it up. The Roman emperors should have had such security."

"How old are the boys?"

"Eight and nine a pair of blonde mop-heads from the reports. They're going stir-crazy cooped up in that room. The matron is devoted but overmatched. She's early fifties, never married, been with O'Farrell a long time."

Torresi nodded and studied his cigar. "Yeah, it wouldn't be right, hitting him in front of his kids. Especially not with young boys like that, they'd never forget it. We don't do things that way. Why not take him on the way to work, get him on the street?"

"I've studied that. He travels with an armed escort. Two bodyguards go with him everywhere, plus a driver and a shotgun rider. None of them are amateurs. They vary the routine: change up the hours, the exits, even the routes they take. I'm not sure, but there might even be a second car running behind them. It's a tight operation, no way to take it down with mere finesse. And then there's the getaway, which could be difficult in the heavy traffic of the city. What do you expect?"

"Did I say we needed finesse?"

"You hired me. Otherwise you could have taken Russo's bright idea and set up a machine gun nest in a window across the street. He's a tough guy. Put him on the job if you want to do it that way. You won't hear me complain."

Torresi's jaw set. "Probably kill a dozen by-standers and still miss O'Farrell. You can imagine the headlines."

"No doubt. So maybe you agree: finesse might be good to try for, huh?"

"Finesse …" He studied his cigar, again with puzzlement. Then he teased the cooled tip with the stub end of his little finger, made a face, and set the stogie down on his desk. Gray and white ash fell off and formed a small pile. He didn't notice this because he was looking at me again, preparing to explain something.

"Out with it," I encouraged.

"Okay," Torresi started. "Not much choice when you think about it. That's fine, but here's the thing: he's not in the state building very often. He has an office there, but he doesn't use it much, maybe not at all anymore. My guy's not sure. He uses an inner office at this address." He pushed a scrap of paper across the wide desk towards me, right up against the bottle of Seagram's. I picked it up and stared at it. "This is where it gets tough. He's on the same floor as the Feds, Hoover's eager boys, plus investigators from Internal Revenue. You know, different groups use that floor, but they're not so much – most of them are accountants or lawyers, college boys, but not all of them are. They've got at least one former Texas Ranger in the group, knows about the hard side of the business."

"Security?"

"Well, it ain't Fort Knox, but it is headquarters for a lot of federal cops and those boys are carrying handguns in their holsters, not slide rules. And there's plenty of shotguns and machineguns laying about too. They may not know how to use them outside of a government range, but then again, they're eager enough …"

"Lovely."

"Maybe there's a Plan B?"

I shrugged unhappily. "This is Plan B."

*

After I left the garage I headed toward the Loop to meet Elinore for an early dinner near the lake. The sky, after we left the restaurant, turned vanilla-orange along the edges as the clouds blew off. Glowing strands of sunlight tethered the atmosphere over the city lights. The days were lengthening steadily in their inexorable march towards the summer solstice. Without speaking, we walked along the half-crowded sidewalk. Her hand was gripped around my arm and then later fell down gently and found my hand. It was natural and comfortable, and for once the little voice in my head was quiet, maybe even resting.

When ten blocks or so had slid beneath our feet, we decided to flag down a taxi to complete the rest of the trip back to her apartment. For a moment I debated on whether to get into the cab with her.

"Just one cocktail," she said, looking up at me from inside the taxi, with her heels still on the pavement. I studied her face. Her lips curled irresistibly.

"Scoot over," I told her. "I'll have the one drink and bet you five you offer me a second."

She giggled and made no attempt at an argument. We rode the distance without speaking again and I wondered if that was because we had nothing left to say or whether all the things there were to say were simply too scary to voice.

*

Elinore stood in her kitchen with a small bottle of Angostura bitters in her hand. She laughed at me and her eyes were happy and dreamy and yet also more alert than the last time I'd seen them. I had noticed the effect at dinner, but thought it might have been the dimmed light at our table. Now I wasn't so sure.

190

"You haven't taken the laudanum today," I told her.

Her smile was bright. "Is that a question? It's three days now. It was tough at first, like you said, but I wanted you to know I could do it. I told you I could. I'm going to be okay."

I nodded, aware of that nagging voice inside my head that was whispering again, its resting time apparently over. "Don't get ahead of yourself. They say to go it one day at a time. And even that might be too fast. The slip-ups always occur when you think there's no chance of one happening. You can't just say it's so and make it be."

"Tell me it will be okay."

"It will be okay, if you will it to be so and don't suffer it. Don't get over-confident. That's when it falls apart."

"No, say it will be okay, no qualifier."

"How can I tell you that?"

"If you say it's so, then it will be."

"That makes no sense."

"Say it. Tell me it will be okay."

My need to take care of her won out. "It will be okay."

"That's better." She set the bitters on the counter and reached for two glasses. "Have a cocktail?"

"Sure. Just the one."

She poured and stirred while I watched the graceful motion of her fingers and the way they touched and held the glassware. She handed one cocktail to me. I sipped but barely tasted it.

"Will you come away with me, away from this city?"

She finished swallowing and set her glass on the counter. "Was that an impulsive question?"

"No. I've had plenty of time to think about it."

Her eyes were large and playful, like a kitten's. "How much thought?"

"Enough."

"Where will we go?"

"Does it matter?"

"No, no it doesn't. When? I might need a week or so to settle a few things."

"Yeah, that's about right. I'm thinking seven to ten days."

Her expression clouded suddenly. Her eyebrows turned in and her lips pouted. "Why? What do you have to do?"

"Never mind. You can't ask me that."

"You have another job on your list?"

I didn't respond. I swirled my cocktail, drank some.

"That's it, isn't it? You have another score in mind."

"It's not like that."

"But there's another job. There's always another job."

"One more."

"Skip it."

"I can't."

Suddenly she spoke with a rush. "Let's go away now. We can go tonight. We have enough money. All that money you've given me, it's right here. I don't have anything so important that I need to settle it up first. I don't know why I said that, I didn't mean it. Let's leave now, right now, this very minute. There's plenty of trains heading out tonight. I'll be happy enough just to be on any one of them, going anywhere with you. Say we will."

"Kid, it's important."

"But there's plenty of money, we won't need more for a long while. This can last us. We'll make it last."

"This one isn't about money."

Elinore stared at me. I drank some more of my bitter-sweet whiskey, and for the first time noticed it was heavy with undissolved sugar crystals at the bottom of the glass.

"It's getting late."

She finished her cocktail. "Stay awhile, please? Reassure me."

She set the empty glass on the counter and moved towards me. The cream-colored skin on her face was young and beautiful, but the desire in her eyes when she leaned toward me was more ancient than the pyramids. I didn't push her away. Her mouth was against mine. There was feral warmth and moisture and when I finally breathed again the sensation stayed with me; I couldn't help myself.

*

Sometime later, much later, she came to the door with me. I opened it, stepped over the threshold, and turned to look at her from out in the hallway.

"Don't go," she whispered. Watching me with wide dark eyes that were oceans I wanted to dive into, swim deep, hold my breath as long as I could, and stay under forever if possible. Instead, I pulled the door shut with a click and headed towards the stairs on the balls of my feet. Every part of my body tingled.

The heartless, blinding light of the early morning sun catapulted over the tall city buildings, mocking me for a fool as I reached the street with my hands trembling in my pockets.

Chapter Twenty-Seven

The Irishman stood in a corner of the Nightingale Club, unaffected by the rhythm of the music that pulsed across the room. I had never actually seen him in his own club before. Girls in white fringing and black garters danced together in a line at one end of the room, just in front of the swing band that was blowing as hard as they could. It was late on a Friday evening and people were cutting loose.

Following Robinson through the crowd, I crossed the room to the small table. It was on an elevated stand so that it held command over the entire room. There were two other elevated stands in other nooks of the large room, but they were not as high. Behind us an original oil painting graced the wall, providing an array of intermingled colors and a glimpse into the lives of wealthy Parisians circa 1890. The table was set with fine silver, silk napkins, and three small dishes of caviar. A bowl of sliced lemons and a vase with a yellow rose centered the table.

"You honor me, Laddie," the Irishman said above the din as I came up to him. He shook my hand and gestured toward the table. "We're drinking champagne tonight, if you approve."

"I approve," I told him, but the champagne was already arriving before I started to speak. Two corks popped nearby almost simultaneously.

We sat, just the three of us, and toasted the wet spring and the flowers that were sure to arrive soon. Robinson wet his lips, though he did not appear to swallow. The Irishman dipped into the caviar with what looked like a small butter knife. It probably had another, more formal name and purpose. He spread the black beads carefully across a thin toast wafer and took an impossibly small bite. Then he chewed slowly and thoroughly before speaking. It was an elaboration of his usual contrived pose.

"Have you seen our friends on the South Side? Surely they too are anxious to bid farewell to this overeager special prosecutor who will generally be quite bad for all our businesses." He was testing me, probing.

I raised my glass in another toast. "To the omniscient Irish."

His smile was modest, almost deprecating. "Well, Mr. Robinson has his sources."

"Then you already know that they thought to hire me for the same job."

The smile did not change. "Did they now? How nice for you. Two paychecks for one bit of work – seems to come out rather nicely for you. I won't begrudge it. Although, you'll need to be careful in your dealings with that group. Seems there is a rumor circling that they attempted to end your days down in Urbana."

I shrugged at that. "Reina might have got a little ahead of himself."

"Well, of course, I wasn't there and don't know how far he tried to take it. There is a story that he had you in the sights of his Thompson machinegun for a brief moment just before you shot him dead. Maybe he was careless or maybe he really was freelancing, thinking to keep that large score from being split too many ways? In which case his finger was slow. Alternatively, one might reasonably wonder if he had the ambition and creativity to develop that idea himself. And if one wonders about that, one might also wonder who put the thought into his head, and then nurtured it to such a fine point."

"I think you're confused about who lured who to that bank. Remember I shot *him*."

"It would worry me if I thought you shot him in self-defense. Maybe I heard it wrong, Laddie. Maybe the wags have a bit too much time on their hands, been drinking turpentine to addle their minds. But what I heard was he'd been promised a nice reward by Mr. Nitti for leaving you in that bank – all the cash he could carry and maybe an internal promotion, if you know what I mean."

I did know what he meant and I had my own uncertainties. It could have been motivated by something other than simple greed. I shut my eyes and then opened them slowly. "So maybe I oughta watch my back, not trust my partners too much, is what you're saying?"

"Only certain partners, my young friend, only certain partners." His smile attempted to be reassuring; it fell flat on the table, sourer than the lemons.

My glass was suddenly empty. From behind me a hand appeared, pointing in towards the center of the table with a bottle of champagne, filling my glass. After it pulled back out of sight, I raised my glass again. "To good partners," I said. "They don't come around often."

"To that."

We drank. The drummer took a solo, Gene Krupa style. The girls kicked higher and faster, bouncing their white fringes. I could feel my old heart racing, unsure if the adrenaline was a product of the performance

196

or the bureaucratic unblinking eyes staring back at me.

"When will you do it?" the Irishman asked. He patted his mouth delicately with a silk napkin.

"Very soon," I replied.

His look was blank, as though he didn't know what I was talking about, and he swirled his champagne a little, frothing the bubbles. Then he dipped into the bowl with the short flat knife and spread more caviar on his toast.

"I'll kill O'Farrell very soon, within a week, ten days minimum," I clarified.

"Tell us the exact day. Eugene will need to make preparations for it." He put the caviar into his mouth.

"I haven't decided yet. I still need more time to scout and prepare."

There was an unusually quiet moment while he finished chewing.

"When will you know?"

"Two or three days, and then I'll know. I'll take him at work. He's not moving around a lot, but I need to be sure of his location within the building. I know the floor, but not the precise office that he works from. Or who else is likely to be around him during the day. I've got to be sure of a lot of little details before I move."

"We'll give you back-up. It will help."

"Don't think I need it."

His flashbulb grin was savage and spiteful. "You'll have it nonetheless and be thankful for it. There are bodyguards to deal with, and at the least you'll need a diversion."

He did not trust me.

"I can handle all that by myself. I've worked it out."

"I'm sure you have, but my men will be there. You'll work the plan with Eugene after I leave the table. He'll tell you how it will come about. And now I suggest we enjoy our caviar and wine. Here's to the mission, a toast, and to our developing ... ahh ... professional relationship."

I raised my glass, though I was in no mood for celebration.

*

Before he left the table the Irishman leaned in close to me and whispered very quietly: "Do not make the mistake of assuming I do not know about it. I do know. You think you'll take the girl with you when you

197

leave. Perish that silly thought from your mind, Laddie."

If Robinson heard what he said, he gave no indication of it. Instead he spent ten minutes explaining to me how his men would assist me in the job, whether I liked it or not.

It wasn't going to be pretty.

Chapter Twenty-Eight

On a bright, cool morning in late May, the 24th to be exact, the lead headline of every newspaper in the city trumpeted the news that Bonnie and Clyde had been shot to pieces by a Texas posse down in Louisiana. I had just started my first cup of coffee when Mrs. Giacalone angrily placed the *Tribune* squarely in front of me and walked back into the kitchen without saying a word. My stomach tightened.

After drinking the coffee and reading the article, I carried the empty cup to the kitchen. A bitter taste settled in my mouth. Mrs. Giacalone stood at the sink with her arms crossed in a self-hug. Her hair had fallen loose along the sides of her face, shielding me from her emotion.

"This isn't about me," I said to her backside and halted in the doorway, half in and half out.

She shook her head by turning at her hips, rocking slightly against the counter. When she spoke her voice was small, narrowed to the point of a sharp pin. "Since you arrived I dread the news, fearing every day that I'll be reading something horrible about you. It seems inevitable."

I didn't know what to say, so I said nothing.

"You never saw it, how you changed our lives here in this small house with your presence. I feared you at first, at least a little. Mostly because I thought I was supposed to. But there was never anything to fear, except for how things will be when you are gone." She straightened and turned around, pushing the hair back from her face to show me the look of bewildered grief. "I don't know who you are. But I have some idea."

I stepped into the kitchen, just far enough to set the empty coffee cup on a counter.

"No. Whatever you might think, you don't know me."

The corners of her mouth trembled in protest. "Yes, I think I do. True, I've got my assumptions, but I'll say this: You're a good man. It is there in you, so evident. Maybe you don't even know it yourself, but its there."

"Mrs. Giacalone," I said, moving closer to her.

She waited until I was beside her and then touched my hand as I placed it on her shoulder. The weight of her fingers was like lilies on a pond. "It might be nice if you addressed me as Maria."

"Maria." I paused. "That's a pretty name. It befits you. Maybe in another time things would have been different …"

"We've been so formal these last few weeks, Mr. Duncan. I don't even know your first name."

This rattled around in my thoughts before I responded. "It's Ross."

"Ross. That's nice. May I use it in the private moments between us?"

I nodded, studying her face and the intent hidden there. Her eyes were weary and radiant and searching at the same time.

"Are you okay?" I asked, wondering too what she saw in me.

"I miss my husband. Having you here has reminded me of how it felt to have a man around. He was a policeman."

"He must have been a good man."

Her posture stiffened. "I'm not quite sure he was. Officially, he was killed in the line of duty – shot by warehouse thieves. They gave him a twenty-one shot salute and I received a folded flag. They said he was a hero. But some wondered why he was at that warehouse in the middle of the night. Some said he wasn't there doing police duty, that he was on the pad, that they shot him because he wanted too much and wasn't satisfied with what they gave him. I don't know. But it could be true, and we live with that. Even if it was true, sometimes you wonder what choices he had, growing up the way he did and putting on that uniform every day to face the things this town threw at him. Tad doesn't know about any of it yet. But someday he'll learn – he'll hear the whispers. And I can't bear to think about how I'll have to make some explanation."

That hung there for a moment while I tried to find some words. She had lost her husband, and, perhaps worse, lost the idea of her husband – both who he was and what he meant to their son. She looked up at me with proud eyes that displayed sadness and intelligence, mingled in with something else, some other powerful nuance I could not define.

"I know," she said, half-smiling for me. "You don't know what to say. There isn't anything to say. There aren't any words that can lessen the pain of it for an old widow. Not now or ever."

"Maria, you're half right. I don't have the words to lessen that pain. But it goes away on its own with time. You and Tad have a chance to recover and to live a good life together. You can be happy, maybe more than you know."

"Yes. We do have that hope. It's there in every prayer I make."

"It's more than a hope. I felt it, staying here these past few weeks. Your home is filled with quiet warmth, caring, and sustaining belief.

You've done well by the boy. He looks up to you."

"You're sure belief is sustaining?"

"Yours is."

"And you're sure God is not utterly indifferent?"

I smiled at that. "I'm pretty sure He's not."

"My family fell apart when my husband was shot. How is that the answer to any prayer?"

"Maybe you're not seeing all of it. You're a real family – you, Tad, and Miss Charlotte. That's more than plenty of people ever have, even people with money and a houseful of blood relatives."

"Do you have a family?"

"No."

Her voice lowered. "Is there a woman?"

I was self-conscious about responding to this question. I felt the blush spread across my face and I wanted to turn toward the window for air. "Yes … well, I'm not sure."

"It's okay. I didn't think that we …" She didn't finish the sentence. She didn't have to. It hung there and floated about us silently.

"It's not just that …" I said, struggling to find the words. "Well, I'm confused about it."

"Do you love her?"

I must have blushed. I could feel the heat of guilt in my face. I tried to hide it with a smile that felt too clever, even to me. "Yes, unquestionably."

Her face tightened with puzzlement.

"What is the problem? Why are you confused? If you love her then you should be with her. Don't allow it to be lost."

"I love her. But it doesn't end with that, I wish it did. I feel responsible for her. She needs me."

"What do you mean?"

"Just exactly that: she's my responsibility. There's no one else to take care of her, and so it falls to me. Maybe there's no words or concepts in our language to explain why an adult woman needs a protector, but she does and it's on me."

"Why you?"

"I made a promise to somebody, a promise that I have to keep no matter what comes. Though it's not only that. You go through life thinking you're alone and then you discover just maybe someone else needs you, and it changes you. I've known her since she was six years old. She was the kid on the block, the one we all looked after and I'm

201

the only one that's left now. It falls to me. She's changed me."

"Oh." Then her expression changed, her eyes spread. "Parents feel that kind of love for their children."

My vision blurred for a moment. Slivers of anxiety cut through me. "I hadn't thought of it quite that way. Perhaps. If it's even possible for someone like me."

"I think it is possible. It's a different kind of love, but you have it in you. It's more than possible. It's probable."

"They're both in there."

"You really don't know which comes out stronger?"

I stifled the blank expression I started to form. This wasn't anything to be casual about.

"How can you know? I desire her. I'm not unsure about that. But the other impulse, the impulse to take care of her, gets in the way. It leaves me ashamed of the other. It cuts against it."

"Oh, you poor thing. You don't know what to do with yourself. Either way, you should be with her."

I nodded.

"You're leaving soon, aren't you? I can tell. I've sensed it for several days now."

I nodded. "Tomorrow."

"When?"

"After breakfast."

Her eyes filled slowly. "Tad and I won't be here in the morning. We couldn't stand it. Miss Charlotte will have to see you off."

"I'll be back again in a few months."

She looked away from me, staring at a distant point over her left shoulder. "No. No you won't, Ross. You won't ever come back … Take care of your girl."

The grief in her voice bore the same hopeless promise as the work whistle of a Pennsylvanian coal mine at dawn. I backed away from it.

Chapter Twenty-Nine

Unusually, I slept through the night, though not without a series of disconcerting dreams that played continuously from one to the next. They were convoluted threads. In the final one, I was on the verge of committing suicide. I sat atop a long, steep slide that would take me forever down to some subterranean place. I could not decide whether to slide with my head or my feet first. Changing my mind, I climbed down the ladder, only to climb back up again. I repeated this ambivalent action several times. When I opened my eyes the dream carried over to my waking state. In confusion, I continued to contemplate whether to end my life on that deadly slide.

A quiet movement on the surface of the blanket near my face brought me out of that dark thought. Miss Charlotte's whiskers tenderly brushed my cheek. She purred with contentment at the start of another day and my momentary presence. I rubbed her white chin and muzzle with my fingertips as she settled down slowly on top of my chest. Her gaze, through half-closed green eyes, was serene and wise.

I let go of the dream.

*

True to her word, Mrs. Giacalone and Tad were nowhere to be found. I had a cup of coffee by myself and then went back upstairs to say goodbye to Miss Charlotte. She slept in a tight curl, positioned against my pillow. Her chin rested upon her hindquarters. A tip of a charcoal tail patted the bed in a gentle rhythm when I spoke her name.

It was harder to leave than I expected it would be. I kissed her once on top of her head, between the ears. She dipped slightly at my touch.

"Bye, Sweetheart. Take care of your family."

Miss Charlotte rose up and looked at me with half-closed eyes before settling down into her curl again with her eyes fully shut. The light sound of a finely tuned motor emanated from some mysterious place within her. I smiled and turned away from the quiet room.

I made three stops after I left the house, including the train station where I stored my bags, and Sullivan's tavern. Jimmy was not there, but I was able to leave him a note. The girl who took it promised me he would get it by early afternoon. As I made my rounds, I took efforts to ensure I was not tailed. The third cab reeked heavily of stale whiskey.

"Fare last night spilled half a bottle of Canadian," the driver told me.

He seemed sober enough that I gave him the benefit of the doubt. I sat carefully and watched the traffic behind and around us.

When I arrived at O'Farrell's building I was two hours early. Lunchtime movements flowed over the street and sidewalks. Across the street a business calling itself 20th Century Liquors advertised fountain lunches and vitamins. They did brisk business with the gray suit crowd. I went in and bought a newspaper and ordered a cup of coffee. From a booth in the back I placed a call to the Blackstone Hotel.

The operator was efficient. Within a minute, Elinore's voice came over the line. "It's been two days. Where are you?" she asked.

"I'm fine. Everything's fine. We go today."

"Are you alright?"

"Yes, absolutely. Today's the day. You know what to do?"

"Of course."

"Meet me at our spot, exactly as we discussed. Don't be early, don't be late."

"Please be careful." Her voice sounded far away and sad.

"You too. I'll see you soon."

*

The plan was simple and old as the proverbial hills. It involved a noisy diversion and an inside man – two of them actually. The Irishman had a local police captain and an agent of the FBI, both stationed near O'Farrell, in his back pocket. They were crucial links of the chain that supported organized criminal enterprise in big cities across the country. It made me smile to think about the fact that I'd never heard of an independent bank robber paying off the police to help rob a bank. It probably happened, somewhere, but it was not the usual way. We earned our stolen riches through hard work and accepted risk, blazing guns and audacious cunning, or so the newspapers would have us all believe.

According to Robinson's plan, the police captain would lead a large number of the law enforcement officers surrounding O'Farrell on a wild goose chase across the city, and thereby reduce the guard. The federal man would open a back door to let me in, and then he would stay out of my way.

A few minutes before two o'clock, I entered the building. I was forty-five minutes early. The lobby was filled with people, most of whom were coming or going. An elderly man with a security badge read the afternoon paper. His eyes focused insecurely and his lips moved. The job was not something that meant a whole lot to him. He was waiting for his shift to end, the beginning of the weekend, a cherished vacation, soon maybe the end of his life. I didn't spot any of Robinson's boys hanging about.

I waited with a small group of messengers and other errand runners, then climbed into an elevator and rode up to the fifteenth floor. There I sat in a stall in the men's room and stared at my watch, urging the hands to circle faster. Again, it was the waiting, something I was used to and a part of the mix I did better than most. When the minute hand finally reached eight after the hour I stretched up and opened my briefcase. It held several extra magazines for my .45, a blackjack, two pairs of handcuffs, a smoke flare, and a U.S. Army issue hand grenade. These I put into my various pockets. I left the empty briefcase inside the stall and headed out to the stairwell.

I took the stairs at medium speed so as not to draw attention to myself or arrive out of breath. When I reached O'Farrell's floor I looked at my watch again. I was exactly ten minutes early. I waited quietly for another minute and tried the door. It was locked, as I expected it would be. Standing to the side of the door I knocked softly, three times with a pause between the second and third knock. That was my signal to the federal man. I hoped he was there on the other side of the door waiting for me, anticipating that I might be early.

At first there was no response. I considered how long I should wait before trying again. While I was playing with that question I heard a low murmur from the other side of the door, and then there was a sharp click. The door opened just wide enough for an eyeball to appear in the shaded crack. It studied me. I shifted slightly to my right so the eye had a better view of my face.

"Delivery," I said.

"Slide it through the door."

"It's flowers, yellow roses."

"Them's the magic words."

The door opened and I saw the FBI agent's face for the first time. He was a tall, slender man with a red face and salt-and-pepper hair that was cut very short on the sides above his ears. His teeth were stained yellow from too many cigarettes and one eyelid hung lower than the other, causing a listless appearance. A pair of reading glasses perched on the end of his nose. I'd seen him before, during my stakeouts and I knew he was the top dog on the floor.

"You're a bit early," he told me.

"Really? Maybe my watch is fast. Let's get on with it, huh?"

But he didn't move. Instead he stared at me with dawning recognition. Perhaps he was calculating whether taking the reward for my capture was worth crossing the Irishman. But he never got the chance to finish that calculation. As his fingers edged toward the revolver in his holster, I sapped him as hard as I could. He crumpled over and hit a filing cabinet on his way down to the floor. The reading glasses skittered across the industrial tiles. I picked him up by the shoulders and pulled him back about ten feet down the spur so that he would not be visible from the main hallway.

I tucked the blackjack into his front breast pocket as a corsage and handcuffed his hands behind his back. The original plan had called for me to make a show of sapping him so that he would appear blameless in the aftermath of O'Farrell's assassination. According to that plan I wasn't supposed to hit him too hard. But I had really creamed him and his head was bleeding. He lay unconscious on the hard, tile floor.

I didn't waste time worrying about him. He was just another corrupt cop to me.

The main hallway was empty and there were few sounds. Moving quickly now, I counted doors until I got to the seventh one on the right.

*

A tingling sensation ran my neck as I peered into the office. A bald man sat at the desk with a pencil held to his lips.

"Mr. O'Farrell?"

The pencil lowered slowly as the man half-turned his head toward the door, while his eyes made up the difference. He allowed a tight nervous smile. His teeth hinted at money and the ivy leagues. He wore cufflinks that glittered and his tie was knotted in an unusually tight manner.

"That's me. Where are my guards? Who are you? How did you get in here?"

I stepped into the doorway and showed him my .45.

"Come with me, sir. Your bodyguards aren't coming back any time soon."

"Who are you? How did you get in here?"

"Men are coming to kill you. We have to get out and we have to do it quickly. There isn't time to explain. I'll lead you out."

"Are you going to kill me?" His voice was dispassionate and I realized he was harder up close than he had looked from a distance. I should have known that went with the territory he waded in.

"No, sir."

"What about my sons?"

"They should come too. I have a car waiting for us down on the street."

"Where are you taking us?"

"We don't have time for that conversation. Pick up your briefcase, now please. Take your most important papers."

I pointed my gun at him to encourage him, but it was unnecessary. Staccato gunshots sounded from some other part of the building, towards the far end of the main hallway. That got his attention.

*

O'Farrell's boys seemed to appreciate the gravity of the situation; they were all concentration. The sound of gunfire has that effect on people, even children.

"Leave your things," O'Farrell told them. "We're going out now. Quickly."

They had blonde hair and somber eyes, and they obeyed their father immediately. Less than sixty seconds after the first gunshot, we were all standing and ready to move. I stepped back out into the hall first and looked in both directions. Without waiting for my signal, O'Farrell came out of the office with his sons right behind him. That was a mistake.

"Hold there."

Twenty feet down the hall stood a man pointing a Thompson machinegun at the floor in front of us. He had a cigar wedged in his mouth. Smoke curled gently off the glowing end of it. Behind him several other men were moving up.

The man with the Thompson wore a badge. From where I stood I could not distinguish which branch he was with, but I didn't think it mattered. He was not there to enforce any laws that I knew of. He started to walk towards us, casually, with the men behind him moving along too. The cigar started to move up and down as his teeth tightened and relaxed on it in steady rhythm.

No one seemed to notice that I was holding a grenade in my left hand. It rested at my side, bouncing gently against my leg below the hip. I'd already pulled the pin and it would explode within a few seconds after I let go. I pointed the .45 with my right hand. "We're going out the other way. You're not going to stop us."

This seemed to surprise the man with the Thompson. There was confusion behind him until a voice rang out: "That's O'Farrell."

"Shoot him," another man yelled. The barrel of the Thompson gun came up in an arc.

I shot the man with one hand and let go of the grenade with the other, rolling it towards them. With my elbow on O'Farrell's chest, I pushed him back against his children into the office we had just come from. There was a loud boom and then a slower roar as dust and debris filled the hallway. My ears rang. I stepped back into the hallway and, with my eyes squinting against the dust, fired the .45 through the haze. My shots were placed low, where I thought Robinson's boys might be if they had survived the blast. I fired the entire magazine and released it to the floor and jammed another one in quickly. The hallway echoed and a high-pitched, anguished moan started up. Someone had survived, but was hurt bad.

"Come on," I said to O'Farrell, grabbing the hand of his smallest child. "Let's get out of here, this way."

We ran down the hall away from the explosion, towards the back stairwell.

*

At street level, a limousine was waiting for us, right where it was supposed to be. I'd leased it that morning and promised the driver a $200 tip if he was in the right spot at the right time. I'd given him $50 in advance just to show him I was serious.

O'Farrell climbed in the back with his sons. I sat in front and placed a small pile of bills on the seat next to the driver.

"Here's the remainder of what I promised you. I'll add another fifty to it if you get us to the train station quickly and without being tailed."

The car roared off. Nobody spoke. I turned to look at the faces in the back seat. The two boys sat still, with their anxious eyes towards their father, watching and waiting for some sign from him. None was forthcoming.

"Where are we going?" O'Farrell asked me. It was the first time he had spoken since our escape. His voice was steady.

"There is a training leaving for New York in twenty minutes. When we get to the station, all three of you will get on that train. The tickets are in my pocket. You'll know what to do when you get to New York?"

O'Farrell nodded and then looked at each of his sons in turn. "Relax Walter, relax Simon. We're going to be okay. This is just a short trip. We'll let Mrs. Sloan know where she can catch up to us in a couple of days."

Simon, the oldest boy, peered up at him through blonde locks. His face was straight and the expression indicated he didn't believe everything he heard. "Those men were going to kill us." His voice trembled slightly, but his eyes were clear and they did not waver. He reminded me of Tad.

"Yes," O'Farrell said slowly. "They were. But they did not, thanks to this man here. He saved our lives. We are safe now."

O'Farrell turned his head to study my face until I became self-conscious. I turned around and watched the street. I positioned the side mirror so that I could see traffic behind us. I kept my eyes in constant motion – the mirror, the side window, the front windshield – all in one seamless flowing triangle, and occasionally a square as I looked to my left. I didn't see anything that worried me. The chauffer drove expertly. He took the shortest route and when traffic was heavy before us, he was inventive about finding alternate routes. In five minutes we were at the train station.

"Wait on the curb for me," I said to O'Farrell, pointing towards a spot back against the wall, and I told him the track we would take. When he and the boys were out of the car and standing far enough away so that they could not hear what I said to the driver, I addressed him: "You performed an important service for me this morning. Thank you. Here is the remaining amount I promised you, and then some."

I placed a fifty-dollar bill on top of the money already piled on the seat between us. The driver's eyes widened as he flipped through the bills, counting them, and he looked up at me quickly, with some surprise. His eyes flickered and then darted back down to the money. His hand tightened around the bills, but he did not yet lift them.

"Look at me. You know who I am?"

He nodded.

"Then you know my reputation?"

He nodded again.

"You may feel temptation to let somebody know about the fare you had today. It might make a good story in about a week. I won't mind you telling that story ... in a week. You're welcome to it, then. You might feel some temptation to tell the story sooner than a week, like maybe today, to somebody looking for me or looking for the other gentleman. Do you know what that would get you?"

The driver hesitated. He started to protest that he would never, but I asked him, loudly, to simply answer my question.

"Dead?" he said.

"No. Dead is what you will wish you were. If you tell anyone looking for me or the other gentleman, you will find yourself in a great deal of pain and for quite a long while and with no hope for release. People you care about will suffer too."

"I won't tell anyone for a week. At least a week."

"Let's make it two, just to be sure." I handed him another fifty. This one I placed directly into his hand. "Just so you don't think I'm all meanness. And I have your number. Maybe there will be other jobs for you when I'm in town again."

He nodded heavily as I backed out of the car. As soon as I was out and the door was slammed shut, he drove off. I turned around, clasping the buttons of my jacket against the cold, sun-filled Chicago air. O'Farrell and his two young boys were waiting on the sidewalk, back out of the sun, under the shadows. Their faces were turned away from the street.

I gave him an envelope. "These tickets take you south. You have a sleeper car for privacy."

He opened the envelope and flipped through the three tickets quickly. "You said New York."

"I'm not sure about the driver."

"And the three hundred?"

"In case you need it."

"I'll have to pay you back."

"That's fine, no rush, though. Maybe you'll have a chance someday."

"What is the correct track?"

I told him. "I'll walk you down there just in case. We have less than eight minutes."

The four of us walked quickly through the train station. The two boys led the way and we kept up. They did not ask questions. We found the line and the car efficiently and O'Farrell got each of his sons set up in a window seat facing each other.

"Stay here until I come back," he counseled them. To me he said, "Talk with me out here."

We stood out on the platform, with wisps of steam skirting around our ankles and the occasional train whistle sounding from somewhere down the track. The lighting was dim and unnatural, even though it was only mid-afternoon.

"Those men were really going to kill me and my boys, weren't they?"

I nodded. "Yes sir, they were."

"Who were they?"

"Just men, bad men. The kind of men who could shoot a man in front of his children and not lose too much sleep over it. You've scared a lot of people in this town. The price on your head is higher than the price on mine."

"Its not supposed to be that way."

"No."

"Who do they work for?"

"Does it matter?"

"You know it does."

"Aren't they all the same?"

"Who? Tell me."

My eyes focused on his. "The Irishman."

"He would kill me, my children like that? Snuff us out like candles?"

I nodded.

"Just for doing my job?"

211

The incomprehension in his eyes expanded into a hard anger. It had never occurred to him it would really be like this. But there it was: a simple hard truth, a truth that had never occurred to him.

"Yes, sir. This is Chicago. It's jungle law here. He thinks you're coming after him for doing *his* job."

O'Farrell's jaw tightened, and then relaxed as he looked at me and stared into my eyes.

"It's a tough business we're in. Chicago is a rough town. Most of my colleagues back in Washington wouldn't understand. Even if they said they would."

"No, sir. They would not."

He continued to study me. "Why did you save me? You could have been killed."

I shrugged, unsure of the answer myself. Fleeting images of an Ohio farmhouse ran through my mind. "What difference does it make?"

"You're fixing something, trying to make up for something."

"I had a friend, a partner, we went back together, way back: childhood, reform school, Joliet prison, and then worse. I owed him everything. He needed me, but I couldn't save him. I had to save somebody. You were the one who came along, needed saving, seemed worth saving. People think I'm a killer and maybe I am when I'm cornered. But they thought I would kill for money, the hard, cold way, and I wouldn't do that. I couldn't give in to them the way they expected."

O'Farrell waited before responding. I wasn't sure if he didn't know what to say or if he thought I was not finished with my explanation.

"I know who you are," he said when he finally spoke. "I knew it from the moment you stepped into my office. I thought you were there to kill me."

I nodded my head. "I understand. I let them believe I would kill you so that I could get in there first."

He nodded. "Thank you. For myself and my boys."

"What will you do now?"

"I know what to do. I'll get to Washington in a few days and talk to the right people. Thanks to what I have in this briefcase, I think we have enough to indict and convict the man you refer to as the Irishman. He may get the chair; probably not, though he should go away for a nice bit of time. I'll make sure of that now. He'll be my first priority."

"If you can find an honest judge."

He smiled wanly. "I think I can, at least one that's honest enough."

I wasn't so sure, but I didn't say so.

Up the track, the whistle blew urgently and the "all aboard" announcement sounded.

"Good luck." I extended my hand.

O'Farrell grasped it tightly. "Thank you. If you ever want to come in, get in touch with me. I'll make sure you're safe and that you get a fair shake from the system. I'll let the court know about how you helped me and my boys."

I tipped my hat.

O'Farrell jumped on the train just as it started to move. He turned and looked at me, but was quickly out of sight. As the cars pulled by I saw the faces of his two boys as they went past, for just an instant. Their eyes were wide with numb shock and fear as their journey began.

I stood there, a man in false armor watching the train depart.

Chapter Thirty

Marshall Field and Company did not entice me to spend my money, but their main retail store, which covered a full city block at State and Washington in The Loop, provided me with a good place to meet when things were hot. My pulse was slow and even. I waited for Elinore in the central court of the South Rotunda looking up at over a million and half expensive pieces of iridescent Tiffany Favrile art glass.

The glass mosaic dome spread sky-like above me for six thousand square feet. It seemed to go on forever. Polished mahogany, hand-carved counters, bronze fittings, hydraulic elevators, and vast miles of carpeting and gleaming tiled floors surrounded me with style. I'd read somewhere that when old Mr. Field had died of pneumonia, after a round of winter golf in 1906, all the stores along State Street had closed. The Board of Trade had suspended afternoon trading in honor of his wealth, while flags across the city flew at half-mast. I wondered if anyone had actually mourned.

My ears buzzed with the sounds and the motion. Hundreds of imperfect statues of human figures moved around me: ladies on day-long social outings, with leisurely lunches and hours in the full-service salons; children pushed about in carriages held large rainbow-colored lollipops, many tired and crying; serious men in carefully tailored suits picked out just the right gift for the special person. It was a whole new society and not one I particularly liked. Even in the late afternoon, the city's wealthiest, prettiest consumers moved about with a tapered frenetic energy. It was not a place that welcomed the poor, the recent immigrant, or the ancestor of slaves. My eyes blinked against it all.

I'd been five minutes early, but now Elinore was over ten minutes late. I looked at my watch again and compared it to the time reported on the large store clocks that filled the rotunda. They matched well enough. Rising, I paced to a stand that sold newspapers and selected the afternoon edition of the *Tribune*. A quick scan of the front page revealed nothing that interested me.

Returning to the spot where I was to meet her, I remained standing. My eyes surveyed the crowd in three directions and searched across the court and down the hallways as far as possible. I turned slowly to look in the fourth direction. There was no sign of her. She should have been here by now. We had discussed this carefully two days ago. To keep her from harm, I had arranged a room for her at the Blackstone Hotel. No one could have known where she was.

I checked my watch again: she was fifteen minutes late. Now I was anxious in a way that had nothing to do with the ostentatious consumerism around me. A nearby bench was empty. I sat down again and opened the paper, staring at the ink, the headlines, the bylines, the photographs, absorbing none of it.

A heavy-set woman with three red shopping bags sat at the end of the bench, wiping her forehead. Her snore-like breathing was heavy. When she caught up to herself she sighed and asked me if I knew where glassware was. I didn't. She moved on.

Every few minutes I stood and completed my visual search of the rotunda again, turning slowly with a growing madness in my chest. Fearing the worst, I started to look for other faces, familiar or otherwise: furtive men with dark intent. Despite all the people around me, I saw nobody. When she was thirty minutes late I started to understand she was not coming, and after another fifteen minutes passed I was sure of it.

It was time to quit waiting. At the Washington Street curb I caught a cab and gave the driver the address to her apartment. As we floated through the downtown traffic of rush hour I sat back low in the seat and rechecked the action on my .45.

My jaw felt as though it might crack under the pressure of my clench.

*

From the outside of her apartment nothing appeared amiss. The street was quiet. Nothing moved. Windows above me offered no clues to anything. I abandoned caution and went into the building.

I came up the steps slowly with one hand flexed and ready in my pocket. At the landing I turned, my eyes lifted towards the varnished oak banister that fronted the entrance to her apartment along the stairwell. Something *was* amiss: a stomach wrenching quarter-inch of dusk-lit air separated the door from the molding of its frame. I stop-started. Bounding the last few stairs I pushed it open and stepped into the withering light. As my eyes adjusted to the dark, I dared not inhale.

Then everything came into focus. But I was too late.

She lay on the couch in a tight curl, much as she had the last time I'd been there with her. A ribbon of red silk nestled beneath her feet. She was an image from a shampoo advertisement: her hair splayed forward over the pillow beneath her cheek, rode back across her whitening forehead, and swept behind her ear, down along her neck. Frail lines of black make-up had melted down her face beneath her eyes. One partially open hand tilted off the edge to dip toward the floor, as if grasping symbolically for something that was not there – an empty bottle of laudanum. It sprawled just out of reach at the edge of a gray-green Persian area rug.

Nothing could have been more still.

Without hope, I knelt beside her and held that soft errant hand. I folded it close to her breast, a more natural position. My face covered hers. I wept. Warm tears did nothing to resuscitate her from the coldness that filled those eyelids.

I whispered her name quietly, aching so very deep in my soul. She died alone, and now lay there in the dark without an angel over her.

I dreamed for a moment of dropping down into that absence of light, that warm eternity, of holding myself with my own arms gripped tight as I sank into the welcomed nothingness that would simply envelope me if I were to let go and take the long, slow fall down that subterranean slide – how I wanted to. That stillness would have been so easy to accept.

The moments passed as I sat there with her. I was recalled from this dream of eternity by a haunting specter of the Irishman, with his tuxedo in perfect order. It floated up hotly behind my eyeballs: there, on the dining table, laid out in waiting for me on carefully folded green tissue, a single yellow long-stem rose. The anger caught suddenly in the back of my throat, a hard bitter pill.

I rose up.

Shaking and with minute stars circling randomly in the periphery of my vision, I went out again, closing the door carefully and gently behind me as if not to wake a slumbering child.

Outside, in the moist night air, I was pounded by the darkness and the sharp, discrete pricks of the city lights as they flickered about me.

Chapter Thirty-One

Imagination suggested my ears heard angels singing. Their voices were high.

By now, I knew my way around the maze of corridors, stairwells, and lobbies on the first two floors of the building that housed the Nightingale Club. I used this knowledge to come upon the Sentimental Thug from behind as he sat facing the street entrance, which I noticed was locked now. With his back to me he looked even bigger than he did from the front. His shoulders stretched his jacket out as a large chunk of unsculpted granite might have.

"Easy," I said to him. "It's a .45 at your back, but I don't want to use it on you. Turn around slowly."

The whites of his eyes were softly bloodshot, but he was clean-shaven and there was no odor of gin or bitters about him. The tips of his fingers trembled slightly as he extended them, palms down and elbows bent, at a level even with his chest. We both noticed it.

"It ain't what you think," he explained. "I haven't hit the sauce in a week or more. I've got the high sugar in my blood."

"Where's your gun?"

"Under my left shoulder, a .38. I go with a revolver because they need less care, they're more reliable, no springs to wear out."

"Uh huh. Stop talking so much. Use your right thumb and forefinger only. Take it out slowly, like you're pulling a long fragile splinter."

He complied and I took it from him.

"What's going on? I thought everybody was friends."

"Friends fall out."

His eyes registered no surprise. There wasn't anything he hadn't seen by now on this job.

I studied his face. "Do you carry a second?"

"No. Never needed one."

"Is he up there?"

"Who?"

"You know who."

He shrugged. His eyes were dull. "Nobody tells me nothing. There's been a lot of cars out there, people coming and going, but I don't know the whos or the whats of it."

"Think about it for a minute. Who am I going to find when I open that door with the brass handle on it?"

He thought about it and then shrugged again. "They'll kill me if I tell you anything … maybe kill me anyway for letting you get by."

"So don't stand around, walk away."

"And go where?"

"Fishing maybe, someplace warm, someplace where you can watch your sugar and keep the doctors from chopping you apart from the toes up. Or friends from fitting you for cement shoes."

He nodded thoughtfully. "Can I bum a cigarette?"

Suddenly, I didn't trust him at that moment. "Do you really need one?"

His eyes clouded a moment before he moved. I swept the .45 across in a backhand swipe as he was bringing one hard fist up. My barrel caught his right cheek and ploughed over his nose. It was a rough blow. Red petals blossomed from beneath his eyes and he staggered against the wall, but did not fall down.

Now I handed him a cigarette and waited while he lit it for himself. He ignored the blood that was spreading down his face onto his collar.

He expelled a lungful of smoke. The trembling of his fingers diminished as the tobacco entered his system and calmed him. "I don't know who's up there. I really don't. I'd tell you if I did."

"Beat it," I said, jerking my head towards the door.

"Thanks for the second chance."

I noticed the angelic sopranos had fallen silent to my ears now.

"You won't get a third."

*

It was seventeen floors up but I took the stairs. I paused at the sixteenth floor to catch my breath. With nothing to lose anymore, I could be patient. I waited until my pulse was even again. While there I stepped out to check the location of the stairwell in relation to the elevator: the stairwell door was across and twenty feet down from the elevator door – near enough for what I had in mind.

I pushed through the door on the seventeenth floor quickly with the .45 in my right hand and the confiscated .38 revolver in the left. There were two men standing at semi-attention on either side of the elevator. Each held a revolver in his right hand, one of them was a nickel-plated snub-nose, but I had them covered. It was the first time I had caught a look at snub-nose's face. He was early middle-aged, maybe around forty, give or take five years of hard time. His eyes were pushed close together and his expression was set firm, like carved mahogany. The skin on his face was worn out, as if from too much sun and wind, or some other kind of coarse living.

"I'm an equally good shot with either hand. Just close your eyes tightly if you believe me."

The man on my right shut his lids and kept them closed. Snub-nose shifted his weight slightly on one set of toes without so much as blinking. Proving my point, I shot him in the heart with the .38. The nickel-plated snub-nose tumbled out of his hand and lay on the floor a couple feet from his dead body. It was pearl-handled and rubbed hard to a fast shine.

"You're going to get me in that room," I told the other man, with no feeling for the one I had just killed.

The man standing in front of me still had his eyes clamped tight.

*

"Open your eyes now. Who's in there?"

"Mr. Robinson, a coupl'a others."

"The Irishman?"

"No. He's left."

"Where'd he go?"

"I have no idea, Mista."

"How many are in there now?"

"Noya sure – probably three, but maybe four or five. I've lost track."

"Set your pistol on the floor, slowly, and lead me down there. When we get there you're going to tell them that you've shot me coming out of the elevator. Get me into that room, whatever it takes. Do you understand?"

He gave a compact nod and complied as instructed, slowly setting his gun on the floor. If he had moved any slower, I might have shot him for that.

"Are you going to kill me?" he asked when he was standing upright again.

"Not unless I have to, but you'll be between me and them, so it's in your interest to be convincing. Quickly now."

I noticed that not a single door down the long corridor had opened to investigate the sound of the gunshot. With feathers under our heels, we moved down the red carpet. We walked fast. When we stood in front of the door with the bronze handle, he took a deep breath before raising his hand to knock. I stood close enough to the man to smell the sweat and the fear on him; it was almost paralyzing.

He knocked twice with a space between, then spoke through the door. "Mr. Robinson … its Al. We've shot a man coming out of the elevator. It might be your'a guy."

There was a long response delay. On the edge of my peripheral vision I was aware of the insulting yellow rose in its usual place outside the door, resting in a vase on the small table. I felt the spiteful anger surge up the middle of my chest, into my throat. Then a bolt on the door clicked and withdrew. The door opened a crack and wavered there. Reaching around the man in front of me, I fired the .38 three times right through the center of the door, and then dropped the gun. Splinters came back on us and I knew they must have hit my human shield in the chest and face.

I kicked the door in and pushed Al forward into the room, past a crumpling body. Two shots hit Al in the side and spun him around and then over. In that freeze-framed instant, I saw two men standing together near the center of the room, as if they had just been in close conference. One of them, a man I'd never seen before, held a pistol with smoke drifting from the barrel. The other man was Eugene Robinson. Robinson stood with his own pistol drawn, though not fully raised. He leaned backwards, under the pale yellow light of the chandelier – chin up, lips contorted thinly – as if unsure for the first time in his life. I shot him in the shoulder with my .45 and put the other man down with two shots that hit him square in the chest. He would have been dead before the second shot him.

The wood-paneled room reverberated from the sudden noise and deadly vibrations. I glanced down at Al. A high-pitched cry escaped his mouth and he tried unsuccessfully to pull himself across the floor, moving blindly towards nothing at all. He was twisted around and bleeding heavily. I doubted there was much chance he would survive.

I stepped over him and walked into the room, stooping once to pick up Robinson's unfired pistol. It was a hand-customized government model 1911 .45 caliber semi-automatic, made at the Springfield Armory. It had a rounded hammer, a slightly beveled ejection port, and an ambidextrous thumb-safety. It was a lot like mine. I stared down at the man, pointing both .45s.

*

Robinson managed to pull himself up by the edge of the desk; just enough so that he could lean back against it while he looked up at me with dazed eyes. His pupils were constricted. Quite a bit of blood had spread along the outside of his evening jacket, staining the black fabric a darker, harsher color. It seeped into the seams of his starched white shirt. His shoulder would never be right again, but he wasn't mortally wounded – unless he bled to death or succumbed to shock. A lock of his hair had shaken loose and hung down over his forehead.

"Help me with this," he said, pulling at his bowtie.

It was an odd detail to be concerned with. I ignored his request but he continued to work the tight black knot. It came untied and unfurled down his chest. After another moment he got the top button loose. His breath was labored, but even. With his head back now, he looked up at me.

"A pox," he sighed. "We didn't figure you to cross us on the O'Farrell hit, thought that would come later … if it was to come at all."

"It didn't sit right with me, being coerced to kill a man in cold blood, in front of his children. I don't know what led you to believe I would ever kill the children."

Robinson nodded with a grimace. The pain was starting to set in and shock would follow if he didn't get attention soon.

"Where's the Irishman?"

Robinson coughed roughly. "He's not here. When he heard you'd crossed us with O'Farrell he left immediately for New York. He had a plane waiting."

"You had to kill the girl? She wasn't part of this."

He allowed himself a slack, unsettling smile. "I figured that was why you were here."

"You didn't have to do that."

"We thought it would draw you out for us."

"You enjoyed it."

"Maybe."

"You did."

"Yes, I did."

"Who enjoys that?"

"Maybe I was born without a conscience." His features became warm putty, sagging under the sickly light. The blood was draining from his body.

"Nobody is born without a conscience."

The expression on his face, the first real one I'd seen on him, was one of triumph. It hung on his face like clown's paint.

"You see what you've done? You traded her life for O'Farrell's. She called me this morning, looking for a fix, maybe she thought she was leaving town, maybe she didn't think you needed to know. We took her as insurance. She wanted laudanum, just a sip to carry her. After you loused us, we gave it to her. You should have seen the way she cried when I forced her to drink the full bottle. She wept like a small child. It was almost pitiful, especially once she was quiet. Was it a fair trade, Laddie? Was it? Maybe you too will now become one of *the others*."

I shot him point blank in the face with this own gun. The blast echoed back on me in the small, blood-splattered room under the pale, distorting light of the chandelier. Scooping the yellow rose from its vase, I laid it across his chest, perpendicular to the row of luminous black buttons. Then I straightened up fully and made a slow turn. My eyes watered, but only from the sting of cordite in the air.

He was right: I had become one of *the others*.

Chapter Thirty-Two

I caught Torresi at his desk. He looked up as I pushed the door open. The garage was empty and he was alone.

When he spoke, his voice seemed to echo in the tiny office. "Heard on the radio there was an explosion and a shooting in a downtown office building – two thugs gunned down dead, several more injured, but no mention of Mr. O'Farrell. They got an APB out on you. What happened?"

"Alvarini warned me this city was unclean. He told me that before I left I would be sorry I ever came."

"Are you?"

I nodded wearily.

"Mind if I sit?"

Torresi pointed towards a chair. I sank into it.

"What happened?" he asked again.

"O'Farrell caught a ride out of town."

Impassive dark eyes stared back at me. They were beads in a mound of ruddy, inert flesh.

"That was your plan all along?"

I nodded.

"Why?"

"Because maybe he didn't deserve to die, because maybe I'm not a killer after all. At least not the way you think I might be. Because maybe it's not too late for redemption."

"Be sure you make the distinction between penance and redemption. You know we gotta come at you now. Why are you here?"

"So you'd hear it from me, and hear it straight."

"I'm listening."

"I had to take out the Irishman's back-up. No one will miss them. I got O'Farrell and his two sons out on a train. They didn't deserve to be killed like that. He might just be one of the good guys, just maybe one of the very few. I was going to skip with the girl. I had her stashed at the Blackstone, but she went back to them for one last fix. Robinson murdered her. So, I paid a visit to the Nightingale before I came here."

Torresi's eyes gleamed and then narrowed further.

"Maybe I turned off the radio too soon. What's the line?"

"The Irishman skipped, but Robinson and four of his men are dead."

Torresi stared at me. Some dark philosophy swept his brow and wiped his eyes clean.

"Might not be so bad for us. You killed that S.O.B. Robinson; we were going to have to do it sooner or later, that evens things for Alvarini. The Irishman's in hiding and O'Farrell's left town. And even if he returns, it's the Irishman he'll be calling for. There may be some pieces we can pick up here."

"Does that mean we're Jake?"

He thought about this and then nodded slowly. "Yeah, more or less, far as I can see. I doubt Nitti will see it differently, or take any further exception. But no keys to the city for you. In fact, I were you, I'd leave Chicago tonight and I wouldn't hurry back any time soon."

"I'm already gone."

"Mind that APB. An All Points Bulletin is not something to fool around with. Somebody recognized you – and they got you by name. Those FBI boys are foaming at the mouth, as if this were another Kansas City. It's ironic – you're hotter with the law than I'll ever be, but I never saved no special prosecutor's life before."

I put on my hat and turned for the door, having said everything I could possibly think of to say.

"Mr. Duncan," I heard behind me. "I am sorry about the girl. Don't go too hard on yourself about it."

Chapter Thirty-Three

Just shy of three o'clock in the morning, that abandoned hour of the night, Jimmy met me at the train station, far down Track number four, behind a large supply cart. He wore a cloth checkered hat and an old brown leather jacket with a shoulder patch. The look in his eyes was a far away dream. In his right hand he carried my briefcase. He didn't ask any questions, just nodded and handed the briefcase to me. I handed him an envelope that I knew contained $10,000 in cash. He didn't even seem interested, just put the envelope in the front inside pocket of his jacket and shook my hand.

"My wife lit a candle for you this evening," he said quietly after a moment.

"Please thank her for me and I'll keep Helen in my prayers. I hope she will be well again soon. And if not, I pray her suffering will ease."

There was a poetic flash of motion in his eyes. It settled as quickly as it appeared. "Where will you go?"

"About as far as that Rider can take me."

"When will you be back?"

I just mustered a smile and shook my head once. "See to your bride, Jimmy."

Jimmy nodded and looked at me with a dignity I had rarely seen in another human being. He nodded again, once, and turned around. I boarded the train and then stood on the platform and leant out slightly to look down the track and watch him return to his wife. I thought that even right there, at that moment, with every thing he had to face, he had more in his world than I could ever hope for again.

*

The train jolted forward and moved slowly. I picked up my suitcase.

"Help ya with that, suh?" The porter was slight and elderly and his accent was from the Deep South. His eyes were rheumy and still gleamed with kindness. "Ya looks mighty worn out, ya do, lemme help ya with that, suh." He showed me to my carriage and hefted my suitcase into the upper rack. The entire time he was whistling a soft melody between his teeth. I didn't recognize the tune. He syncopated it with slight head bobs.

"Dinin' cah opens at six for breakfast, suh."

"Thank you. I didn't expect to be greeted by a porter at this hour of the morning. Wouldn't have blamed you if you slept through this stop."

The gentleman smiled and bowed his slightly. "Ah might not ah come out, but I seen through da winder that you looked tired and jess 'bout bluer than blue. Said to mahself I best come do for ya, efen ah can help sum."

His words resonated with me and I was grateful. I said so. Then I said, "How long have you worked for the railroad?"

"Don't quite remember, suh. Reckon almost forty yeahs. Came up from 'Bama as a young 'un."

"Seen a lot in that time?"

"Jess 'bout eveythin'. Not all ah it good." He smiled patiently and shrugged.

"You holding up?"

"Every day's a blessin'."

"No complaints?"

"Can't say ah do. Anythin' else, suh?"

I looked around the car.

"No. I think I'm settled fine."

"You have a blessed evenin', suh."

"Just a minute. How much you make in a year?"

"Just 'bout nuff, ay spose."

"How much would that be?"

He named a low, round figure. I reached into my breast pocket and found a sheaf of bills. I gave it all to him.

"Brother, take a few months off if you like."

"That's mo money'n ah's evah seen at one time."

"What's your name?" I asked.

"Solomon."

I extended my hand. "Mine's Ross."

He grasped it.

His eyes had clouded with a soft puzzlement. "Nobody in these cars eveh did that before?" And he wasn't referring to the money I'd handed him.

"'… whatever you did not do for one of the least among you …'" I wasn't referring to the money either – he really could have slept through

228

the stop, most porters would have.

"Matthew twenny-five. Dey Good Book."

Solomon tipped his cap as he backed out of the sleeper car.

*

The train moved out past the city line, gathering momentum slowly, ineluctably, clicking and grinding heavily in its metallic stride against the tracks as it picked up speed. I was lost, a failure, overcome with grief and exhaustion. My eyes filled with tears. I sat back in the turned-down bed of the sleeper car, with the gentle creaking of the carriage around me, and stared out of the window into the blackness, searching for the first emerging points of light off over the horizon, and waiting for the soft, cool respite of dawn.

THE END

Acknowledgments

I am deeply grateful to: my agent, Sonia Land, for all her steady encouragement, thoughtful guidance, and dedication to my writing career; my father-in-law, Gene Pellegrin, for his support and professional advice; and Leila Dewji with Acorn Press for her invaluable editorial contributions to the current work.

About the Author

Christopher Bartley, a pen name, is American with a PhD in Clinical Psychology and is presently a Professor of Psychology at the University of Hawaii and Director of Clinical Research at The Menninger Clinic in Houston, Texas. The teaching responsibilities and consultancies in worthy and prestigious establishments are too numerous to list here. He still finds time to sit on a large number of editorial boards and is a reviewer of countless psychiatric, behavioural research, mental health, obesity, depression and anxiety (to name but a few) journals and academic papers. He has had his works published in letters, papers, in journals and scholarly books, often making scientific presentations, and has written for media such as *Time* and *The Huffington Post*. He directs research and conducts clinical trials on chronic combat-related posttraumatic stress disorder mostly with prisoners and combat veterans, working to improve their mental health and separate science from quackery.

He has had an interest in American history since hearing a first-hand account of the Battle of San Juan Hill from his great-grandfather as a child, and then learning later of his father's military service in Vietnam. He is also fascinated with the history of jazz, gangsters, bank robbers and baseball, all of which seems to converge in the 1920s, '30s and '40s. Writing noir crime and thriller novels set in the period just after prohibition affords him an enjoyably different aspect from his work and allows him to delve into research of one of his favourite periods.

Made in the USA
Lexington, KY
10 August 2013